VOICES

VOICES

A Novel

by

Bill Lamperes

New Visions Publishing
Glendale, Arizona

VOICES
A Novel

Published by: New Visions Publishing
6146 W. Quail Avenue
Glendale, Arizona 85308
(623) 680-1792 or (623) 236-9663

This is a work of fiction. All the characters, names, incidents,
organizations and dialogue in the novel are either the products of the
author's imagination or are used fictitiously.
ISBN: 13: 978-1469968834
ISBN: 10:1469968835
Printed in the United States of America
Suggested retail price: $14.95
New Visions Publishing April, 2012

Cover photo: Rebecca Reynolds (Amococo Labyrinth Luminarium)
Cover design: Christopher Ostermeier
Interior layout: Jeff Smith

Dedication

To Rosel:

A well-read friend who shares her thoughtful insights

and criticisms about my work with a delightful blend

of dedication and a pinch of impish, quirky humor.

Acknowledgments

I delight in the skill and competence of my friend and grammar editor, Karen Parris. Her talent for finding errant commas, misplaced words or grammatical mistakes amazes me. Karen's attention to detail and ability to fine-tune a completed novel brings life to my work. She is a rare gem who makes a huge difference with her brilliance and methodical mind. Thank you for adding class to my world.

Rosel Sersante, to whom I dedicate this novel, is a voracious reader. She consumes every possible genre for the sheer joy of discovering new stories and creative writing. Her understanding of style, character development, plot expansion and dialogue has turned the woman into an unpaid, expert reading critic for me. Rosel's experienced, self-trained eye has made her an ardent word merchant who can analyze and critique every aspect of a novel. Rosel's feedback encouraged me to improve, kept my ego in check and made me realize, at best, I am still learning the art of writing. However, her support has given me confidence about my passion for spinning tales. After completing this novel, I believe I have developed into an "advanced-novice" author. Thank you for coaching and encouraging me, Rosel.

My dear friend, Rebecca Reynolds, has provided steadfast support for my desire to write. Her refusal to read or discuss any part of the manuscript or its characters until I finish my first draft motivates me to stay on task and complete my work. Rebecca wants to read my entire story with fresh eyes and be surprised by every scene and chapter. She has become my holistic reader and lets me know what part of the tale needs elaboration and which character requires additional work.

I want to thank my friend, Marcia Fitzhorn, for showing me pictures of the "ghosts" she discovered in the recesses of dark caverns when her family took the lantern tour of Cave of the Winds near Colorado Springs. These eerie digital snapshots present the casual observer with an unexplained phenomenon: cloudy circles of a presence hiding in remote corners of the cave. Her photography set my imaginative mind in motion so I could create a possible playground for my paranormal spirits. Thanks, Marcia.

I want to extend a special thanks to Ginger Mohs for helping me understand the nuances of forensic evidence and for being such a great private investigator. She helped me craft the story's conclusion. Ginger had a brilliant mind, a gentle soul and a delightful personality. Her presence will be missed.

Members of my writers' group proved to be invaluable assets as they applied their red pens and carved up each of my initial drafts. Eduardo Cervino, Jeff Smith and Charles Mallory patiently reviewed my writing and offered meaningful insights to refine the manuscript. My fellow writers pushed me to become a better author. I thank them for the time they spent testing the thickness of my skin.

Donna Morey, another avid reader, diligently examined my final manuscript for details and errors that may reveal inconsistencies. She often found fine points my familiarity with the document overlooked. Thank you for both your exquisite skills and dedication to read my unfinished work.

Special thanks go to my group of "beta" readers. After receiving valuable feedback from many sources, I rewrote the manuscript and asked Janet Pearce, Dawn Hurley, Rich Goldhaber and Rosel Sersante to examine my revisions and answer my questions about character development. This group helped me refine the parts of the book in which I asked readers to suspend belief and to step into the arena of paranormal activity.

Grateful thanks goes to Melanie Tighe, co-owner of Dog-Eared Pages bookstore in Phoenix. Melanie, the brilliant author of *The Mistral Tale*, written under the pen name Anna Questerly, reviewed my final draft. She inspired and encouraged me by saying, "I'd love to put this book in my store."

Finally, I want to thank those kindred, musical artists who created the songs I have used to convey clues in the story. The lyrics offering powerful messages include:

- "Blinded by the Light," Artist: Manfred Mann,
  Writer: Bruce Springsteen, Producer: Thrill Hill
  Productions
- "Light My Fire," Artist: The Doors, Writer: Robby
  Krieger, Producer: Black on Gold Label
- "Fearless," Artist: Pink Floyd, Writer: David Gilmore and
  Rogers Waters, Producer: Pink Floyd
- "Light On," Artist: David Cook, Writer: Chris Cornell and
  Brian Howes, Producer: EMI Blackwood, Inc.
- "Beginning to See the Light," Writer: Jack Reed and The
  Velvet Underground, Producer: The Velvet Underground
- "Light Surrounding You," Artist: Evermore,
  Writer: Dann Hume, Producer: John Hume and
  Jon Alagia, Warner Label

Introduction: The Voices We Hear

We hear voices every day. The *primary voice* we listen to is our own. People mentally talk to themselves and their conscience; the inner voice speaks back. Humans accept the presence of this inner voice and are comfortable with it because it has been there for as long as we have been alive. That voice collaborates with all the analytic functions of the brain to synthesize information, make judgments and direct short-and long-term actions. Our inner voice reminds us every action leads to either a punishment or a reward. Consequently, this voice serves as a moral guide and attends to basic survival needs. Such brain activity happens in nanoseconds and plays a continuous part of our day.

For most people, the inner voice has become a trusted friend. That voice helps us formulate thoughts to share with others or promotes actions as various insights emerge. Even when alone, most of us engage our inner voice in personal conversations and often enjoy debating the merits of random ideas and notions — all a part of the human process.

Children, unencumbered by the social limits of culture, have added substance to their inner voice by creating imaginary friends with whom they converse on a frequent basis. As people mature, an imaginary friend often transforms into "an angel sitting on their shoulder" watching over them. They feel comfort knowing they are not alone in the world.

A *second kind of voice*, heard more randomly, disturbs us because of the discomfort the one-way conversation causes. A stranger often absorbed in an argument with an invisible voice only he or she hears, scares us and becomes someone to be avoided. Such encounters are not part of the everyday experience, and these one-way interchanges suggest the speaker may suffer from some delusional affliction, perhaps is under the influence of excessive amounts of alcohol or is completely insane. We usually react by giving the speaker a wide berth.

One summer day, I sat on a park bench watching the sailboats in the San Francisco Harbor. A woman dressed in a down-filled parka and ski pants sat down at the far end of my bench and began talking to some invisible listener. A lively, albeit one-sided conversation ensued.

I glanced in her direction and decided to interrupt. She informed me she was communicating with her authority on the planet of Odeonus and pointed to the approximate area where the North Star appears in the night sky to help me locate her home.

We chatted about her purpose for coming to planet Earth. The woman informed me she had helped William the Conqueror plan the Battle of Hastings, Gutenberg invent the printing press and more recently showed Jonas Salk how to cure polio. She told me San Francisco presented her with a time-travel portal to return home, and her departure to leave was soon.

I sat quietly analyzing her words when she began to stir. She gathered her things and walked down the promenade toward the cable cars. I watched her move at a slow, unsteady pace.

My traveling companion returned, and I quickly shared my experience. I turned to point out the woman I had been talking with, but she had disappeared … much too quickly for her slow-moving gait.

My acquaintance smiled, shot me a skeptical look and then offered another scenario to ponder. She asked me if anyone else had passed the bench when I was chatting with my new friend. They hadn't. She suggested people may have gone out of their way to avoid an obviously crazy or drunken man, talking to himself on a park bench. Perhaps my unique "bench mate" could only be seen by me. I hadn't thought of the possibility. Such a conundrum presents a dilemma for thought and future investigation. It may lead to a different kind of novel, one that explores quantum mechanics and characters who move between various time and space dimensions, but not as the major theme of this book.

A *third type of voice* provides the plot for this novel. It is the kind of voice you only hear in your dreams. It is the voice of strangers, friends or family, both living and dead, who materialize as images in one's dreamscape. Many psychologists believe such voices help the resting mind work out problems or impart warnings of some future event. Often, the messages offer sound advice.

What is the source of these voices? Are these the voices of spirits who cannot be seen by our limited human vision? Are they the voices of "guardian angels" who have accepted the task of protecting us? Could a ghost speak to us in dreams or leave signs to guide our decisions?

The potential power of these voices fascinates me. As a fiction writer, I often listen to the voices of my characters as I sleep. They beg me to craft specific dialogue they want to speak in my novels. Are their voices real, imagined or merely part of my thinking process? As I construct my manuscript and re-read the dialogues I have typed, I wonder if I captured their message. Are the words mine or thoughts channeled through me by the voices I hear?

Given my experience with a variety of paranormal encounters, dreams or people who talk to themselves, I decided to use *voices* in this novel to help my central character, Jack Weston, deal with his personal grief. These voices offer Jack clues to solve his wife's murder. Their efforts only make sense to him after he finds a balance between his emotional side and his logic.

I invite the reader to step into a world where this third kind of voice plays a significant role in the story and provides a link between logic and the inner voice. I believe we humans often ignore many signs and omens these unexplained voices share every day, and miss their attempt to nurture and guide our quest for knowledge. Perhaps this novel will encourage the reader to listen more carefully to the soft sound of other voices they may faintly hear. Enjoy the story.

A Thought to Begin:

Ships that pass in the night, and speak each other in passing,

only a signal shown, and a distant voice in the darkness;

So on the ocean of life, we pass and speak one another,

only a look and a voice, then darkness again and a silence.

—Henry Wadsworth Longfellow

Part One: Agony

Only in the agony of parting do we look into the depths of love.

— George Elliott

Chapter One

"You have to be crazy to live out here in the damn desert," the driver shouted as excessive heat flooded through his vehicle's front window. Phillip Slocum fought a losing battle with the rental car's broken air conditioner. He cursed his decision to leave the comfort of Los Angeles and make this trip into hell. With growing exasperation, he asked himself: *What difference would a personal visit make?* Beads of sweat continued to trickle down his face as the 100-degree day offered no mercy. *How can it be so hot in May?*

Slocum had already spent an hour on the highway when he entered Desert Valley and faced the challenge of locating Jack's house — somewhere out there, off the beaten path, north of Cave Creek Road. After negotiating remote, steaming ribbons of asphalt and bouncing along pothole-littered gravel roads, he arrived at a two-story home resembling more a Roman villa than a desert dwelling. Rows of Corinthian columns lined the entrance, and the remnants of a well-manicured garden, now weed-infested, greeted him. A walkway leading to a detached garage, lined with Lombardy poplars, added a feeling of grace to a vine-covered trellis. An infinity pool on the east side of the house presented a commanding view of the surrounding area.

The man hoisted his excessive body out of the vehicle and wiped his face again with an already-soaked handkerchief. He surveyed the area and became aware of a deafening silence. A wisp of wind blew loose sand across the driveway and allayed the fears he had lost all hearing. *I would go nuts with this kind of isolation,* he thought. Phillip turned toward the building and spotted the ornate, hand-carved wooden door at its entrance.

Reaching the marble-lined walkway leading to the main entrance, he felt pangs of anger rise in his chest. "After all my support, I can't believe Jack shut me out," he muttered. "What did he say on the phone? ... 'I can hardly stand my agony!'" *Well,* he thought, *showing my anger may not be the best way to get him back into the fold. Be cool about it, Phil.*

Phillip Slocum, travel editor for *Western Trails Magazine,* slowly lumbered up the steps of the desert mansion and turned to study the landscape below. He could see for miles as tremors of heat danced in the noonday sun. They all but obscured a view of the stately saguaro cactus and lowly scrub brush struggling to survive in the parched terrain. The sun played tricks, creating a mirage of water-filled lakes, glistening in the distance. The spectacular view failed to impress him. Phillip turned toward the house and kicked at a lizard scampering to find a place to hide in the shade.

He needed to meet Jack face-to-face and determine if his writer should be fired or rescued. Only a gut check in Jack's presence would dictate the decision. He rang the doorbell and stepped back. No response. Phillip knocked on the door, and it opened to his touch. He walked in and yelled, "Jack? Jack, it's Phil. Are you here?"

At first, silence greeted Phillip's calls. The editor walked into the living room and spotted empty bottles of booze covering the tables and floor. The place reeked. Pizza boxes, dirty glasses and empty snack bags littered the area. A host of flies covered half-eaten food smashed into the carpet. The stench of soiled plates, rotting cans of spaghetti and moldy cheese filled the air. The television had a picture, but no sound. Phillip located the remote and turned off the power. For a second time, he shouted, "Jack, Jack, you home?"

Phillip stood listening to the silent house and then heard glass shattering upstairs. Uncomfortable with his intrusion, Phillip yelled again, "Jack, is that you? Are you all right? Do you need help?"

"Phil, … Phil, … Phil, …. what the hell are you doing here?" The words seemed distant, foggy, slurred.

"Yes, Jack, it's me. I came to talk with you. Are you okay?"

"Yeah, yeah, … okay, okay. Gimmee a minute. I'll be down … down in a minute. That's it, I'm comin' down. I promise. It's true. I promise."

Phillip covered his nose to fight the nausea stuck in his throat. The house looked like a garbage pit. Neglect would have been a kind description. Phil discovered a greater disaster in the kitchen. The filthy glasses and dirty dishes, piled high in the sink, defied gravity. The sink was surrounded by more empty bottles of whiskey, scotch and gin, like glass soldiers protecting Jack from dealing with his personal agony. *Hell, the man's lost and wallowing in self-pity.*

Phillip shook his head, did an about-face, stepped back into the living room and opened all the windows. A blast of hot, desert air rushed in and attacked the foul odors dominating the room. He gathered most of the obnoxious trash and tossed it into the garbage bin behind the house. When Phil returned, he found Jack's disheveled body weaving in the kitchen doorway.

Phillip gasped at Jack's appearance. Barely able to stand, a bedraggled human form clung to the doorframe for support. Unshaven, with a three-week-old beard, Jack looked terrible. His bloodshot eyes lay in sunken orbs framed by an ashen, emotionless face.

"My god, what's happened to you?" Phillip asked.

"Haven't you heard?" Jack muttered. "Taylor's dead."

"I know. Man, I know," Phillip replied. "But, Jack, she's been dead for three months. You're still alive! You've got to stop this shit and get on with life."

"Why? Who says?"

"I do." Phillip curtly responded, practically yelling at the wretched, human heap barely remaining upright. "Yes, Taylor's dead, but you need to snap out of it. You're a talented writer. Write about your pain. Write about her life, whatever, but write again. People will understand."

"Who cares?"

"Your stories have touched thousands of readers. People hunger for your words. They live vicariously through you."

Phillip's reasoning fell on deaf ears as Jack searched for a bottle with remnants of liquid comfort. He found the dark, pacifying fluid in the bottom of a Jack Daniel bottle, took a huge swig and grabbed the counter to steady his body.

"Tell your readers I'm dead. Nobody feels the pain like I do. They won't understand. … Oh, god, Phil, it hurts so much. I can't stand it. Nobody gets it."

"It's true. Nobody feels the pain like you, but you've got to get past this agony of yours and start living again."

"I'll never get past it. I … I can't live without her. I don't want to live without Taylor!"

"That's the booze speaking. You have to sober up before we talk. Now go shower and shave. Obey your editor. Understand? I'm still your boss." Phil gently pushed the man toward the stairs leading to the master bath.

"I don't want to be sober. I don't want to feel more pain."

"Listen, Jack," the editor shouted as he grabbed the intoxicated writer by the shirt and shook him, "don't make me strip those filthy clothes off your body and throw you in the shower myself!"

"Okay, okay, don't push me around. I'll go. … I'll go."

Phillip put his arms around his friend and gave him a hug. The foul-smelling man almost made Phil puke. However, he regained control of his gag reflex and practically carried his favorite writer up the stairs to the bathroom. Jack stood in front of the shower, weaving from side to side.

"If I don't hear the water in the next five minutes, I'll hose you down and scrub your naked ass myself. Got it?"

"Yeah, yeah, yeah. … I'm going. I'm going … into the shower … promise."

Phillip closed the door and stood outside. Once he heard the water running, Phil started downstairs to finish his cleanup job. He negotiated the steps, piled high with dirty clothes and un-read newspapers. His eye caught the gallery of incredible pictures covering the walls — all of Taylor and Jack together or alone. The photographs had a refined skill — sensitive to both of them. Nothing staged. None of the pictures showed the couple facing the camera in artificial poses. They smiled, joyful and carefree, and the camera revealed their total bliss.

He walked through the living and dining rooms and admired a dozen more photos of the pair hung on the surface of each wall — all remarkable for their ability to capture Jack and Taylor's euphoria. Like the ones on the stairs, most of the pictures caught Jack or Taylor in action shots or sharing intimate glances. It broke Phil's heart to see such contentment and unbridled delight destroyed by the tragedy.

Phil dismissed his sadness and returned to the kitchen. He started coffee, emptied the contents of partially filled bottles down the sink, stuffed the dishwasher and scrubbed the counters. Within minutes, he had worked a small cleaning miracle. Phil, pleased with his impromptu housekeeping project, felt satisfied with his intervention. Out of character for the hard-nosed editor, the effort made him feel useful in this uncomfortable situation. He poured a cup of coffee and waited for Jack. He shook his head as he spotted more pictures strategically hung in the nooks and crannies of the kitchen.

Phil exercised immense patience, waiting while Jack took most of the morning to shower and shave. Then the pushy editor forced Jack to down five cups of coffee. After an hour, the writer began to look human, but still unable to talk or listen. Phillip watched Jack slowly return to reality and let him sober up before talking business.

When Phil sensed Jack could reason, he began a rehearsed speech. "I came here to fire you today. I've waited three months, and I need a writer. If you can't do it, I'll hire someone else. I can't stall the publisher much longer. Do you want to keep the job, or not?"

"I don't care. I have nothing to write about. If I ever muster any energy, all I want to do is find the bastard who killed her. The scumbag left Taylor in the road to die. As long as he's out there, I don't care about anything else. You understand, boss?" Jack's voice cracked as he spoke. His

7

bloodshot eyes glistened as pools of new tears formed and yielded to the force of gravity.

"The truth is, Jack, I won't fire you. I refuse to abandon a good friend, especially at a time like this. You've grieved enough. You need to return to what you know and let Taylor's death take care of itself — in its own time."

"I can't," he paused. "I can't," repeated the submissive man. His bowed head looked absolutely pitiful to the editor. Phil's arrival had been one of a long-awaited executioner, paying his last respects. The self-imposed prisoner had accepted his fate. Like a condemned convict, already blindfolded, Jack stood quietly against an imaginary wall, pleading to make his life end quickly. The executioner, however, couldn't order the firing squad to shoot. Phil had to try one more time to save the life of his personal and professional friend.

"Let's go get something to eat," Phillip suggested. "You need food — some real food. You can't make a good decision on an empty stomach."

Chapter Two

On the way to the restaurant, Jack quietly slumped in the front seat and stared out the window. The uncomfortable silence permitted Phil to reflect on his remarkable years with Jack. At their first interview, the writer appeared bright and enthusiastic, and Phillip liked him from the start. In fact, he smiled at Jack's passion and delighted in his new writer's first submissions. The words sparkled with flare and immediately fostered a loyal readership.

#####

Long before Taylor became part of Jack's life, he honed his active imagination spinning scary stories on Boy Scout trips. As an adolescent, Jack frightened the most hardened teen with tales, causing campers to zip up their tents as shadows filled the surrounding woods with unfamiliar noises. His vivid words created sinister images of creatures lurking at the edge of the foreboding darkness. Jack's ability to tell flamboyant stories provided an early glimmer of his future career. In school, teachers often read his compositions to inspire less creative classmates. When he graduated from high school, they voted him the prestigious "Hemingway award."

Jack often bragged about being an only child. His well-educated parents offered him the implicit benefits of old-school money and financial abundance fulfilled most of his early desires. His mother's failure to set boundaries could have spoiled the young man, but his father's stern, consistent expectations kept Jack's life in balance.

To expand his worldliness, Jack's mother took him on trips throughout the United States, and occasionally, Europe. At an early age, she introduced him to the theater and taught him to become aware of the ebb and flow of life as captured in stage performances.

His father established Jack's educational goals and reviewed his son's school work. He critiqued everything his son wrote and demanded Jack replace bland adjectives, adverbs and nouns with expressive language. The young writer learned to use active rather than passive verbs with everything he penned. Only after completing these revisions would he be allowed to play with other children. Throughout childhood, "Mr. Thesaurus" and Jack became best friends.

Phil liked sharing time with Jack. His "chickmagnet" appearance turned women's heads. The man's flashing blue eyes mesmerized females who longingly gazed at his features. His natural athlete's talent and a lean six-foot frame transformed him into a sports star. Women delighted in twirling their fingers through his sandy brown curls on the back of his neck. Jack emerged into adulthood as one of the beautiful people whose presence brought joy to others.

Jack attended college at Arizona State University and published a book of short stories ranging from little-known sports heroes to early frontier pioneers. He became the editor of the campus newspaper and its literary magazine. His father's trust fund enabled him to attend school without worrying about securing a part-time job. After graduation, Jack pursued a commitment to become a writer.

He tried to pen fiction novels, but after two years of rejection letters and constant rewrites, his two manuscripts failed to get published. Critics said he could spin a good tale, but needed more seasoning and deeper life experiences to make his characters believable. Waiting for life to catch up with his imagination, he applied to write for *Western Trails* and immediately bonded with Phil. Within a year, Jack's descriptive prose added more financial rewards to his abundant lifestyle.

Phillip's career began to parallel Jack's success. Over the next four years, the two spent more time together playing in Las Vegas, Mexico and San Francisco. Similar tastes in sports, women and alcohol forged a personal and professional bond, sealing their relationship.

Jack shunned living in Los Angeles, the company's home office, and chose to return to Phoenix. The close proximity to the desert reminded him of the Old West, and he wanted to surround himself with a more open environment. Residence in a desert area removed the temptations of a city like Los Angeles, providing the quiet space necessary to refine his craft.

Phillip encouraged Jack to write articles appealing to weekend travelers, so they could vicariously enjoy adventures through the author's unique perspective. Given his innovative mind and an eye for detail, Jack became the most popular writer at *Western Trails*. Readers claimed Jack's prose turned him into their personal tour guide, sharing new experiences in unfamiliar places. He tantalized readers with eloquent, refreshing and velvety language. When Jack wrote about meals, prepared in unique, off-the-beaten-path restaurants, readers swore they could taste the flavors in each dish. Eventually, restaurants, bed and breakfast, and small-town hotel owners begged the magazine to send Jack to write about them.

#####

Now, in the depths of Jack's despair, Phillip's friendship and professional connection would be tested. How could the editor find a way to relieve Jack's misery and bring him back into *Western Trail's* fold? Phillip had to exercise tolerance and encourage his writer to step away from the brink of his own personal disaster.

Chapter Three

Phillip glanced at the sleeping writer and smiled. *God, he loved Taylor.* Jack's uncontrolled energy now seemed so far removed from the lump of humanity crunched down in his passenger's seat.

Jack told him the story of how he met Taylor at least a hundred times. He'd share it whenever the opportunity arose. Even though the writer moved to the desert, Phil continued to maintain his friendship, and they talked frequently. The Jack and Taylor saga became embossed on his memory.

#####

Jack and his college roommate, Tom, rented a house in Glendale, Arizona, located in a subdivision on the seventh tee of Arrowhead Legend Golf Course. Tom spent most of the week working in San Diego, which gave Jack time to concentrate on writing and being the domestic caretaker of their shared home. Jack used the backdrop of rugged mountains and rich, green golf course lawns as motivation to compose his travel articles.

On weekends, Jack and his buddies played golf and attended a variety of professional sporting events. Always on the lookout for a quality watering hole, Tom suggested the group drop by Zendejas Grill. Joaquin and Nanette Zendejas, the owners, created the perfect setting where soft recessed lighting seductively enhanced the black and maroon décor of its two bars and dining area. Strategically placed tables complimented booths upholstered with a matching crushed velvet material.

Joaquin, a former NFL kicker, knew how to cater to sports-oriented customers, and Nanette scheduled a continuous calendar of weekend entertainment. The usual top shelf brands of tequila and flavored vodkas added a touch of class to the selection of beers on tap. Afternoon hors d'oeuvres, an extended happy hour and a half-dozen oversized flat screen televisions completed the bar's relaxed, but intimate atmosphere.

The first time the foursome walked into the bar, Tom's well-trained eye spotted the attractive bartender. Her short blonde hair framed a soft, beautiful face. The woman's alluring body, dancing blue eyes and warm smile immediately captured his attention.

"Hello, my name is Tom, and this is my first visit. Who hired an angel to serve drinks?"

The woman looked up, smiled and said, "My name is Michelle. How are you doing today?"

"My day just got a lot better. If you keep smiling at me, I'll join your legion of admirers," said Tom. "Life would be heaven if you also poured me a tall beer." Turning to his golf partners, whose attention had been distracted by the menu, Tom continued, "These other three guys are Jack, Pete and Fred. You decide if you want to know anything about them. I can't vouch for their character, but I'm really the most important one to know."

"Thanks, good information, Tom. If any of them forget to pay their tab, I can always count on their spokesman to lay out the cash, right?"

Tom's companions laughed at their self-appointed leader and gave Michelle a thumbs-up sign.

"What can I get for you, gentlemen?" she asked the other men.

"Another three lookers like you, dear," blurted Pete, who also admired the woman's charms.

"Now cut that out, guys," Jack said. "We meet Michelle for the first time and you hit on her like Neanderthal troglodytes. Take it easy, Pete, I live in the neighborhood and may want to come back."

"I'm sorry, dear lady," Pete said, clasping his hands together in mock apology. "I've just spent eight hours playing golf with this riffraff and forgot my manners."

"I guess I'll forgive you once, especially if you order a second beer," Michelle smiled.

"Simple enough. To make up for my caveman behavior, I'll buy the first round for my thirsty friends," Pete announced.

Michelle brought out the drinks and continued to cut limes. Pete and Fred drifted into a discussion about their golf game and Tom became engrossed in a Diamondbacks rally taking place on television.

Jack studied the bartender for a minute and asked, "How long have you worked here?"

"I came to Phoenix from Montana with my husband and started bartending a couple months ago. He's a golf pro for the Palms Resort."

"You married a professional golfer?"

"Yeah, he plans to join the tour soon. Arizona's warm weather gives him more time to practice than he had in Montana."

"It's probably difficult to hit par out of a snow bank. I wish him luck."

"Thanks, I'll let him know he's got a rooting section."

"Do you enjoy bartending?"

"It's okay. I became a bartender as a college student. It's a good fallback job."

"It sounds like you'd rather be doing something else."

"Actually, I want to become a photographer, but it's difficult breaking into the profession. The phone book's packed with pages of them."

"Are you any good?" Jack asked.

"Of course, I have an eye for composition. I don't like to brag, but I shoot great action shots of people and have a knack for capturing their moods."

"Really," he responded. "I'd like to see some of your work. When can you show me your portfolio?"

"It's a bit difficult to pour beer and show pictures at the same time, but I'll let you see some if you're really interested."

"Perhaps I'll hire you if I ever need your services."

"What do you do?" she asked.

"I'm a freelance writer for magazines. I write travel articles. Have you read anything by Jack Weston?"

"Probably not. I don't often read travel magazines. Which ones publish your work?"

"I mostly write for *Western Trails Magazine*."

"Sorry," she smiled. "Perhaps you can bring in your portfolio, and I'll examine your stories," she quipped.

"Touché," Jack grinned.

"You get paid to travel, write stories about places and encourage people to go — sort of a Rick Steves or Arthur Frommer, right?"

"Exactly, but my stories focus on out-of-the-way locations. It's fun and keeps me from getting into trouble."

"Doesn't your wife or girlfriend mind when you're on the road?"

"No problem. I'm single and have no responsibilities … other than taking care of these guys."

"Except for that, it sounds exciting. If you need pictures of those places, let me know. I'll go along as your photographer."

"We can become partners after we validate each other's credentials," he said. They both smiled.

"In the meantime, if you ever want someplace to hang out, come back here. Nanette brings in a band every weekend. Entertainment coupled with dinner specials. We have a blast."

"I'll keep it in mind."

Chapter Four

Jo Ellen Field had been best friends with Taylor Simmons since elementary school. They shared intimate secrets, spent most of their time together and bonded for life. Jo Ellen and Taylor ran on the same cross-country track team, shared clothes and doubled-dated.

When Taylor earned enough money to live on her own, she and Jo Ellen became roommates. They moved into a condo near Jo Ellen's school, a place close enough to Loop 101 to give Taylor quick access to jobs in Phoenix. Jo Ellen enrolled in Midwestern University's dental hygienist program and supported herself with a part-time job at Zendejas Grill.

She introduced Taylor to Jack on a whim and delighted in how romance exploded after their first meeting. Now, however, sadness stalked her waking hours. Devastated by Taylor's untimely death, Jo Ellen had only fond memories to soothe a troubled heart. One of those memories included how she had set up the meeting between Taylor and Jack.

#####

Jo Ellen, an exuberant brunette with an appealing figure, attracted many men with her bouncy hair, long legs and sharp wit. All were fascinated with her ability to act like one of the guys. Her own special talent never forced Jo Ellen to compete with Taylor.

Whenever the golfing buddies came into Zendejas, Jo Ellen's humor always challenged them. Pete, a committed macho man, constantly put a move on her. To everyone's amusement, Jo Ellen rebuffed him so effectively he became the butt of constant jokes. Jo Ellen toyed with his bravado and kept patrons laughing, mostly at Pete's expense.

"You've probably never been out with a man like me," Pete suggested one afternoon.

"No, you're right," Jo Ellen smiled. "My momma warned me about older men like you."

"But, times have changed, and you're all grown up."

"I know, but you haven't and probably never will."

Michelle offered the wounded male another draft and a sympathetic pat on the arm.

Pete pursued another path. "What kind of a man interests you, Jo Ellen?"

"Tough and toned. I'm a runner and like to stay in shape. Can you run five miles a day?"

"No, but I shoot in the low seventies on the golf course and bowl a mean game."

"Right," Jo Ellen said. "You drive an electric cart around a golf course, step off to swing a club seventy times, while you drink beer and tell off-colored jokes. It's the perfect kind of activity to keep you fit."

"Hey, I burn a lot of calories with my practice swings." retorted the faux athlete.

"And, when did bowling become an official athletic sport?"

"Come on, cut it out," Pete protested. It takes a lot of skill to knock down all those pins with consistency. I usually average around two-fifty a game,"

"I've been to a few bowling alleys in my day," Jo Ellen continued. "It doesn't take skill to knock back a beer every frame. It keeps your gut nice and firm. Don't you fellas down a beer every time you stay out of the gutter?"

"No, no, only the fifth frame — designated as the official beer frame, low man buys."

"The fifth frame really needs to be called the spare tire bonus," she smiled, patting Pete on his protruding stomach. Everyone laughed.

"If you want a real workout," Jo Ellen said, "why don't you join me and my roommate on a morning run? Perspiration flows, muscles burn and you feel invigorated, lean and mean."

"I don't ever want to get as mean as you," Pete said. "You hurt my feelings. I can't even order a beer …."

Michelle sensed his not-so-subtle request and placed another cold one in front of the drooping man. "Here, Pete, this should pick up your spirits."

"How far do you and your roommate run?" Jack asked.

"About five miles or so. We live in the neighborhood and run on the Thunderbird trails. If you think I'm in good shape, you should meet Taylor. She's one toned chick."

"Why don't you bring her in and let my charms impress her?" Pete said.

"Because she has too much class for your lecherous talk and out-of-shape body," Jo Ellen sneered. "I think she'd be more attracted to an intelligent fellow like Jack. Good mind, handsome and a fit body."

"Thanks for the compliment, but I'm not looking for a girlfriend," said Jack.

"Correction, you haven't found the right woman yet," said Michelle.

"Maybe not, but in the meantime, I'm content with my three friends here … of course, with one exception," hitting Pete on the arm.

"I think we need to invite Taylor to meet us for a beer some afternoon," Jo Ellen suggested.

"Perhaps we do, perhaps we do," responded Michelle.

#####

Taylor Simmons was born gorgeous. Immediately after her delivery, nurses and doctors surrounded the basinet and gazed at her delicate features. All through childhood, people stopped her parents to marvel at the beautiful child. Deep green eyes, cupid lips and dimpled cheeks drew admiring looks from everyone. By the time Taylor entered grade school, she displayed a refined grace and personality complimenting her beauty.

In high school, Taylor's striking features intimidated most males her own age but always turned the admiring heads of adults. Her five-foot-ten-inch willowy body glided when she walked and caused her thick brown hair to bounce in an alluring way. Unaffected by her own beauty, Taylor exuded a friendly smile and made everyone feel comfortable in her presence.

After graduation, Taylor enrolled in modeling school, catapulting her into a high fashion career. Agents begged her to pose for magazines and photo shoots in the competitive markets of New York, Paris and Los Angeles, but she rejected these offers. Taylor remained dedicated to family and friends and stayed in the Phoenix valley. Her agent secured a contract with Macy's Department Store where she modeled their seasonal clothing line and appeared in the annual catalogue. She became a symbolic centerpiece for store events.

By the young age of twenty-one, Taylor had earned more than a hundred-thousand dollars and demonstrated maturity beyond her years. She asked her parents to invest the money and set up a fund to pay her a monthly allowance. Fame and fortune had little impact on her personal values.

On the Saturday she met Jack, she enjoyed a break from modeling and accepted Jo Ellen's invitation to join her for a drink at Zendejas. Jo Ellen told her about a group of funny guys who usually became the afternoon's entertainment. Jo Ellen remembered Taylor smiled and said she would like to participate in the rare diversion from her hectic schedule.

Chapter Five

The four golfers, now regulars at Zendejas, arrived for happy hour late Saturday afternoon. They spotted Jo Ellen and Michelle surrounding a woman whose beauty caused Jack to stop speaking in midsentence. He could only stare at her lovely features. Momentarily stunned, Jack slowly recovered and extended a hand toward the striking female. Everyone felt the instant electricity.

"Hello, my name is Jack Weston. Excuse me for being so bold, but you are the most beautiful woman I have ever seen in my life."

Accustomed to such compliments, she smiled, ignored the come on and extended her hand to him. "Well, thank you, my name is Taylor Simmons."

"Makes a great first impression, doesn't she?" Jo Ellen interrupted.

"Oh my," the only words Jack could muster as he looked at her in awe.

"I can see why Jo Ellen keeps you a hidden secret," Pete said.

Not distracted by Pete's comment, Jack said, "I'm sorry, Taylor. I usually don't react this way when I first meet someone, but you caught me off-guard."

"I'm flattered, Jack. No need to apologize," she smiled.

"Um … this may sound trite, and I'm not trying to hit on you, but can I buy you a drink?" he asked.

"Absolutely," she responded. "Michelle, please mix a cosmopolitan, and I'll run it off tomorrow."

"This event calls for a more upscale drink for me, too. Michelle, please make a Rusty Nail," Jack said and placed a twenty-dollar bill on the bar.

Pete didn't permit the obvious to go unnoticed. "Michelle, get your camera. We need to capture the premier episode of this steamy soap opera." Jo Ellen and the others swatted Pete on his head and shoulders to shut him up.

"Knock it off, Pete!" Michelle yelled. "Can't you see you're interrupting a special moment here?"

"I get it, I get it," Pete pleaded.

Ignoring the frivolity, Jack leaned close to Taylor and whispered, "You know they're right. This is a special moment. At least I feel it, do you?"

"Yes, Jack, I feel the same energy. But, this isn't the most convenient time, especially with an audience. Here's my card. Why don't you call, and let's find some alone time to talk."

Michelle observed the exchange but said nothing. Jack's eye caught Michelle's glance as she nodded with an approving smile.

The evening continued with conversation, laughter, more drinks and war stories about Jack. The group had already heard all of them, but felt compelled to share Jack's adventures with Taylor. She laughed at every tale, much to the delight of each storyteller. The festive mood became a celebration of Jack and Taylor's new connection. Jack had met someone who captured his heart, and they enjoyed watching Taylor and Jack make an instant connection.

The group created a spontaneous rooting section for Jack. The three women exchanged knowing looks and smiles throughout the evening. Everyone recognized the fact the women did not orchestrate a collective bathroom break. In most social circles, this event becomes the *deal breaker* for every new couple. Sequestered behind powder room doors, woman share their judgment and offer advice about why the union can't and won't work. This afternoon, however, the feminine judges only offered approval.

Taylor left the party first, informing everyone she had a photo shoot in the morning. Jack walked her to the parking lot, gave her a gentle hug goodbye and promised to call. When he returned, five sets of eyes greeted him, followed by unsolicited clapping and cheering.

Jack blushed, ordered another drink, threw up his hands and simply said, "What?"

Chapter Six

Like a brilliant comet streaking across the night sky, everyone talked about Jack and Taylor's spectacular romance. The two local personalities became a fixture at the valley's most prestigious social events. They made a stunning couple. Jack, a former Arizona State University basketball player, enjoyed the notoriety of being a favorite local athlete and well-known writer. Taylor's frequently photographed face and body brought her instant recognition as the Macy Girl. The couple attracted attention whenever they appeared together in public.

Spotted at a variety of sporting venues, Jack and Taylor's pictures graced the society pages of *The Arizona Republic* and *Phoenix Magazine*. Their love affair consumed people's attention. Once the paparazzi discovered the identity of the tall, slender model, they followed the couple with heightened interest. The notoriety enhanced Taylor's career, and she became an instant celebrity. In typical Taylor fashion, she handled the increased attention with modesty and charm.

#####

Jack once shared an intimate story with Phil, an anecdote to let him know how deeply they loved each other. Now the memory filled the man with sorrow.

After making love one evening, Jack and Taylor lay wrapped in each other's arms. Jack gazed at Taylor and said, "I have never been happier. Your love has filled an empty space in my life. I never felt such bliss."

"Jack, I'm so content. I love you so much." Taylor's hands caressed his face as she looked deep into his eyes.

"I'm in awe."

"Do you think some mystical force brought us together?" she asked, twirling the hairs on the back of his neck.

Jack pressed his head into her hand. "No, but I am grateful you and Jo Ellen stayed friends after high school." He smiled and kissed her forehead.

"Never doubt the power of love."

"I don't know how it happened, but I am connected to your spirit, your soul," Jack said.

Before leaving the house each morning, Taylor slipped into Jack's study and typed a poem or love note on his computer screen. Every message let Jack know how much she loved him and how mystical and eternal their love had become. Jack eagerly anticipated reading these messages before he started writing for the day. He told her they inspired his imagination.

To show his love in return, Jack filled the house with dozens of multi-colored roses. The sweet scent of these delicate blooms confirmed their passion and became the symbol of their union. Every Friday, Jack greeted Taylor with a carpet of soft rose petals beginning at their front door and ending in a cascade across their bed. "The softness of rose petals and their fragrance will always remind me of you," he confessed. "Even when I'm here alone, their scent helps me stay in touch with you."

"Jack, you're a silly romantic. I love being surrounded by roses and their heavenly bouquet." She smiled and pressed her body against him in a lingering hug. "I want you to remember this moment, darling, and savor our love forever."

#####

With Taylor in his life, Jack's writing revealed an intense passionate side, reminding readers of vivid chapters in a romance novel. Women waiting in line at the grocery stores grabbed copies of *Western Trails Magazine* and flipped to his stories. They wanted to experience Jack's sensuous descriptions. His words expressed the wonder of a world awash with a *joie de vive* — the ecstasy of love the couple experienced.

Phil thought about how happy people had been when the couple announced their marriage plans. Joaquin and Nanette hosted the engagement party at Zendejas Grill. The celebration filled the nightclub and spilled onto the outdoor patio. Fifty dozen roses, the symbol of the couple's union, adorned the room. Joaquin and Nanette hired a musical combo and prepared tasty appetizers for the occasion. The couple paid for the event and gave generous tips to the waitstaff and special gifts to Jo Ellen and Michelle for orchestrating their introduction.

Jack and Taylor offered Joaquin and Nanette a thousand dollars to release Michelle for the week before the wedding. Instead of shooting pictures on the wedding day, Jack and Taylor wanted their favorite bartender to take candid shots of them throughout the week. Michelle accepted a five thousand dollar donation and became the couple's official photographer. She enjoyed eavesdropping on their wedding preparations and saved everything for a digital record. Michelle took hundreds of pictures of the couple: shopping, playing, dancing, and relaxing at home — all capturing their intimacy and love.

The wedding and reception, held in the courtyard of the Marriott Hotel near Desert Valley, entertained three hundred guests, including parents, relatives and friends. Jack and Taylor hired three bands to perform throughout the day and provided an open bar for the revelers. Heralded as the social event of the year, newspapers and local magazines ran several articles detailing every aspect of the celebration.

To guarantee their privacy, Jack and Taylor purchased a house near the outskirts of Desert Valley in a remote area overlooking an expansive view of the desert. The multi-million-dollar mansion, originally built for an eastern businessman, had been on the market for a year. The couple swooped up the property, redecorated it to meet their needs, and turned the home into their private desert sanctuary.

Life settled into predictable patterns. Every morning, Taylor quietly slipped out of bed before sunrise to run the isolated roads in the area and enjoy the radiance of each sunrise. Jack, on the other hand, snuggled deep into their warm bed and slept an extra half-hour. Still groggy, he'd rise and prepare breakfast for her.

After breakfast, they'd shower and dress, unless Taylor had a photo shoot. Then, Jack would send her off with a kiss, replace the roses in the house and return to the love note she'd always leave on his computer screen. Life evolved into a beautiful circle until the day of Jack's great agony.

#####

The memory of their joy made Phil's heart sink. He glanced again at the crumpled form of his writer. Unaccustomed to showing outward signs of emotion, he quickly wiped a stray tear from his cheek.

Chapter Seven

Jack stirred in his seat. Almost sober now, the memory of the fateful morning invaded his brain. It had become embossed on his mind, a permanent weight he carried every waking moment. The solace of alcohol let him temporarily forget grief, but Phil's intervention jarred opened the tragedy once again.

That cool February morning began like most others. Jack awoke, looked at the clock and realized he had overslept. He hurriedly got out of bed, dressed and raced into the kitchen to start the coffee and cut vegetables for Taylor's favorite vegetarian three-egg omelet. She loved a big breakfast and had a ravenous appetite after her five-mile run. Jack opened the newspaper, poured a cup of coffee and waited for his gazelle-like sprinter to return. She took care of her body, and even though he disliked running, Jack tried to get to the gym three times a week to work out. He wanted to stay in shape for the love of his life.

Before going to bed the night before, Taylor told Jack her photo shoot would last most of the day, and she wouldn't have time for lunch. Her cameraman promised to bring in pizza, but Taylor never liked stuffing herself with carbohydrates, especially when she modeled clothes. They made plans to meet for dinner at Zendejas around 7 p.m. and catch up with the day's events before coming home for their evening walk in the desert.

The morning grew late, even for Taylor. Jack stopped reading the newspaper and squeezed fresh orange juice. He popped two slices of wheat bread in the toaster, beat the eggs into a frothy mixture, added some white cheese and lightly grilled the vegetables. With everything ready, he grabbed a second cup of coffee and anticipated she'd burst through the kitchen door at any second. Like other days when she worked, he'd give her a warm hug and kiss before she trotted off to take a quick shower, giving him the opportunity to put all of the breakfast ingredients together. Jack had become familiar with her daily pattern. By the time she wrapped her hair in a towel, he'd be ready to greet his love with a fresh rose, a kiss and then a gourmet breakfast.

At 7:30 though, Jack began to worry. Sometimes Taylor felt energized and turned a five-mile run into ten. But when it happened, her perspiration-drenched body rushed through the door, and with an enthusiastic look, she'd beg him to forgive her tardiness. At such times, Taylor wrapped her arms around Jack and showered him with kisses to let him know she loved and appreciated his patience. She enjoyed sharing her physical accomplishments with him. Although Jack anticipated such a celebratory entrance, he worried whenever she broke her normal pattern.

Today, especially with a photo shoot scheduled for midmorning, it would be unlike Taylor to run the extra miles. Jack paced the kitchen floor.

By 8:00, Jack grabbed his car keys and headed out the door. Something had gone wrong. He sensed it. *She had never been this late before. Perhaps she turned an ankle or stepped on a rattlesnake.* Fear lacks words and creates irrational images.

Where would she run this morning? He took the first gravel road to the south and followed it to an asphalt highway leading to Desert Valley. *No,* he thought, *she doesn't like running along paved roads.* Jack located another gravel road and headed north toward their home. Five miles turned into ten and still no sign of her. Jack spotted a third road she ran from time to time and traced its jagged path into the desert. Still, no sign of his love.

Jack turned down another gravel road paralleled to the one he had just left, stopped his car, got out and called her name. As he climbed back into his vehicle, his eye caught sight of several turkey vultures circling less than a mile away. Panic siezed him. He gunned the engine and showered the area in a cloud of dust and rocks.

Perhaps she's really hurt or unconscious, he thought. *Perhaps she's bleeding and has no way to contact me.* "I'm on my way, love," he shouted into the windshield as if she could hear his voice. *If she fell and broke a bone, I'll need to rush her to the hospital.* He opened his cell phone and discovered this remote area had no reception. He raced along the road with no caution for his own safety. The car hit loose gravel and caused it to fishtail several times. The road forced him to overcompensate to retain control. The drive to the circling birds took a matter of minutes, but it seemed much longer to the fearful man.

The car swerved into a sharp curve, almost out of control. Surprised by the unexpected sight, Jack slammed on the brakes and steered the vehicle toward the ditch to avoid hitting the crumpled body in the center of the road. "Oh, god, it's her!" The car barely missed the victim and it slid sideways into the shallow drainage ditch just beyond. Jack jumped out and ran back, shouting, "Taylor! Taylor! Taylor! Oh, no, no, it can't be!"

Taylor lay in the road on her back, eyes open. The serene look on her beautiful face made it appear as if she had laid down to rest. Jack knelt at her side. He touched her cold body, nudged it, and then let out a wail, "Oh, no, god, why Taylor? Why did you take her from me?" Within seconds, his trauma moved to anger and then rage. Then, a feeling of helplessness settled into the depths of his mind. He gently closed Taylor's eyes, embraced her limp body and wept. Jack stood up and carried her lifeless frame in his arms. He aimlessly walked around and kicked at the dirt. He wept with uncontrollable pain and whispered, "Wake up, Taylor, please wake up."

The reality of her death descended and crushed the remnants of hope in his soul. Almost in a daze, he placed her body back in the roadway and released gut-wrenching screams. Birds that once led Jack to her body, now scattered in flight. Angrily, he kicked at the loose gravel and gouged huge divots in the road. Jack yelled, "Please, anybody, please help me." His cry, swallowed by the emptiness of the desert, went unanswered.

Jack picked up Taylor's body and placed her in the front seat of his car. In a daze, he fastened her seat belt and steered his vehicle toward home. He touched her arm in hopes she'd wake up and smile at him — this all being a bad dream. Numbed to reason, Jack carried her limp body into the house, laid it on the living room sofa and tucked her under a blanket. He left her head exposed. *Perhaps she'll wake up after a short nap.* At 9 a.m., he acquiesced and surrendered to reality. He called the Desert Valley Police Department.

The rest of the morning became a blur as police officers followed the paramedics. A forensic team investigated the crime scene and found it difficult to process evidence due to Jack's frenetic activity. The area had been contaminated, and any clues left by the hit-and-run driver were destroyed. The afternoon brought the media, followed by a host of friends and family, all trying to console the devastated man.

The emotional shock caused Jack to withdraw into the depths of his mind and shut out everything. He fell into a tortured, self-imposed isolation. Anguish and pain consumed him. Taylor, his love and soul mate of two years, had been taken from him. He sat at the kitchen table, tortured by grief. No words of consolation, sympathy or solace mattered. Whenever someone tried to help, Jack responded with one word, "Why?"

Chapter Eight

Jack demanded to supervise every detail and required absolute perfection. With head bowed, he sat alone and concentrated on the silence before others arrived. Tears flowed in unchecked rivulets and dropped with abandon on his pressed trousers. Grief respects no boundaries, and he despised showing such deep emotion in front of people. He longed to disappear, to become invisible, and to let the weight of Taylor's loss devour him.

He hated the public invasion of his space — their space, and gave specific instructions to leave three empty rows behind him. He chose to be alone. If people needed closure, he wanted no part of their requirements. How could he ever say goodbye to Taylor?

Michelle and Jo Ellen walked up the steps to the church. Each carried a dozen burgundy roses.

Tom's moist eyes reflected his sadness. "Hi," Tom said with a deep sigh.

Michelle gave him a quick hug and asked, "How are you doing?"

"Okay," he responded, taking in an uneven breath.

"How's Jack?" Jo Ellen asked.

"Completely lost — hasn't spoken all day." Tom looked at the roses and added, "I'm sorry. I'll have to take those."

"Why?" asked Jo Ellen.

"Taylor loved roses," Michelle said.

"Jack made it clear — absolutely no roses today. Not at the funeral or the cemetery. Something about roses symbolized their love. Now the sight and scent tortures him."

"Oh, god, Tom. It doesn't sound good. What can we do to help?" Jo Ellen asked.

"He wants to end this charade and be left alone. Please honor his request," Tom said.

Shaking their heads, Michelle and Jo Ellen deposited the flowers in a container by Tom's side and went into the church. The tragedy evoked more sadness, and sounds of whimpering and sniffling filled the sanctuary. For Jack, the church memorial droned on in an endless stream of nonsense, an exercise in absurdity. *How can life be honored with a celebration of death?*

At the end of the service, Pete escorted Jack to a waiting limousine. The ride to the cemetery became a blur of light as his attention remained riveted on the hearse carrying her remains. More words at the cemetery, followed by hugs failed to register with Jack. Finally, the archaic public ritual came to an end.

Back home and alone, Jack succumbed to total exhaustion. He poured a tall glass of scotch … then another … and a third. Finally, fatigue and alcohol subdued his pain and pushed him into a disturbed sleep. Overwhelmed with gut-wrenching grief, Jack began drinking when the sun rose and continued throughout the day until he fell into another stupor. For the next three months, he paused only for an occasional pizza delivery or to heat up a frozen meal or a can of food. Alcohol became his daily anesthetic.

Jack's depression smothered hope of recovery or a return to anything normal. Unable to accept Taylor's death, a veil of slumber and booze disengaged him from the world. Despair and denial became Jack's housemates — constant companions supporting his agony. Visions of Taylor's limp, lifeless body stalked him. Jack felt emotionally impotent and welcomed his own demise. Even though excessive amounts of scotch, bourbon and gin take years to kill a human, Jack chose this method to slowly suffer through his pain until death would finally embrace his pathetic body. Weeks turned into months, and finally the arrival of Phillip shook the reluctant man back to life.

Chapter Nine

A small café in downtown Desert Valley beckoned Phillip's attention. He shook away the memories of the past and pulled into an empty space in front of the restaurant. He roused Jack and guided him to a table. He ordered eggs, pancakes and a pot of coffee for them. When the food arrived, Jack ravenously consumed everything in sight and Phil ordered an additional side of sausage, bacon and grits. Jack's newly awakened appetite responded to long-neglected physical needs.

Phillip watched Jack slowly step back from the abyss of self-destruction, and he silently congratulated himself. His intervention had been perfectly timed. He watched as Jack, finally satisfied, patted his stomach, heaved a deep sigh and drifted back into his solemn isolation.

Phillip studied Jack and reflected on his unaccustomed role as "lifesaver." His visit seemed out of character. He had worked his way up the corporate ladder for twenty years and developed the reputation of being a no-nonsense, hard-driving boss. Consistency and perfection marked his business life. When staff members couldn't meet his expectations, he fired them with no fanfare or second chance. But, Jack, ah, Jack had been different. Earlier this morning, Phil intended to fire him as well, but the sight of his friend's condition made him discard the thought.

He flashed back to his own childhood and recalled an incident that broke his heart and jaded his perspective on life. Phil remembered how he found a small bird with a broken wing. The bird's pathetic peeping encouraged him to cuddle the wounded creature and take it to his father. *If anyone could help,* the eight-year-old Phillip thought, *it's got to be my dad.* The optimistic child revealed the injured creature safely cradled in his hands, and his pensive father took the bird to the garage. Without a word, the older man grabbed a hammer, killed the bird and threw the feathered victim into the garbage can. The man looked down at his shocked son and said, "In nature and life, you can't waste time on cripples. If they can't do what God intended, they're not worth saving."

The horror of this life lesson turned Phillip into a cold, unemotional boss, an outer shell he retained until Jack's buoyant articles touched his heart. His professional relationship with the young writer turned into a deep friendship. Now, Phil sat in an isolated restaurant in a remote desert town. This time, Phillip chose to ignore his father's philosophy and put his hammer away. He chose to save this wounded bird.

"Since I have your undivided attention, are you ready to make the choice to live or die?" the editor asked.

Placing his elbows on the table and balancing his head in his hands, Jack responded in quiet tones. "I don't have a clue. There's nothing to live for. Taylor was my life. Without her, I'm lost."

"Jack, there are many reasons to stay alive. You need to help catch the bastard who did this, and you need to keep writing. Your soul has been trampled by an incredible loss, but your writing will give you an outlet, a voice to help you heal. Write about your pain."

Jack stared at the wall behind Phillip's head. He didn't hear the logic. The words made no sense to the unfocused man. Phil stopped talking as Jack exhaled and turned away. Slowly, his eyes returned to the editor.

"Phil, I don't have a voice left inside me to write. I can't get past the pain. I still see her body lying in the road ... so lifeless."

"Look, Jack," shouted Phil. He grabbed the writer's arms and pinned them to the table. "I don't know why these things happen. I'm not a religious man, but I *do* know Taylor's death shouldn't end your life, too. If you pick up the pieces, dig down deep and find yourself, you'll become a stronger person. Someday you'll find peace. C'mon, man, you've got to snap out of it!"

"I don't know where to start. How do I glue my life back together?"

"First, my friend, you've got to stop this excessive drinking. You can't drown yourself in booze. Then, you need to seek help from a professional grief counselor." Reaching into his pocket, Phil pulled out the business card of a psychiatrist he knew in the valley. "Here, call him now and set up an appointment."

"I don't know."

"Me neither, but damn it, once you clear the booze out of your brain, you'll start thinking straight again. If you hold onto this kind of shit, it will only kill you. The shrink may help you find a way to deal with this."

Phillip nagged Jack until he finally took out his cell phone, dialed the number and scheduled an appointment with Dr. Joseph Aberdeen. The renowned grief therapist had an excellent reputation for successfully treating emotionally troubled survivors of unexpected tragedy.

#####

During the next five months, the sessions with Dr. Aberdeen slowly helped Jack make sense out of his life. At one appointment in October, Dr. Aberdeen offered him a glimmer of hope to accelerate his progress.

"Tell me about your week, Jack."

"I'm sleeping much better now. I'm exercising, playing golf, although still alone, and eating a couple meals a day."

"Sounds good. Have you been able to write anything?"

"Not much. I start, but every time I sit in front of my computer I see Taylor in the road, and cry. When I can write anything, it's shit — pabulum Phil has to hide as a sidebar."

"Does crying make you feel better?"

Jack pondered the question. "No, but it helps relieve the total helplessness I feel about my inability to save her. If I had only been out there sooner; if I would have followed my instincts and acted on them, I could have …."

"Stop it, Jack. It's time to replace despair and vulnerability with something more tangible."

Dr. Aberdeen handed Jack a triangular chart with emotions listed on it from top to bottom.

Surprised by the psychiatrist's tactical change, Jack asked, "What do you mean by tangible?"

"Do you see the emotional words listed on the top of the chart?"

"Yeah, what about them?"

"Joy, love, freedom, passion, eagerness and optimism — all feelings expressed by a few well-adjusted people. These individuals enjoy lives filled with happiness."

"None of those words describe me, Doc."

"I know, but it used to describe your life with Taylor, didn't it?"

Jack tensed, "What's your point?"

"Move to the middle of the triangle. Words like boredom, pessimism, frustration, doubt and worry describe what many people who walk around the planet feel like every day. It's considered normal behavior."

Following the chart to the bottom of the page, Jack said, "These words down here describe me the best, Doc." He read aloud: "guilt, depression and despair. That's me, where I'm at — right at the bottom."

"I agree. Those are the feelings that paralyze your emotions," Aberdeen said. "However, there's hope. Take a look at the words on the chart just above them."

"Anger, hate, revenge — so what?" Jack asked.

"My approach may seem a bit unorthodox, but I want you to stop wallowing in the feelings listed at the bottom of the chart and move to the next level. I want you to get angry, feel hate and, perhaps, seek revenge."

"What kind of a shrink are you, anyway?"

"Look, Jack, feelings of anger are also not healthy, but at least those emotions will get you back on your feet again. You need to take charge of what you feel. It's the key to helping you get better."

Jack studied the words and said nothing.

"For the past several sessions, you've only talked about your powerlessness, guilt and insecurity."

"So? It's where I am. How I feel," Jack said.

"I know, but the road to emotional stability requires you to move your emotional vibrations up to the next level. Concentrate on how you feel about the guy who killed Taylor. Stop talking about how bad *you* feel. Tell me how you feel about him."

"I want to kill the asshole. I want to rip out his heart. I want to cut out his insides and make him die a slow, painful death."

"Good. You get my point," the psychiatrist said. "I want you to have a reason to stop feeling sorry for yourself. Leave your pity party and go after revenge."

"Isn't revenge pretty negative, Doc?"

"In this case, you need to jump-start your emotions, feel some rage, hate, anger. You shouldn't stay there for long, but it may be necessary to feel something different instead of grief or helplessness. We'll worry about moving up the chart as things get better."

Dr. Aberdeen paused to let his words seep into Jack's brain, giving his patient time to analyze the implications. Aberdeen removed his glasses and waited until Jack's eyes met his.

"Have you heard anything from the police investigation yet?"

"Nothing. They already labeled it a cold case: no leads, no clues and no witnesses. They've given up."

"How does it make you feel, Jack?"

"Helpless. Oh, I see where you're going. I accept being a victim and live with the emotions at the bottom of the chart."

"Correct. Only you have the power to change your feelings, Jack."

"I know, but what can I do?"

"Let me make a suggestion. I have a friend, a private detective named Sarah McShay. Why don't you hire her, an independent third party, to conduct a preliminary investigation for you? If her analysis confirms the police report, you can trust the authorities have done everything possible. However, if Sarah uncovers new clues, it may motivate you to get involved and, more importantly, feel *angry* about her death."

"You're right, Doc. I can either hire Detective McShay or swallow cyanide. But, if she can offer another approach, I'll get pissed off enough and go after the killer myself." He paused and smiled, "Besides, I'm getting tired of making the monthly payments on your Lexus. No offense, Doc, but you get paid big bucks to listen to my incoherent chatter."

The two men laughed, shook hands and ended the session. Jack changed his appointments to meet with Dr. Aberdeen only once a month. He hired Sarah McShay and hoped for the best.

Chapter Ten

The small Glendale office smelled stale and musty. Piles of papers and an unfinished lunch sat in the middle of her desk attracting a cluster of flies. The clutter assaulted his senses, and he wrinkled up his nose. Disheveled file folders occupied the remaining space. A huge, boxy computer covered with dust, dirt, fingerprints and food stains crowded the remainder of the desktop. It looked as if she had not touched her link with modern technology in months, and he wondered if the detective had the skills to do the job. The office reminded Jack of his current writing area. A month ago, he hired Sarah over the phone and had no idea she was such a novice, fly-by-night investigator.

Did Dr. Aberdeen owe her a favor or was she a relative? I've stepped back into one of those 1940s dingy, black-and-white P.I. offices like the one in the Maltese Falcon. At any moment, Humphrey Bogart will step into a scene and the director will yell "cut" from behind some hidden camera. He snickered as he stared across the desk at a boyish-looking Sarah McShay.

All of twenty-six, clothes hung on her body as if thrown together by convenience rather than style. She wore loose-fitting slacks and a thick-ribbed sweater, obscuring any hint of substantial breasts. Lack of makeup told Jack she rejected traditional female trappings. *Hmm, she's an independent woman, most likely single or possibly a lesbian.*

Sarah's plain features, however, offered a natural, pleasant appearance. Strangely, the look aided her profession because she could easily slip in and out of social settings without drawing attention to herself. Jack reasoned a private detective needed such a nondescript image to move about unnoticed.

The P.I.'s rumpled appearance accentuated her short, curly brown hair, exercising a will of its own. Sarah's habit of brushing a hand through a tussle of hair dangling over the front of her face drew Jack's attention. Her continuous fixation with the clump of rebellious locks suggested she suffered from a nervous disorder. Jack also had difficulty following her frenetic speech pattern, spit out like rapid gunfire. The woman's ideas ricocheted to and fro, much ahead of her thinking.

Regardless of these distractions, Sarah had a refreshing manner. The woman didn't inspire confidence, but her mischievous eyes and pleasant smile invited his trust. She wasn't the stereotype femme fatale he associated with a mystery classic. But, in spite of the eccentric behaviors, her enthusiasm for the case attracted him.

She frequently shifted her body in the chair, and its loud squeaking provided a constant testimony to the struggle to keep her unbounded energy in check. Whenever Sarah made a point, she'd balance her hands on the arms of the chair, lift her body and swing her legs underneath her frame. Another annoying habit, but Jack ignored this additional behavior and listened to Sarah reveal the details of her initial investigation.

"Here's another interesting quandary," she said, swinging her legs out from under her body, causing the chair to groan. "The autopsy report showed marks on the back of her legs indicating she was hit from behind, below her knees, and never saw or heard the car coming. Scrapes on the bottom of her running shoes indicate the sudden impact sent her flying backwards."

"I know Taylor liked to listen to music when she ran. It helped her set the pace. I now remember hearing her iPod still playing when I found her body. I forgot about that."

"The autopsy also showed she flipped over the hood of the car at an angle and hit the back of her head on the gravel road. It's what killed her, Jack, not the car. A blunt trauma to the head would have given her … perhaps, fifteen to twenty seconds of life before she lost consciousness and died. Basically, the ground paralyzed her body, and she felt no pain before death occurred."

"Nobody told me," Jack said, attempting to hold back tears. "It frightened me to think she lay in the road for hours, slowly dying, and I wasn't there to save her."

"Rest assured, you could do nothing to help her. But, here's part of the unsolved mystery," she said, trying unsuccessfully to straightened the fluff of hair, again.

Jack leaned forward.

"She had a nasty scrape, a contusion on her left shoulder with some unknown pieces of glass embedded in it. Forensics said it came from glass in the gravel road, but they couldn't tell for sure."

"What does it mean?" asked Jack.

"Don't know, but the forensics report indicated it had no impact on the case."

"I heard they had nothing more to go on," responded Jack.

"Something seems strange about the investigation," said Sarah. "They closed the case too quickly. These things usually take more time."

"Sarah, are you telling me the police have totally given up?"

"Looks that way, but you can't jump to conclusions." Sarah tried to adjust her hair again and failed. "Call it female intuition, but my gut says there's more. I just can't figure it out."

"What do we do now?"

"Nothing much," added a nonchalant Sarah. "It's your call, mister. Let me know what you want from me. I'll put your file right here on my desk so it stays fresh in my mind."

Jack watched the woman add Taylor's file to the six-inch stack of stuffed manila folders clinging precariously to the edge of her desk. If the moment wasn't so serious, he would have laughed at her antics and archaic filing system. However, he suppressed the thought and looked at her with a blank stare.

"I'm officially off the clock and will send you my bill. But if you get something new, call me, and I'll check it out."

Jack walked down a flight of stairs and stepped into the fresh morning air. He paused and reflected on his encounter with the eccentric detective. His initial appraisal of Sarah prevented an understanding of the qualities lying under the surface of her idiosyncratic façade. However, in time, her presence would be essential. For the moment, he remained unconvinced his expense produced any tangible results.

Frustrated, he stood by his car door and pondered his next move. He reached in his pocket and pulled out a pack of Camels. With Dr. Aberdeen's approval, he replaced drinking with smoking, a strategy to remain rational and deal with his frustrations. He lit a cigarette and inhaled deeply.

Jack exhaled and became conscious of a different emotion stirring in his gut. For the first time in months, Jack felt anger. Sarah had planted the seed. *Why can't the police do something about the hit-and-run? Desert Valley isn't a big town. People talk about things like this all the time. Surely, someone would give it up. I hate their lack of commitment.* He slammed his foot against his car door and left a visible dent as a testament to his frustration.

The private eye observed him from her second-story window. *He's one frustrated guy,* she thought. *I'm not sure he'll make it.*

Chapter Eleven

Sarah observed Jack's actions to assess the unspoken workings of his mind under pressure. Like the rest of her life, Jack's dilemma represented another puzzle to understand. She loved solving mysteries, a trait she learned from her parents. Sarah's mother worked crosswords every day and always laid out a three-thousand-piece jigsaw puzzle on a card table in the dining room. Anyone who passed felt compelled to study the scattered picture and try to fit in at least one piece.

Her father, Richard, loved reading murder mysteries and delighted in sharing obtuse clues with his precocious daughter. He often challenged Sarah to discover the culprit in each "whodunit" before the book ended.

"Sarah," he'd say, "if the killer in my novel leaves a matchbook at the scene of the crime, how would you track him down?"

"Easy one, Dad. I'd check for fingerprints, and if I came up with nothing, I'd go to the bar or restaurant on the cover to see if they could make a connection between the victim and the killer's identity."

"Nice start," he'd say. "Now keep thinking. I'll tell you how the detective in the book figures it out."

Sarah's father also loved welding. On trash day, he and Sarah scoured the neighborhood looking for odd pieces of metal for his latest lawn decoration. Richard, a gifted "metal Picasso" waiting to be discovered, never achieved such fame. He taught Sarah how to use an arc-welder and emphasized the importance of creativity to solve the mysteries of perception.

"Dad, how do you know what you're making?" Sarah once asked, holding two uneven pieces of metal for her father to weld.

"I concentrate on my intuition. The metal speaks to me and shows me where it wants to go."

"How does the metal speak to you?"

"Sarah, everything in the universe is alive. Every particle has a vibrational energy. Use your senses — trust your feelings to learn what each object tells you. Listen and observe to understand. It will help you solve many mysteries in life."

Adored as a child, Sarah relished being spoiled. Her inquisitive nature and proclivity to challenge authority, especially at school, thrilled her father. Sarah's parents often attended disciplinary conferences hosted by irritated teachers or the school principal. When revelations of her shenanigans became known, her parents appropriately reprimanded her in public. In private, however, the couple praised her audacity and encouraged Sarah to discover what motivated people.

"Why do you think we had to attend your conference today?" Sarah's father once asked.

"Because I did something wrong?"

"Your behavior didn't require a parent conference. They should have handled it at school."

"Then, Daddy, why did they ask you to come in today?"

"It's a mystery for you to figure out, dear. You tell me."

"I think I embarrassed them, and they had to punish me in front of you."

"Why didn't they punish you at school?"

"Maybe, because they were frustrated and needed to tell on me, like we're all little kids or something."

"Pretty good, dear, but you need to learn that power is the secret. They have the authority to make the rules at school, but when someone challenges their power or discovers how to sabotage policy, they panic and need parental support. Insecure people always look for others to justify their actions."

"Kids like me never stand a chance, do we?"

"Remember who you challenge before doing anything stupid."

"I will, Daddy. I will."

"And don't take crap from anyone. You know as much as they do."

Growing up, Sarah played the tomboy and shunned prissy-looking clothes and the expected feminine manners. Dressed in blue jeans and plaid shirts, Sarah spent most of her time playing in the dirt and enjoyed an ability to wrestle and whip every boy in the neighborhood.

In high school, she showed few female interests. She played tackle football with the guys and mocked the cheerleaders. Sarah refused to participate in choir and got dropped from home economics after starting a kitchen fire. This rugged approach to life isolated her from traditional social circles but endeared her to a more streetwise group. In time, Sarah dropped out.

"I've decided to quit school," she announced one night at dinner.

"But, darling, you only have one more year before earning a diploma," her mother pleaded.

"The traditional high school isn't working for me. I can't stand the boredom."

"What other choices do you have?" her father asked.

Given permission to think for herself, Sarah spoke her favorite phrase, *"Okay, okay, here's the plan,"* a signature statement she'd use throughout adult life. "I'll enroll in the district's alternative school, complete my GED, move on to junior college and get trained to do something I like."

"Sounds like you've got it figured out. Nothing more to say, except go for it," her proud father responded.

"Yeah, I'm never going to get brainwashed again by small egos that make stupid rules to control my life. I promise."

Giving up on formal schooling, Sarah enrolled in the Phoenix Law Enforcement Academy — a path to an action-oriented profession. Sarah's athletic, wiry body and assertive attitude positioned her to become a successful candidate for the Phoenix police force. She developed into a model officer, earned the respect of her peers and moved up within the department.

Sarah's conflict with the police force began when her favorite captain retired, replaced by a sexist, ego-centered militarist who believed women police officers were inferior to men. Under his command, the captain created policies and encouraged female officers to quit or opt for transfers to desk jobs.

Her defiant personality immediately clashed with the captain's leadership style and led to an eventual showdown. Conflicts escalated with every new order or policy change.

She reverted to her high school days, forgot the lessons she previous learned about challenging power and publically mocked his decisions. Her actions fomented discontent among her peers. The squad room became a battleground — a test of egos — a contest Sarah could never win. Her rapier wit constantly embarrassed the arrogant captain and entertained her attentive peers. In short time, these exchanges became grounds for insubordination. After several verbal and written reprimands, the captain designed an improvement plan Sarah could never hope to fulfill. Rather than being fired, she decided to quit the force and become an independent private eye. Now Jack Weston's case promised to test her skills, patience and intuitive thinking. How could she help resolve his agony?

Part Two: The Voices

*Solitude is such a potential thing. We hear
voices in solitude, we never hear in the hurry
and turmoil of life; we receive counsels and
comforts, we get under no other condition.*

— *Amelia E. Barr*

Chapter Twelve

Thanksgiving and Christmas passed with no new clues to Taylor's death. Jack attempted to write, but the bland, mediocre articles he sent Phil reflected an exercise in futility. On the anniversary of Taylor's death, Jack sat all day in front of his blank computer screen. He couldn't find a voice to express in words. Finally, he made a phone call to push his life in a different direction.

"Phil, this is Jack. I need an assignment. I can't write in a place filled with so many memories. I have to get out of the valley and find a reason to discover new stories. I need to travel as far away from here as possible. Please, give me something to get me out of this goddamn place."

"No problem, Jack. I think you could write terrific stories again," said the editor. *At last, he's made a breakthrough. We'll get back to the quality articles he used to write,* Phil thought. "Give me a chance to meet with the editorial staff here in L.A., and I'll call you back with a new assignment."

"Oh, and, Phil, thanks for caring. Doc Aberdeen saved my life."

"It's what friends are for. I'll get right back as soon as I can." *A year is the longest I've ever given anyone,* he thought. *If you consider Jack's talent, my patience has got to pay off.*

Another week passed, and Jack started thinking about his immediate future. He had called Sarah on a regular basis, but nothing changed. Lack of new information and police inaction added to his growing discouragement.

His lack of power fomented more anger. Jack took his emotions out on the several cords of wood he diligently chopped for a fireplace he never used. Physically exhausted by his new activity, sleep came easier. Jack's emotional stability fluctuated between waves of sadness to deep-seeded hatred for the unknown driver who had left his love to die alone. Only revenge would satisfy the emotional chaos consuming his mind and body. Alive and almost functional as a human being again, he detested the feelings still gnawing at him every day. He looked forward to leaving town — something, anything to redirect his anger.

Phillip finally called. "Hello, Jack, sorry for the delay. The editorial staff would like you to spend a couple of weeks on the road to develop a series of stories."

"Terrific, what do they have in mind?"

"They want you to visit a few haunted hotels in the southwest and write several stories to get readers interested in exploring the phenomenon on their own."

"Easy enough."

"While you're at it, nose around and add a few sidebars about places to eat, shop and hang out for entertainment."

"Not a challenging assignment, but it will get me out of here."

"And, Jack, tell us where you'll be, and we'll pay for the room and meals in advance."

"What could be better? Thanks, Phil. I'm glad you stuck with me." Jack exhaled deeply.

"No problem, my friend. I've released an injured bird."

"What bird?"

"Oh, nothing. Just a childhood memory. I'll share it with you sometime." The editor hung up.

Jack searched his computer for haunted hotels of the southwest. *The Copper Queen in Bisbee is pretty famous for its ghosts,* he thought. *But, its story has been overdone. And less than a month ago, a reporter for The Arizona Republic wrote an intriguing story about the ghost tour at The San Marcos Hotel in Phoenix. He focused on Marilyn Monroe's ghost. Old stuff.*

He decided to write from a different perspective. His readers deserved to experience a unique adventure into the paranormal. People might enjoy reading about haunted hotels from the ghost's point of view.

Jack's thoughts drifted to Taylor. *This will be my first trip alone since I met her. I'm not sure how it will work without her by my side.*

"I'll pretend we'll do this together," he said aloud. "If Taylor and I wanted to leave the valley for a get-away weekend and add some spice to the trip, where would we go?" He searched the Internet again and selected places renowned for their romantic setting. He chose the Hassayampa Inn in Prescott, the Grand Hotel in Jerome, the Hotel Monte Vista in Flagstaff, and Santa Fe, New Mexico's La Fonda Inn. He'd search for others to visit if time permitted, but the initial choices offered him core destinations. Located in cities offering rich historical backgrounds to explore, the hotels would provide an architectural charm to compliment each city's tourist attractions.

He sent Phil a list of destinations and decided to leave the next day. Jack planned to spend a couple of days at each location and get a flavor for the hotel, the town and its amenities. He'd mingle with locals, ask a lot of questions and let his creative mind do the rest. After a quick review, Phil approved the plan. He hung up, and Jack smiled. *Phil would have agreed to any idea, just to help me write again.* "He's been a good friend," he spoke aloud.

Jack wanted to get an early start in the morning, but sat on the front veranda to soak in one last evening before leaving the valley. The sun slipped below the horizon and filled the sky with a glorious pattern of gold, orange and red. In time, the night turned cool, and Jack slipped on a jacket to fend off the desert wind. Quiet and serene, the silence soothed his soul. A year ago, he would have been in a drunken stupor, oblivious to everything. Tonight, however, he sat in the darkness holding a half-finished can of Pepsi and a lit cigarette.

The evening sounds comforted him. An owl hooted and landed on his roof in search of a companion or, more likely, a snack. A forlorn coyote howled in the distance and then a second animal answered back. Jack lit another cigarette and watched it glow in the darkness. Dr. Aberdeen encouraged

Jack to replace alcohol with nicotine, and now he had successfully acquired a new addiction.

"Thanks, Doc," he said. "I wonder if it's one of those unorthodox techniques he learned in nut-school training or just made it up to keep his patients hooked."

He smiled and flicked the dead butt into the desert as his mood turned somber. Unchecked tears streamed down his face, and he felt the emptiness of Taylor's loss surround him. He missed everything about her, every moment they shared together. Jack remembered her radiant smile, the smell and feel of her hair, and the warmth of her body cuddled up to him on the wicker couch he now occupied alone.

Jack took a deep breath, held it and counted slowly … one Mississippi, two Mississippi, three Mississippi … until he'd let it out at fifteen Mississippi. Jack gasped for air and moaned, "And that's how long it took for her to die." *Was she in pain?* he wondered. *Did she know she was dying? What were her last thoughts? Was she afraid?* More tears fell, and then another surge of anger tightened his muscles.

Why can't the police find the bastard? It's been over a year and nothing, not even from Sarah. Overcome with fatigue, Jack shook the half-consumed Pepsi over the rail, tossed the can into the dark desert and went inside. Fully clothed, he plopped on his bed and within minutes fell into a fitful sleep.

The morning sun disturbed his slumber. Jack struggled out of bed, undressed and headed for a hot shower. When he came downstairs to make coffee, the wall clock chimed seven times. He planned to stay at the Hassayampa Inn tucked away in the mountain town of Prescott. Located only a short eighty miles to the northwest, the drive would take around two hours, so he figured he could move at a leisurely pace.

Jack drove down the gravel roads successfully isolating his home from the world and pulled onto Happy Valley Highway. He traveled west until the road intersected with I-17 north and stopped at a gas station to top off his tank. From the station, he noticed the green road sign with its white letters:

VOICES

Happy Valley Exit. How ironic, he thought. *It's exactly what I'm doing, leaving happiness behind.*

He drove out of the station and approached the interstate. As his car entered the access lane, he saw a petite woman hitchhiking. A red bandanna held matted, greasy-looking dreadlocks in place. Her oversized peasant blouse and ruffled skirt betrayed a lack of fashion sense. She reminded Jack of images he once saw in magazines of the 1960s flower children frolicking in a park. He smiled at her as he passed. *She could have learned a few things from Taylor,* he thought. He ignored her outstretched hand.

However, as he passed the woman, he caught a glimpse of her sweet, innocent face with its impish, permanently affixed smile. The woman's eyes pleaded with him; the look left an impression.

Within the hour, he exited the interstate at the Sunset Point rest stop and parked his car in an isolated area. He and Taylor had come here often, a favorite spot to watch the sun collapse behind layers of mountains and bathe the two lovers in the myriad of colors. At such times they walked, talked and communed with God. It became the perfect setting for Jack to propose. He closed his eyes and recalled the radiance in her face when she said 'yes.' Now, alone in the parking lot with the sun high at his back, Jack waded back into his sorrow.

He remained transfixed for almost two hours. Returning to reality, he continued on his trip. By the time Jack reached the Prescott turnoff, the day had moved past noon and pangs of hunger tugged at his body. Having left home without breakfast, he began to search for a fast food oasis to satisfy his desire.

A McDonald's Restaurant caught his attention, and he pulled into the parking lot with visions of a "Quarter Pounder" and fries dancing in his head. As Jack stood in line waiting to order, he glanced around and spotted the same hitchhiker he'd seen earlier in the morning. She had finished lunch and looked wistfully out the window. The full light of day enhanced her features. *With some attention to hygiene and makeup, she could be attractive*, he mused. She must have sensed Jack's stare because she unexpectedly turned and smiled at him. Embarrassed, he looked away and pretended to study the menu. After he ordered, Jack found a table and scanned the room. The hitchhiker was gone.

Chapter Thirteen

Jack filled his gas tank again after lunch and found the road to Prescott. Before accelerating, he noticed the "hippie chick," as he thought of her, standing by the road with an extended thumb at the end of a tired arm. Her forlorn look attracted scant attention from other motorists. After he honored Taylor's memory at Sunset Point and took care of his hunger, Jack felt a sense of benevolence toward the young traveler. He slowed the car and mumbled into the windshield, "We're practically friends. I ran into her twice this morning. As Taylor used to say, be kind to strangers when you can." *Give her a ride. It will take your mind off your troubles.*

His vehicle came to a halt about thirty feet beyond the woman, and she ran after him, a sort of an unspoken obligation for hitchhikers. Jack lowered the passenger window and leaned across the console, "Where are you headed?"

"Hi, Jack, at least as far as Prescott tonight," she responded.

"Me, too," he smiled. "Jump in."

She threw a soft bag into the back of his car, settled into the passenger seat and looked about with curious eyes.

"Mind if I smoke?" he asked.

"It's your ride."

Jack shook a Camel out of the pack and put it to his lips. Instead of using the car lighter, he struck a match. The woman abruptly raised her hand to shield her face from the tiny flame.

Curious reaction, he thought. *I wonder what that's about.* He let his curiosity go and returned to a more pressing question, "How did you know my name is Jack?"

"Lucky guess, … well, not really. A lot of us hitchers call truck drivers and people we meet 'Jack' so we can make a personal connection. You know, like the waitresses who call their customers 'honey.' Same thing."

He accepted her explanation, and they drove on in silence for a few miles.

Jack finally disrupted the quiet and said, "My last name is Weston. Jack Weston. Sorry, you never told me yours."

"It's Pandora."

He looked at her and smiled, "Pandora what?"

"Just Pandora. Mother never believed in last names."

"Your mother must have had a strange sense of humor. Do you know what Pandora means?"

"Oh, yeah," she giggled. "My mother liked Greek mythology. Told me I looked like mischief the first time she saw me. So she named me Pandora. Just Pandora. She said the name says it all!"

He smiled at her explanation and added, "You know the Greek myth tells us Pandora unleashed all sorts of sickness, pain and trouble into the world. Being named after such a legacy can't make you very popular."

"I know the story, but it doesn't bother me. I only create positive energy."

"Good news," Jack grinned. "Does it mean I can relax?"

"Yes, you can," she laughed. "But to tell you the truth, until I turned five, I created a lot of problems for my parents. From then on, I brought good things into the world."

"You were a handful until you started kindergarten?"

"Sort of," she responded.

"What happened to make you change?"

"Well, just like the mythical Pandora, I learned to help people."

"Really? How?"

"I use my smile to give others a lift when they need it. Mama used to say I had a guardian angel on my shoulder and everyone could see it. Now people who spend time with me feel better. I help them find the silver lining behind dark clouds in their life."

"Fascinating. Care to tell me how you make that happen?"

"Nope, not important right now. Just think of my presence as a gift, like some medicine you'd put on a wound. I'm like a potion to help heal your recent stress."

"How could you possibly know anything about my stress?" Jack snapped. "Is that your sense of humor?"

"Honest, it's no joke," she offered. "My mission is to help people replace anxiety with optimism. Nobody's immune to pain and hurt, so I've got a lot of work to do."

"Why do you think I'm stressed?"

"I have wonderful intuition. I meet a lot of people, and it's easy to spot someone who needs me. Take you, for example. Your body language tells me you're really sad."

Jack gave her a quizzical sideways glance.

Pandora ignored the look and continued. "You need to experience something positive. If not, your future will continue to be difficult with no place to run or hide from your loss."

This conversation invaded his life and made him uncomfortable. The woman's wisdom, well beyond her years, made him feel uneasy. She answered his questions, but already seemed to know a lot about him. "This is weird, lady. Am I being set up? Do you work for Dr. Aberdeen? Did he send you to keep track of me?"

"I don't know him. Just remember, I'm Pandora." She smiled without reacting. "Think of it this way: The ancient Greek gods sent Pandora as a gift to the world, and now I'm kind of a gift for you."

Jack leaned back and grabbed another cigarette. *I picked up a wacko woman who spouts nonsensical, gibberish bullshit. I hope she gets out soon.*

He lit a match and, out of the corner of his eye, noticed her flinch again. *Very strange*, he thought. *Calm down, Jack. This is not about me. She's clueless. Pandora's got a refined intuitive skill, nothing more.*

Jack concluded he must have telegraphed his emotional vulnerability, and her heightened sensitivity picked it up.

That's probably how con artists identify easy marks, he thought. He shook his head. *Cool it, Jack, I'll soon be free of this crazy woman.*

Jack stopped speculating and asked, "Do you mind if I turn on the radio?"

"Of course not, it's your car."

Jack flipped to an old rock station, and Manfred Mann's version of "Blinded by the Light" gushed out of the speakers: *Blinded by the light, dressed up like a duce in the middle of the night. . . .*

Jack turned down the volume and spoke again, "That song's always confused me. I have no idea what the lyrics mean."

"Yeah, you can interpret those words in lots of ways," she said. "Some people claim it's a drug song while others say it's about old cars. I guess you have to really listen closely to the words and decide for yourself how they fit your life."

Jack looked at his passenger and thought, *How they fit my life?* Confused by her rambling, he decided not to delve into Pandora's idiosyncrasies. So, he managed a taciturn smile and glanced in her direction.

She returned his look and said, "Well, here's where I get out. I'll see you around. Thanks for the lift."

Thank god, it's almost over, he thought.

They entered Prescott city limits, and Jack maneuvered his vehicle to the curb. Pandora got out, and he pulled away. He scrutinized her image in the rearview mirror and saw her flash a two-fingered peace sign as she waved goodbye. *How did she know I'd be watching? She's one weird, but interesting chick,* he thought. *I have no idea where she came up with all of those crazy ideas.* "Forget it, Jack," he spoke aloud. "You're a bit paranoid, aren't you?"

He steered his vehicle toward his final destination: The Hassayampa Inn on Bailey Street. Dismissing Pandora, his thoughts turned to his assignment. He now imagined Faith's ghost waiting for him to check in.

Chapter Fourteen

Jack's reservation specifically requested suite 426. According to legend, a newlywed couple stayed in this room shortly after the hotel opened in 1927. After checking in, the husband, a man much older than his bride, left to purchase a cigar and a bottle of brandy, no small task in the middle of Prohibition. He never returned. Three days passed, and the young bride panicked. Out of desperation and fear, she hung herself from the room's balcony. Faith's death and the stories about her paranormal antics became the center of Jack's investigation.

An affable desk clerk greeted Jack as he walked into the Hassayampa lobby. "Good afternoon, sir. I hope you had a pleasant trip."

Jack read the man's nametag and responded, "Thank you, Jerry. Yes, a short drive up from Phoenix. I'm Jack Weston. Is my room ready?"

"Yes, Mr. Weston. We were expecting you. The reservation indicates you're doing a story on Faith, one of our resident spirits. I'm sure she'll look forward to meeting you," he added with a tongue-in-cheek smile.

"Yes, I plan to camp in the room for a couple of days to see if the two of us can *chat* about politics, sports, life and death. You know the usual things you share with a ghost."

Jerry smiled and handed him a pen to register. "Mr. Weston, if Faith's unavailable to talk, we have a couple of other spirits milling about the place. They hang out in our restaurant and basement. I don't mean to discount Faith's claim to fame, but female ghosts can get fickle and ignore interested gentlemen."

"Jerry, I think your statement may be the most important lesson you'll ever learn about women." Both men grinned at his pronouncement.

Jack picked up an electronic key and found the elevator. He turned to admire the lobby's attention to detail and elegant appearance. The reception area featured hand painted, wood-beamed ceilings complemented by embossed copper wall panels. One side of the lobby featured a Talavera tile fireplace, quite stylish in the height of fashion in the 1920s. The lobby's rich carpets showcased exquisite Castilian walnut furniture, and the room contained several etched-glass chandeliers.

Jack concluded the Hassayampa Inn would offer a charming ambiance for a romantic weekend. It may appeal to nostalgic readers who yearn to experience the atmosphere of a slower, more elegant time. Satisfied the hotel offered him an ideal location to write; he looked forward to beginning his research.

The writer entered the restored vintage elevator and let the tension created by Pandora evaporate. He reached room 426, slipped the key in the lock and heard the electronic mechanism release. Pushing the door open, Jack greeted his potential roommate, "Hello, Faith, I'm home. I've come to spend a few days with you so I can write a story. Hope you don't mind my intrusion." Smirking to himself, Jack set the laptop on the desk and unpacked his suitcase. *Pretty stupid,* he thought. *Now I'm acting like the kook I met on the road.*

Jack unlocked the door to the balcony, stepped outside and looked down Gurley Street toward Whiskey Row. He saw the courthouse and the gentle rolling hills surrounding Prescott. His mind drifted to Taylor. *She would have loved this place.*

Returning to his assignment, he speculated, *I wonder if Faith ever joins couples who stay here for romantic weekends.* He smiled to himself and said, "C'mon, Jack, a ghostly threesome? You're not a fiction writer."

Jack decided he'd try to get close to Faith by replicating her husband's actions the night they registered. He showered, shaved and dressed in a pair of dark blue dress slacks with a white, open-collared shirt. He completed his semi-formal look with a charcoal gray herringbone blazer with black elbow patches. After a splash of cologne, Jack grabbed his notebook and headed for the door. Before leaving, he turned and spoke into the empty room, "I'm going out for dinner

and a cigar, Faith. I'll be back in a few hours, sweetheart."
Really lame, mister writer.

When he stepped onto Gurley Street, the cool mountain air greeted the author. He shook off the slight chill and headed directly for the Palace Saloon across the square on Montezuma Street, the heart of Whiskey Row. The noise level, magnified by the ancient restaurant's high ceilings, offered proof customers enjoyed the place. Jack took a table directly across from the huge bar. He scanned the historic saloon and admired its ambiance, decorated with relics from the Old West and autographed pictures of popular western movie stars. The menu included a huge assortment of food choices ranging from simple bar fare to dinner specials, all prepared by the Palace's award-winning chef. Jack selected the Tom Mixed Grill and added a small Sagebrush Salad. He also ordered a glass of the house chardonnay to upgrade his frontier dining adventure.

Erica, a member of the waitstaff, became a genial host and an informative conversationalist. She shared historical tidbits about Prescott and the Palace Saloon. Jack and Erica's conversation soon focused on his writing assignment.

"Erica, what's your take on Faith, the Hassayampa ghost?"

"To start, I don't believe her husband would have run off and left her," she said.

"Why not? Why do you think he disappeared?"

"I grew up in Prescott, and my grandpa Franklin worked here at the Palace."

"Is this a job handed down through the family?"

"Yes, our family knows the owner. Grandpa Franklin used to tell me stories about the place. He said Whiskey Row and the Palace Hotel went through some hard times during Prohibition. The owners couldn't make ends meet by just serving food, if you catch my drift."

"Are you suggesting the Palace Saloon became a speakeasy?"

"Nothing of the sort. Such a thing would have been illegal," she winked. "A lot of knowledgeable, ... um, ... shall we say, assertive businessmen lurked about, ready for possible financial opportunities. You know, the sale of a bottle of hooch on the side could supplement your income."

"Do you think Faith's husband found a source to score a bottle?"

"Possibly. Nobody in town knew much about him," Erica said.

"Do you think he fell in with the wrong crowd and got shanghaied?"

"According to Grandpa Franklin, there used to be a hidden speakeasy outside of town, and if you asked the right people, they'd take you there for a price."

"You're thinking Faith's husband went to look for an extra honeymoon present and found trouble instead?" Jack conjectured.

"It's the story my grandpa tells. But, back then everyone in town suspected strangers who asked too many questions. The husband's curiosity may have cost him his life. Maybe the locals thought he was too nosey, acted like a Federal revenuer. Or, it's possible he flashed a big wad of cash and got rolled for it."

"Yeah, in World War II, the phrase *loose lips sink ships* said it all. If the husband pretended to be an arrogant showoff with his money, he could have become an easy target."

"Exactly," added Erica. "It's also possible Faith's husband drank with the locals, had too much, got mean and pissed them off. Maybe they had a fight, hit him on the head, took his money and dropped his body down a mine shaft."

"And Faith, the loving bride, steadfastly waited for him to return."

"Maybe she had poor self-esteem and thought he rejected her, changed his mind or ran off with another woman," Erica continued. "She'd have trouble explaining his absence to her parents and friends."

"Alone, filled with fear and guilt, suicide became the only option. In those days, a soiled woman got labeled a floozy, or worse, a whore."

"You might have to figure it out, mister. Gonna write it in your story?"

"Can't decide. I just got here and haven't talked with Faith yet."

"Good luck," she said and added, "any coffee or desert?"

"Nope. Just the check and the directions to a smoke shop and liquor store."

Chapter Fifteen

Jack returned to the hotel, unlocked his door and shouted, "Hello, Faith, I'm back!" The writer turned on the lights, took an inexpensive bottle of E & J Brandy out of the bag and poured a glass. He unwrapped the 5 Vegas Gold cigar, lit it and watched billows of white clouds fill the non-smoking room.

Unaccustomed to smoking cigars, Jack had asked the sales clerk for a mild one, pleasing to the taste. However, the harsh bite of the tobacco burned in his throat and lungs and made him cough. He opened the balcony door to air out the non-smoking room, not wanting to set off the smoke alarm and be joined by Prescott firemen. Jack didn't have enough brandy to share, and a crowd would discourage Faith from attending his planned rendezvous.

Jack walked onto the balcony, sipped his brandy and tried to relight the cigar. "I hope you're not offended by the smoke, Faith." He sat in a wicker chair to enjoy the brandy and forced a few more puffs on the cigar. A light breeze caused the smoke to vanish, and the stogy's gray ash fell off. "Did you do that, Faith? I'm enjoying myself, but if you want to talk, I'll stop."

Jack listened for a second and lit up again. He exhaled and then heard the distinct sound of moans coming from inside his room. He cocked his head and strained his ears to identify the source. Transfixed by the sound, he tossed the cigar over the rail and walked into the room. He closed the balcony door to eliminate street noise and sat on the bed, anticipating he'd hear another moan.

"Hello, Faith. Are you in the room?"

Silence greeted him as he sat motionless, waiting for a sound. Jack heard the moan again and paced the room to locate it. Finally, he walked to the balcony doors, listened again and smiled. The wind seeped under the crack around the two wooden doors and had created human-like noise.

False alarm, he thought. *Faith doesn't want to be interviewed.* He shook his head at the notion he could communicate with Faith's ghost by merely copying her husband's behavior. *Pretty silly,* he mused.

"Okay, Faith, I'll be patient and wait. But I need your help to write an article about you and this room. You have to fill in some of the details."

More silence followed.

"Can we make a deal? Let me know you're here, and I'll write nice things about you."

Jack's proposal went unanswered, and he stepped onto the balcony to light another cigar, changed his mind and threw it over the side to join its half-smoked twin. "Nasty, vulgar habit," he spoke into the night air. He drained the last swallow of brandy and prepared for bed. Jack slept lightly, hoping his slumber would be interrupted by the sounds or sight of Faith's ghost. But, nothing bothered his sleep.

He awoke in the morning, yawned and stretched. He whispered to a silent room, "Ms. Faith, I am disappointed. I wanted to hear your story, and you ignored me — not neighborly. If I offended you with my cigar smoking and brandy drinking last night, I apologize. Tell me I'm forgiven."

Jack only heard more silence. He made coffee in the room's two-cup, automatic Cuisinart and took a quick shower. As the hot water cascaded over his head, Jack recalled the stories his grandmother used to tell him about her encounters with ghosts. At first they scared him, but as he grew older, Jack enjoyed such tales and often embellished them in his writing. The presence of Faith, although a long shot, would please more than frighten the writer.

Before refocusing on Faith, Jack wanted to gather more background information about Prescott. If Faith failed to materialize, and eliminated the centerpiece of Jack's article, most of it would have to be filler about the nostalgic amenities of the town. A great ghost story would turn into a mundane travelogue. Jack dressed and put his wallet, money clip and car keys in his pants, but couldn't locate the room key. He searched everywhere, but failed to find the errant plastic card. He convinced himself it must be under something in the room. He decided to stop by the front desk to get a duplicate made instead of conducting an extensive search.

He left the room and turned to check the door. Surprised, he saw the plastic key card sitting in the door lock. His room had been unsecured all night. Anyone could have walked in. He reviewed the sequence of his actions as he returned to the room the night before. He distinctly remembered putting the key in the paper bag holding his brandy and cigars. *Quite odd,* he thought. *The key should have been in the sack. I never left the room again.* He rummaged through the trash and unfolded the used paper bag — nothing in the bottom but a receipt. *Jack, you've got to pay closer attention to details,* he scolded himself. *How could I have left the key in the door? It's not like me ... how careless.* He shrugged it off and headed out.

He spent the day walking the streets of downtown Prescott and took note of restaurants, antique shops and other amenities. The courthouse square beckoned visitors to explore its huge block-wide grassy area. Although still dormant from winter, mature trees would provide visitors with a marvelous canopy of shade in summer months. Tourists could then enjoy major events of Prescott's history chiseled into cement pavement blocks in front of the court house.

He meandered through the town to locate bed and breakfasts for those couples who preferred another kind of adventure, and ended his tour with an examination of amenities provided by historic Hotel St. Michael on the corner of Montezuma and Bailey streets. After Jack finished his extensive self-guided tour, he had enough details to write a generic article about the city. It would be sufficient, but disappointing. Jack wanted, no needed, more information about Faith and a real encounter with her ghost to make his words turn into a spellbinding article.

By mid-afternoon, Jack returned to his room, turned on his laptop and began to compose the story. Without Faith's voice, the words emerged in a flat, unimaginative style. He deleted several attempts and stopped. He poured a healthy glass of brandy, stepped onto the balcony and berated himself. "I have lost my touch," he whispered into his glass. "I used to be good at this. My words used to be exciting, but without Taylor, I can't write anymore." He downed the dark-colored liquid and paused. Had he just heard the faint sounds of weeping from inside his room?

Surprised, Jack turned and looked through the balcony window. *No one there. Of course, it must be the wind,* he thought. He stood motionless to confirm his suspicion, but no air stirred. Jack listened and tried to locate the sound coming from within the room. Again, he heard the faint sobbing of a woman. He opened the door and stepped in. "Faith? Are you here?" he asked. More silence. Quiet, like a prayerful moment in church.

Jack returned to his laptop and gasped at what he saw. In the middle of the computer screen, a poem had been typed. *How did this get here?* He read each line with care:

Dead? Not to thee, thou keen watcher, — not silent, not viewless, to thee,

Immortal still wrapped in the mortal! I, from the mortal set free,

Greet thee by many clear tokens thou smilest to hear and to see.

"Faith, is this your message?" He looked at the screen and shouted, "No! It's not from Faith. … It's got to be from Taylor. … Taylor always left love notes on my computer screen." *This is crazy,* he thought. Jack stomped around the room. *My attempt to write an article about an eighty-year-old ghost — my reporter's séance has now shifted to my dead wife.* Jack's mind raced. *If the other side exists, I may have broken through with my desire and pain? Whose words are these on my screen? Faith or Taylor's?*

Jack googled the first lines of the poem and discovered Edith Matilda Thomas had penned a poem titled, "Spirit to Spirit." She died in 1925, two years before Faith hung herself. *Why*, he thought, *would this partial poem appear on my screen? Is this a message from beyond I need to understand?*

He pondered his questions and finally mumbled, "Okay, man, get a grip. You're going to have a breakdown. Knock it off!"

Unable to handle the confusion, Jack grabbed his coat and left the room. He decided to get some fresh air. He needed time to think outside the confines of his haunted hotel room.

Chapter Sixteen

Jack wandered across the courthouse square and walked into the Palace Saloon. Erica, now behind the bar, noticed her guest. "You look terrible. What's the matter?"

"Give me a shot of Maker's Mark. I've been with a ghost."

"Isn't that what you wanted? You writer types have such overactive imaginations." She shook her head. "Okay, tell me about it."

"I'm not sure, but I was outside on the balcony and heard a woman crying. When I walked into the room, I found a message typed on the computer screen."

"Now there's a new one — a ghost who uses modern technology to haunt the living."

"I'm a bit confused about it myself."

"Well, I'll tell you, Jack, life's too short to question such events. Here's my advice: take a deep breath and go back to your room. If you can channel a spirit, don't get freaked out. Remember, you stalked her first. Get in touch and write your story."

"True," Jack said. "I have to take advantage of this unexpected opportunity. If I can get something from Faith's spirit, my readers will love it!" Jack downed his drink, left ten dollars on the bar and returned to room 426.

As Jack left, Erica shouted, "Just don't write anything kinky about her. It would spoil my image."

Jack returned to the hotel and clicked on his laptop; the poem had disappeared. However, the words rolled around in Jack's mind. *Dead? Not to thee. What does that mean?* He sat down to write the article. In a breakthrough session, words flew from his mind onto the screen, as if he took dictation. He stopped and read the finished article. Packed with some of his best prose, the paragraphs alluded to Faith's passionate love, prematurely cut short. Jack found it easy to personally relate to Faith's fear of life without her spouse. But, unlike Faith, who killed herself, Jack wanted to stay alive to solve Taylor's murder. Pleased with his work, but fatigued, he hit the "save" key and turned off his laptop. Just before lying down, he checked the bedroom door to make sure the key had not been left in the outside slot again.

Jack enjoyed a deep, dreamless sleep until he awoke with a start at 3 a.m. He felt the presence of someone sitting at the foot of his bed. He rolled over and nudged a form with his foot. It had substance. Jack bolted upright and peered into the darkened space. "Hello, someone there?" he asked and waved his arm into the shadows. No response. Jack wondered if it had been a dream or if Faith's spirit actually occupied the room. Jack swung his feet over the edge of the bed and snapped on the table lamp. The room flooded with light, and Jack squinted, using his hand to block the blinding intrusion. He hopped out of bed and nervously paced the room. He stepped into the bathroom and then the walk-in closet. Still alone, Jack whispered, "Not a good way to begin a relationship, Faith. If you want to communicate, don't startle me."

Jack poured a shot of brandy and downed it. He stared into the deserted streets below and stood motionless to settle his rattled nerves. Then, Jack returned to bed, turned off the light and said, "Okay, Faith, no more tricks."

He had not been asleep for more than an hour, when he again woke up and sensed a presence in the room. This time he decided to lay still and let the spirit, Taylor or whatever aberration appeared initiate the next move. To his surprise, a warm hand touched his feet under the covers. Jack's muscles tensed as the strange anomaly invaded his personal space. He waited to see what happened next. The touch turned into a gentle foot massage, and it felt soothing. *Should I speak to her? Will she disappear?* The hotel's *Ghost Register* described how Faith often massaged the feet of female guests. But her actions didn't make sense. *Why me? I'm a man.*

"Faith, are you here?"

"Shh," filled his ears.

Was that the wind or Faith? He lay still with his eyes wide open and felt the warmth of the massage move up his calves. *This has got to be real.* He lost track of time and somewhere in the process drifted back to sleep, leaving many questions unanswered.

Jack woke at 7:30 a.m. and immediately recalled his experience. *Was last night a dream? Had Faith visited his room twice and massaged his feet on her second trip? Did she guide my writing?* Jack sat on the edge of the bed in a sleepy fog. He shook his head, unable to make sense of it, and jumped into the shower. *Just my imagination, a dream,* he thought.

After breakfast, Jack returned to his room to revise and finalize his article. He added more insights and sensitive reflections to his final draft. He pushed back from the screen and admired his work, the first good piece he had written in more than a year. Jack lingered over the artistic words and touching phrases. The language reflected softness, revealing a different, more poignant side to the writer. Jack's words moved him to tears. *Readers will develop a love affair with Prescott and an empathy for Faith,* he thought. In vivid detail, Jack's article described the anguish of a lost love. "Thank you, Faith. I really understand your feelings," he said in a reverent tone.

Jack felt uplifted. His encounter with Faith gave him a glimmer of hope, reinforcing his talent to accurately express thoughts and feelings again. He toasted Faith with another glass of brandy: "To Faith, you helped me believe in myself again."

The article complete, Jack decided to leave a day early and drive the twenty miles to his next destination: Jerome. He changed his reservation at the Grand Hotel, the next stop, and packed his bags. Finally, he checked the article he e-mailed Phil. Before he shut down his laptop, Jack noticed an unfamiliar word document on the desktop. He clicked on the icon, opened it and read:

> *Dead? Not to thee, thou keen watcher, — not silent, not viewless, to thee,*
>
> *Immortal still wrapped in the mortal! I, from the mortal set free.*

"How did this get here again?" he said aloud to the machine. "I remember thinking about the poem last night. I know I didn't save it, yet must have. Or else … no, no, … too bizarre." Confronted with another unexplainable phenomenon, Jack put the laptop away, shook his head and said, "Time for me to leave."

He spotted Erica walking into work at the Palace and made a point to thank her. Jack bought Erica lunch and shared his nocturnal experience along with the second appearance of the poem on his computer screen.

"Interesting, but don't get any ideas about romancing a spirit. They don't have much substance, nothing to squeeze, and they can get pretty scary if you piss 'em off."

"You know, Erica," Jack said, "You've just planted an unpleasant image in my brain. That thought never crossed my mind."

They shared a last beer and engaged in small talk about the town. By late afternoon, Jack figured he had spent enough time in Faith's haunted lair and headed for Jerome.

Chapter Seventeen

The road to Jerome wanders through low, treeless hills north of Prescott before its dramatic climb into the mountains. Jack switched on the radio and anticipated a pleasant drive. He thought about his destination and recalled the background information motivating him to select the Grand Hotel as his next stop. Jerome, an abandoned mining town until the 1970s, began to flourish again when a group of hippie artists turned it into a tourist destination. Jack decided to spend the next couple of days at the Jerome Grand Hotel. It sat on top of Cleopatra Hill at five thousand feet, overlooked the town and offered guests a sweeping view of the Verde Valley.

Jack recalled some of the ghost stories reported at the hotel. The West Coast Ghost and Paranormal Society investigated the Grand several years back and had officially certified it as a legitimate haunted building. The thought intrigued him because the possibilities of another encounter like his experience with Faith could add luster to his next article. He negotiated another curve in the highway, but slowed his vehicle to a crawl when he spotted Pandora. *What the hell. What's she doing here?* He brought the vehicle to a stop, turned down the radio and lowered the passenger window.

"Hi, Jack," she said with a bubbly smile. "Did you have a good visit in Prescott?"

"Pandora, were you waiting for me?"

"Not really, just lucky," she said with a smile. "I'm heading to Jerome to visit friends."

"How did you know I would be driving there today?" he asked. "No, don't tell me. Let me guess, you're actually a psychic."

"Just call it a hunch. Sort of woman's intuition."

"Luck or coincidence, it doesn't matter. Jump in."

"Thanks. You're so sweet."

They rode for a few minutes in silence. Jack pondered the odds of meeting Pandora after his two days in Prescott. Logic failed him.

An inquisitive Pandora interrupted his pensive mood. "Didn't you find Faith amusing?"

"What?" he asked. "How do you know about Faith?"

"Come on, everyone who lives in Arizona knows about Faith. Did you experience her spirit?"

Jack hesitated for a second and then decided to be honest. "Yes, I think I did." He glanced at his passenger to see if she thought he was joking. "We shared a drink, and she gave me a foot massage. We definitely didn't get together for a date or a heart-to-heart chat, if that's what you mean."

"No, you're certainly not ready for that," she smiled.

"And, just what does that mean, young lady?"

"Nothing. Just nonsense."

More silence followed.

"Jack," Pandora now spoke in a quiet tone. "Seriously, did you learn anything from your encounter with her ghost?"

He gave her another quick glance, studied her face for a moment and then answered. "Yes, as a matter of fact, she taught me a lot." He looked at Pandora, who seemed to be waiting for a more detailed explanation. "Actually, my interaction with Faith," he paused, "renewed *faith* in myself."

"Cute," she smiled. "How did she do that?"

"Faith taught me love is never-ending, sort of immortal. Once you discover the love of another, even death can't destroy it."

"Wow, I'm impressed. Quite profound."

"There's more." He carefully selected his words. "By taking her life, Faith cheated herself out of the potential to love again. You know, like it's important to love yourself before you can love another."

Pandora smiled and nodded at him as if he had tapped into some deep universal truth. "That's an excellent insight. It's important to realize every encounter with the living and the dead gives us meaningful messages. An astute person will take the time to hear and interpret them."

Jack focused on the road for a moment and said, "How did such a young woman become so philosophical?"

"Don't ponder my thoughts too much. Most people think I'm a pain, but it is part of my purpose."

"I won't dwell on it," Jack said. "More importantly, over the last two days, I rediscovered my ability to express my voice with words again. It's all I need for now."

"Good for you." She leaned forward and turned up the radio, ending the philosophical discussion. The Doors' song "Light My Fire" filled the car. When the lyrics reached the chorus, she shouted out the words and made a valiant attempt to carry the tune. "Come on, baby, light my fire. Come on, baby, light my fire. Try to set the night on fiyah!" Then she hummed the melody, unable to recall the remaining lyrics.

Jack smiled at her antics.

She blushed and said, "C'mon, Jack, sing." She turned up the volume so the sound drowned out all thought. In a playful mood, Jack threw his head back and belted out the tune with Pandora. Both sang at the top of their lungs. They reached the last line together, and along with Jim Morrison, warbled the final words to copy the vocalist.

The car swayed on the highway as the two rocked together with unbridled enthusiasm. Jack laughed at Pandora's exaggerated gestures, and in turn, Jack copied John Travolta's *Saturday Night Fever* move with his right hand. The car shook with his body movements.

Outside of Jerome the song ended, and Pandora abruptly turned serious. "Jack, this is where I need to get out. Keep singing. There's meaning in the lyrics of every song. Just listen for it."

He pulled the car over and let her out.

"Thanks."

"No problem, Pandora. I'll probably see you down the road again."

"Oh, you can count on it." She smiled at him and waved goodbye.

Did she mean that as a promise or a threat?

Chapter Eighteen

Jack lived in Arizona for a good part of his life but never visited Jerome. To his amazement, the dilapidated, century-old buildings still maintained their grip on the edge of steep hillsides like autumn leaves struggling to remain affixed to their branches. On the way to the hotel, Jerome's narrow streets, designed for horse drawn wagons more than modern vehicles, tested Jack's driving skills. The Grand Hotel, a five-story Spanish architectural edifice, commanded an incredible view of the town and valley below. Built on a cement foundation and poured at a severe angle, it confidently clung to the mountainside.

Originally, the building served the town as the United Verde Hospital, a state-of-the-art medical facility. Jack stepped out of the vehicle to admire the sweeping panorama spreading out for miles below. The view extended to a point where the horizon and sky became indistinguishable. Temporarily mesmerized by the incredible view, he stood in awe for several minutes.

After he registered, Jack rode a vintage, self-service elevator to the fourth floor. The confined space made him feel claustrophobic. However, the sensation disappeared as the antique cage jolted to an abrupt stop at his floor. Jack released an anxious breath and stepped out into the hallway. After putting his things in the assigned room, he headed to the hotel's restaurant. Famished, he wanted to experience the grandeur of the hotel's eatery, famed for its delectable culinary choices and incredible view.

He entered The Asylum, an attractive dining area furnished with a touch of elegance. Jack chose a table by a window offering a spectacular view of the valley, ordered a Rusty Nail and studied the menu. David, a distinguished, middle-aged server, approached and rattled off a list of chef specialties for the evening. Jack relaxed over his cocktail and studied the room's rich interior. He felt comfortable in its stylish surroundings and looked forward to a leisurely dinner.

David returned and noticed Jack's empty cocktail glass.

"Care for another Rusty Nail, or are you ready to order, sir?"

"Yes, I'll have another, and then you can bring me the Chicken Tenderloin Alfredo with a garden salad for dinner."

Few patrons occupied tables for the early dinner specials, giving Jack time to chat with his waiter. "How long have you worked here, David?"

"Six years."

"I'm writing an article about haunted hotels for *Western Trails Magazine*. Ever read it?"

"Occasionally," he answered. "You must be the fellow the manager alerted us to …."

"Yes, I'm Jack Weston."

"Pleased to meet you. I understand you'll be here for a couple of days. The manager copied one of your articles to prepare us for your visit. I liked the style."

"Thanks. What can you tell me about the ghosts who haunt the Grand?"

"Oh, Mr. Weston, I can tell you they *are all* quite real and regularly attempt to scare us. You know: heavy breathing, doors slamming, lights going off and on, water running. And the damn elevator … well, sometimes it has a mind of its own."

"You ever afraid?" Jack inquired.

"Nah! I've worked here too long and got used to them."

"Which ghost intrigues you the most? I want to write an interesting story for my readers."

"Um, …you'll want to write about Claude Harvey's ghost."

"Why Harvey?"

"He used to be the Grand's resident handyman. In 1935, they found him with his head crushed in at the bottom of the elevator shaft. Some say he was murdered. More likely he got drunk, got careless, and the elevator killed him."

"What do you think, David?"

"Can't say one way or the other, but it's a good story. You're the reporter, ask him yourself," the waiter smiled.

"You know, David, I might. Do you know if he's available for an interview?"

"Only if he wants to talk with you," David quipped.

That night, sleep eluded Jack. Aroused by a growing sense of curiosity, he left the comfort of his bed, dressed and headed for the elevator. He pressed the button for the lobby and rode the old Otis to the first floor. It creaked and groaned with every movement. *Nothing special about the ride,* he thought, and exited the small capsule. He found a sleepy desk clerk making a valiant attempt to tend his post.

"Good evening," Jack interrupted.

The man's head snapped to attention.

"Oh," stammered the surprised clerk. "Good evening, sir, may I help you?"

"Yes, I want to visit the basement and chat with Mr. Harvey."

"You must be Mr. Weston, the magazine writer."

"You've got it. Can I check out the area?"

"Sure, go through the door on your right and take the stairs down to the floor below."

Jack followed the directions and entered a part of the hotel showing the least attention. *Out of sight, out of mind, ... old cliché, but true in this case.* Only a bare 100-watt bulb illuminated the stairs, but once he stepped on the cement slab, Jack stood in the cool, dimly lit underbelly of the hotel. He pointed a pocket light into the shadows until he located the base of the elevator shaft. He knelt down and felt the approximate location where Claude Harvey's body had been found. He pulled a digital camera out of his pack and snapped several pictures of the floor area and the elevator structure.

He stepped into the empty elevator shaft and looked up. Without warning, the elevator lurched and sprang to life. The unexpected movement caused Jack to jump out of the way, an unnecessary reaction because the ancient lift moved with slow irregular movements. *Who besides me would ride the elevator at this time of night?* Jack watched as the elevator moved up three floors above the basement. Even though Jack felt safe, his heart beat rapidly as an adrenalin rush tightened his muscles. He let out a gasp of air, listened and observed the elevator. The creaky equipment descended to the second floor where it abruptly caught on the cable, remained suspended for two to three seconds, slipped on the cable another few inches and caught again. Its short trip ended with a quick, head-snapping jerk on the second floor.

Jack heard the elevator's two passengers yelp. The woman let out a small scream, followed by a man's belly laugh. "It must be one of Harvey's tricks," he explained to his frightened companion. "Go away, Claude." Both laughed nervously as they exited.

Jack looked back to the spot on the floor where Claude's body had been discovered years earlier. "Well, Mr. Harvey," he spoke into the darkness, "there is no way in hell you couldn't have heard the elevator and safely jumped out of the way."

Jack examined the basement and noted the six-inch gap between the floor and the elevator stop. He snapped pictures of the area and walked around to get a broader perspective. Finally, he returned to where the handyman's body once lay and whispered, "Mr. Harvey, I believe you were murdered and not the victim of your own carelessness. The elevator crushed your head after you were already dead. The murderer must have dragged your body into the shaft to make it look like you fell into it."

Jack returned to his room and looked at digital images in his camera. He clicked on "photo view" to inspect the shots taken in the dark. Disappointed with the results, he realized the camera didn't have enough light to take clear pictures. Even though a murky cloud around each photo could be detected, he blamed the phenomenon on the lack of light. Disheartened, Jack deleted the images. "Not even a good ghost picture in the lot."

VOICES

The next day, Jack walked the three streets defining the town's business district, gathering information about its shops, restaurants and bed and breakfasts — more sidebars for his readers to enjoy. Jerome presented tourists with another location for a pleasant weekend getaway.

He sat in the restaurant and typed a second article for *Western Trails Magazine*. His words flowed with a lyrical rhythm, but still left the author feeling incomplete. His accurate descriptions added an interesting flavor to Jerome, yet the article lacked an essential hook to grab the reader's attention. He had not talked with the ghost of Claude Harvey or experienced anything close to his encounter with Faith.

The story included pictures and tales of the historic "cribs" used by the town's former prostitutes. These tiny shacks, sequestered behind legitimate business storefronts, stayed hidden from the more gentile residents. A narrow path, constructed between a set of buildings, required customers interested in negotiated affection to pick their way along a steep incline to reach the cribs in the alley below.

In spite of a congratulatory e-mail from Phil praising Jack's article about Faith and Prescott, he still wrestled with his thoughts about Claude Harvey's demise. He needed to know more about the man to satisfy his curiosity and add a rich verve to this article.

Harvey's ghostly shenanigans had never been harmful or mean-spirited to the hotel's present-day guests. His translucent form darted through the halls, and the guttural moans or unexplained elevator lurches mostly amused patrons. *So, why did Harvey's ghost still haunt the place?*

Frustrated, Jack went to bed. Around 2 a.m., a cool breeze blew through an open window and woke him. He shut the window and jumped back under the covers. The writer believed he had fallen asleep again, but as Jack recalled later, a vivid, realistic dream invaded his sleep. He dreamt Claude Harvey sat in his room sipping a bottle of beer. Harvey looked at Jack and shook him awake.

"Care for a beer, boy?"

"No, thanks, I need to rewrite a story and want to keep a clear head,"

"Well, suit yourself, young fella. Ain't too often I get a chance to indulge in a cold one like the old days."

"That's a new one. I didn't know you ghost-types liked beer."

"Old habits don't always die when you do. So, while I sit here and enjoy my brew, you can ask me your questions?"

Jack sat up and grabbed his notebook. "Tell me, Mr. Harvey, what happened to cause your gruesome death?"

The ghost reached up and felt the huge hole in the back of his skull. "You're right, son. Ain't no way to die."

"They say you were crushed under the elevator? I don't buy the story. The lift makes such a racket; you should have heard it and jumped out of the way."

"You're damn right, sonny! It's obvious. Can't figure out why the police didn't think so, too."

"You know you were murdered?"

"Any fool could understand it."

"What happened?"

"I was greasing down the cable. When I stepped out of the shaft, someone hit me on the back of the head, and my brains went flying."

"You never saw the murderer?"

"Nope, when you're hit from behind with an iron pipe, you only see death. Someone hiding in the basement didn't want to be discovered. But, the authorities never called it murder. They accepted the accident theory. They thought I was drunk."

"Were you?"

"Nope, never drank on the job, but I could sure put 'em away off duty."

"Too bad, Mr. Harvey. It makes for unfinished earthly business, doesn't it?"

"Yup. It's the only reason I stick around. Listen to me, boy, when someone's murdered, it's important those left behind seek justice. Not revenge, mind you, but justice."

"Is that the reason you keep haunting the hotel?"

"Right, I try to make sure people won't forget me."

"Didn't it make you angry when no one tried to find justice for you?"

"Oh, yeah, I was angry for a couple of decades, but let me tell you, sonny, anger never solves anything. Listen carefully. This is what I know: a man can't think straight when he's angry. Anger gets in the way of solving problems. So, don't accept Doc Aberdeen's ideas for too long."

"Aberdeen. How do you know about him?"

"Hush, boy. We're not here to talk about your headshrinker. Get back to the interview."

"Sorry for the distraction." Jack looked puzzled but returned to his notes. "Anybody ever open the case again?"

"A couple of you writer folks nosed around from time to time, but after all these years, the memory of Claude Harvey has faded. Can't blame 'em. I was killed a long time ago. I'm only a funny ghost story now."

"How did you get rid of your anger, Mr. Harvey?"

"No secret formula. Justice only comes after you replace negative energy with patience and logic. If you ever hope to find justice for Taylor's death, learn how to exercise patience."

"Taylor? You know about Taylor, too?"

The telephone rang and interrupted Jack's sleep. He sat upright. "God, only a dream," Jack cursed and answered the phone on its fifth ring.

Chapter Nineteen

Phillip Slocum's voice enthusiastically greeted the dreamer. "It's Dr. Phil checking in on my personal rehab project." Phil lapsed into silence as if assessing Jack's mental stability.

"Phil, I'm doing fine, but I just woke up. Don't worry about me, boss."

"Really?"

"Yes, it's one of the best assignments I've ever had. I'm relaxed and enjoying the unique souls I've met along the way, both living and dead — they've kept me going." The comment prompted another long silence. The stillness caused Jack to intervene. "Hello, Phil, you still there?"

"Jack, don't make me fret again. I'm not going to ask for an explanation about what you said, but whatever's going on has improved your writing. The editorial staff loved your story about Prescott and Faith."

"They'll get better, Phil. In fact, I want you to discard the Jerome story I e-mailed you yesterday. I had a dream last night and can now add a new dimension to Claude Harvey's tale."

"You mean the dead guy, one of those hotel ghosts you mentioned in the story?"

"Exactly. I've got more to say about him. My replacement story will be stronger and focus on his reflections about anger and justice"

"And you got this insight from his ghost?"

"Yes. I have a knack for talking with spirits in my dreams."

"I'm not going there, Jack. Just consider it done."

"Great, I'll e-mail the story before noon."

Jack finished his article, and this time it flowed with a magic, capturing the feelings and emotions of those who lived and died at the hotel. His words offered heart-tugging descriptions with prose that could awaken sympathetic feelings in the most calloused reader.

Later in the day, Phil called and added more effusive praise. He said the editorial staff felt like Harvey's ghost had spoken to each of them. "Marvelous work, Jack. Absolutely excellent."

"Thank you, boss. Claude inspired me."

"In spite of all this weird talk, your writing has evolved into something extraordinary. We're planning to revamp next month's edition to feature your adventures for the magazine's flagship article. Select a good topic. Your work has moved up several notches."

"Thanks, Phil. I like what I'm writing now."

"Is your research complete in Jerome?"

"Yeah, the last article sums it up. I'm ahead of schedule, so I think I'll drive to Sedona for a short visit."

"Why Sedona?"

"It's a personal side trip, a special place for Taylor and me." Jack didn't share his real reason for the diversion. "I'm going to explore the power of vortexes to see if they can energize my words. Don't call me crazy, Phil. I want to see what vortex power is all about."

"I'm not going to question your sanity, but if you can improve the quality of your first two articles, go play in all the energy fields you want. Just don't let any extraterrestrials kidnap you, buddy." His joke evoked no response and an awkward silence followed. "Okay," Phil said, "I'll let you go.

"Give me a call when you reach Flagstaff."

"You've got it, Phil."

Jack jumped out of bed, showered, paid his bill and left the Jerome Grand. He negotiated his car through the town's winding, one-way streets and down the mountain toward Cottonwood. Out of habit, Jack searched the roadside and expected to find Pandora, but no hitchhikers appeared. He spotted a couple of serious bicycle enthusiasts peddling toward Sedona, but no sign of Pandora. *It's strange, but I miss the tiny muse.*

By 10 a.m., he checked into the Best Western Motel. Sedona seemed busy even for early March. Timeshare sales booths, jeep tour outlets and discount tickets for hot air balloon rides lined the main drag. These agencies provided a strange contrast to a plethora of T-shirt shops, chintzy tourist stores, restaurants, bars and art galleries. This odd collection of businesses made Sedona resemble a carnival midway. An occasional palm reader's neon sign added to the eclectic image.

Jack ignored the town's disquieting ambiance and settled into his room. The balcony faced south and offered a magnificent view of Oak Creek Canyon and the river two hundred feet below. He walked outside to admire the huge red sandstone outcroppings dwarfing the human activity. The late morning sun had turned the formations into glorious shades of ochre and crimson. He sighed and soaked in the beauty. He remained in a reflective trance for almost an hour until he recognized the melancholy feeling casting a pall over him. Jack shook off the negative mood and grabbed his jacket to look for *their* favorite restaurant.

His mind flooded with memories of the wonderful weekend he and Taylor spent in Sedona three years ago. They had just started dating, and the three-day weekend evolved into a golden experience. Jack stepped into the Oaxaca Restaurant and Cantina and spotted the corner table where he and Taylor enjoyed brunch on that Saturday morning so long ago. Filled with a glimmer of a joyous future, they lingered over breakfast and giggled like small kids on a picnic.

A waiter brought a bowl of chips, homemade salsa and a menu. He ordered a raspberry margarita, Taylor's favorite, and selected the Red Rocks Enchilada for lunch, the same meal he and Taylor enjoyed on their date. The memory saddened him, but Jack remained determined to repeat all of their actions.

His plan depended on the ability to recreate those memories. He ordered another margarita and a shot of tequila to subdue his sorrow. The buzz helped him regain control and recall how they had spent the rest of their special Saturday.

Whether spawned by alcohol or his recent encounters with the spirit world, Jack added more detail to his bizarre plan. He wanted to use his new clairvoyant power to have a conversation with Taylor. *What if,* he thought, *the energy vortexes in Sedona could open communication channels between me and Taylor? I could use my ability to contact my beloved wife.* "It's possible," Jack said aloud and downed a second shot of tequila.

It's so simple, he thought. *I've exchanged messages with Faith and listened to Claude in my dreams. Perhaps I could be like Jennifer Love Hewitt, the cutie actress who plays the ghost whisperer on TV. But she had to follow a script, and I … I have tapped into real psychic powers.* He smiled at his clever bit of reasoning. *Taylor's death wasn't so long ago. Perhaps her spirit may be waiting to talk to me. She may not be far away. I can tell her how much I loved her and still do.*

With another margarita, his mind flowed with blurred, illogical thinking. *The vortex energy could provide an extra boost so I could talk with her like we used to do at breakfast,* he concluded. "She can identify her murderer," he spoke into his half-empty margarita glass, "and she can tell me how to find him. I'll catch the bastard and then kill him. Just like that …." He snapped his fingers.

Jack's slurred self-talk grew louder, and the people sitting two tables away frowned and sent him disgusted looks. He ignored their scoffs and failed to notice them abandon half-finished meals and leave early.

"I can even the score and have my revenge."

Jack jumped up and wobbled toward the cashier. She took his credit card, looked into the excited man's face and misinterpreted his inebriation for a buoyant attitude.

"You seem pretty happy. Doing anything special this afternoon?"

"You bet," Jack slurred. "I'm going to find a vortex and talk with my dead wife."

The cashier hesitated and looked up to see if he joked. His fixed stare and swaying body revealed no humor. Uncomfortable with further small talk, she hurriedly asked

Jack to sign the receipt and returned his credit card. Oblivious to her distress, Jack stumbled out the door. Several sets of eyes peered at him through the window and turned away. The cashier rolled her forefinger in a circle around her ear. "The guy's nuts."

#####

After a short nap, Jack cleared his head enough to negotiate his vehicle south on 89A toward the Papago Shopping Center. He pulled into the Mystic Rock's parking lot and stared at a small, white clapboard building. It showed signs of neglect and begged for new paint. Jack stepped through the door, and the pungent smell of burning incense assaulted his nostrils. He gasped for air and inhaled small breaths to counter the unpleasant aroma. A thin curtain of glass beads failed to obscure the disarray of randomly stacked books, tarot cards, crystals and various clothing items scattered throughout the showroom. Obviously, effective marketing strategies had not been one of the owner's priorities.

God, I've stepped into a time warp and landed back in the sixties. His eyes slowly adjusted to the dimly lit space, a dramatic contrast to the sundrenched parking lot. Out of habit, he scanned the area in anticipation of seeing Pandora, but no such luck. He smiled at the thought.

A slight man in a dingy-white poet's shirt sat behind a low counter. He reminded Jack of a poster he had seen on a visit to the Haight-Ashbury district of San Francisco. Small, rose-colored glasses sat perched on the end of his nose, and he concentrated on a page from Herman Hess's *Siddhartha*. The man barely moved as Jack approached.

How fitting, Jack thought. *In front of me sits an authentic counter culture refugee, a relic frozen in time. This store was in vogue more than fifty years ago.*

"Excuse me," Jack began.

The man looked over his wire rims and glanced at the intruder. "Yes?"

"Can give me some information about the vortexes in Sedona?"

The clerk's body language let Jack know he preferred reading rather than engage in small talk about vortexes with another tourist. He pointed to a corner of the store and in a monotone voice said, "All of the vortex books are on the table over there, and the rack by the wall contains maps of hiking trails to each one." The man finished his drone sentence and reconnected with the index finger marking his place in the book.

"Thank you," responded Jack. "I don't want to read about the vortexes; I want to talk with someone who knows their power. Are you such a person?"

The man looked up, set his book down and removed his glasses. "Yes, I am." He let out a deep breath and said, "I've lived in Sedona twenty years and have meditated at all the vortex sites. What do you want to know?" He released another sigh.

"My name is Jack Weston, and I am a travel writer for *Western Trails Magazine.*"

Immediately, the man's face lit up and his demeanor changed. "*Western Trails* … I've read that magazine — nice pictures. Are you writing an article about the Sedona vortexes?"

"Possibly …."

The man's voice revealed the first signs of enthusiasm. "Well, welcome to Mystic Rock. I'm Seth Reagan, the owner." He stuck out his hand. He smoothed his long ponytail and tried to tame some stray hairs. Seth cleared his throat and spoke with an air of authority as the impromptu interview continued. "I'd say I am the area's best authority on vortexes. If you do a story about them, you'll probably want to take pictures of me and the shop."

"Pleased to meet you, Seth. I'm doing some research before I write a story. What does a novice like me need to know about a vortex?"

"Plenty. I have discovered the energy from a vortex makes it easier to embrace your higher senses and sharpen perceptions."

"How does vortex power work?"

"A vortex contains an energy field, either electric or magnetic. Vortexes have either an up flow or a down flow of energy — sort of a yin and yang impact on people."

Seth explained upward flowing vortexes like Bell Rock and Cathedral Rock provide a spiritual boost to people who meditate. "An upward flow vortex elevates thought," he said. "These places make you feel like your soul blends with the clouds. Your mind rises above problems and connects with the sky, even heaven."

"What happens in a downward flowing vortex?"

"A downward vortex produces pensive, introspective feelings. People who meditate in these vortexes open their minds to inner fears, doubts and uncertainties."

Seth claimed the entire city of Sedona sat in a downward vortex, but because of traffic and building congestion, the city had become too noisy for anyone to find a place to meditate.

"So, if you want to be reflective, go find a magnetic vortex. If you want to heal an inner hurt or handle a past-life memory, avoid the upward flowing vortexes. Such an energy boost will conflict with your need to find inner peace, and it won't work."

"I guess most tourists don't know the difference."

"Nope. During the day, they climb all over Bell Rock or Airport Mesa and fall in love with the area because they feel connected with the natural beauty enhanced by the positive energy. At night, they return to their motel rooms and enjoy a restful sleep caused by the downward flow of energy. The Chamber of Commerce loves it because people rave about the serenity they find in Sedona."

The two men smiled at the notion. Vortex power had inadvertently provided a lucrative, albeit unplanned marketing plan for the city.

Jack thought about his need to talk with Taylor and asked, "What if a person wants to do both: resolve some past issue and develop greater energy to handle the future?"

"Ah, that's easy. You head for the Boynton Canyon Vortex."

"What's so special about Boynton Canyon?"

"People around here call it the 'twilight zone.' It's a mystical place where the waking world blends with the dream world. Hikers see colored lights and trees shimmer and vibrate. Electric energy flows through your body and opens awareness to possibilities. Whenever I meditate in Boynton Canyon, I get in touch with my tension and can release most of it. The canyon's my favorite place."

"I guess I need to go there," Jack concluded.

Seth showed the writer how to find Boynton Canyon, and in turn, Jack promised he'd mention the Mystic Rock Shop in his next article. To satisfy Seth's ego, Jack took several candid photographs of the dilapidated structure and more photos of its owner posed in front of the building.

Satisfied with his potential fame, Seth sat on the store's front step, located his page in *Siddhartha* and watched Jack wheel his car out of the parking lot toward Boynton Canyon.

Chapter Twenty

Boynton Canyon, the Yavapai Apache's ancestral birth place, offered special healing powers to all who entered. Some locals claimed you could feel Boynton's sacred nature the moment you approached the box canyon. Jack anticipated he had the best chance of contacting Taylor in such a location.

Jack reached the parking lot and began the two-mile walk to the entrance of the canyon. The trail meandered past the upscale Enchantment Resort and Spa. Its pristine, manicured gardens lined the heavy metal fence running parallel to the trail. *The fence keeps the riffraff out, and the foliage placates the hikers,* he thought.

Five hundred yards into the canyon, Jack experienced the first glimmer of its energy. Enhanced by the crimson, orange and cream-colored walls soaring into the sky, the canyon's size dwarfed him and drenched his body in a strange, unexplained sensation. The sounds of the wind and trickling water beckoned him deeper. The trail passed a sandstone spire called The Kachina Woman, and soon Jack found himself surrounded by a thick forest of juniper trees and mahogany-bark Manzanita shrubs.

He stepped off the trail into a clearing and noticed what Seth had described: a shimmering light glittered on the leaves and branches of the foliage in the area. He walked into the trees and observed the same spectacle from different angles. He waved his hands across nearby shrubs, and the sparkling continued. Fascinated, Jack sat for several minutes and watched the glistening waves of energy vibrate.

"This twilight phenomenon must be a conduit to the spirit world," he said aloud to a nearby tree. Jack surmised he had walked into the magnetic source of the vortex and decided to sit in a shady, level area on the side of the trail to absorb the experience. *If I can communicate with Taylor, this will be the spot.*

Jack removed his backpack, took a long drink of water and began to meditate. After sitting in silence for almost thirty minutes, Jack opened his eyes. The afternoon sun had bathed the area in a pleasant, warm glow. The gentle breeze offered a soft backdrop for the twittering birds as they flitted through the trees. Jack had been quiet so long most of the forest critters ignored his presence.

In a whisper, Jack called to his deceased wife. "Taylor, Taylor, I love you, honey. Please talk to me."

Jack waited. Five minutes elapsed and then another five before he tried again.

With greater urgency, he mouthed the words, "Taylor, I miss you so much. It's been so difficult without you. Please talk to me."

Jack's eyes filled with tears, but he choked them back. *I must be strong about this*, he thought. *It's not about me or my loss. I need to concentrate on her.*

Time passed, and the silence continued.

"Taylor, please help me find the man who killed you. Please talk to me. Help me resolve my hurt."

More silence.

"Crap, I did it, again," he shouted. "I asked her to help me take care of my sorrow. Jack, you selfish son-of-a-bitch!"

The sound of his voice scared two birds, previously ignoring his Buddha-like pose, and they flew out of the tree above his head. "Damn it, where's the serenity I felt an hour ago? Concentrate, Jack. You can do this!"

He closed his eyes again and attempted to recapture his initial sense of peace. Too agitated to relax now, he tried a different approach.

"Taylor," he whispered softly, "did you know I have talked with two spirits this week?" he began. "Faith taught me to understand my feelings about fear and disappointment. Then, Claude Harvey taught me about persistence and patience. I won't give up trying to find your killer, dear. I know I can't solve the problem if I'm angry. I'm working on putting my anger away, but I still feel such intense rage when I least expect it."

He paused, took a deep breath and released it. The negative emotions refused to budge, and Jack fought back several urges: to cry, to yell, to tear up the trees and shrubs around him. He shouted into the empty space, "Am I on the edge of insanity with this ghost-talk nonsense? Taylor, I don't know how to cope without you. I need your help to solve the murder."

More silence. No sound except a gentle breeze in the treetops. Now completely sober, Jack became disillusioned with his experiment. Emotions held in check for hours flooded his consciousness. Heartbroken, he lay back on the grass and looked skyward. Blurred by tears, he lost sight of the azure sky with puffs of white clouds framing the deep verdant pine needles. Finally, he ran out of tears and fell into an exhausted sleep.

He woke abruptly. The sun had set and falling temperatures reminded him of the human need for warmth. Shivering, he stood up, rubbed his arms and stomped about to increase blood flow. The vibrating lights had disappeared and the air turned nippy. Stiff and cold, he sprinted toward the parking lot and his waiting vehicle. Dusk created unusual shadows in the canyon and evening dew filled the air. Jack hurried past the resort and ignored the sweet fragrance of roses lingering in the air.

Jack reached his car and simultaneously turned on the engine and its heater. The chill had penetrated his body and disturbed his mind. He reacted to his experiment with anger. He hit the steering wheel and shouted, "What the hell was I thinking? Nobody can actually speak with the ghost of his dead wife. It's all bunk."

On the road back to town, Jack flipped on the radio. Someone dedicated an old Pink Floyd version of "Fearless" to a lost love. The words spilled out of the radio as Jack listened to the melody. With a touch of frustration, Jack said, "Those words ... all day, I wanted to hear you whisper those words to me. You could have spoken the same lyrics to me:

flying above the trees and clouds and listening to the words I shared with you today. "But, you didn't say anything, Taylor," he shouted.

He let out an exasperated breath. Angry again and lonely, he snapped off the radio. *If Taylor could have sent me a message, any message*, he reasoned, *I would have been satisfied.* "I wasted my whole day," he yelled into the front window. "What a fool to think Taylor could talk to me. Enough nonsense," he sighed. "Tomorrow I'll head for Flagstaff and get back to work."

Chapter Twenty-One

By mid-morning, Jack checked out of his hotel and drove toward Flagstaff through Oak Creek Canyon. The winding, narrow road followed the meandering stream through green pines, aspens and rock outcroppings. The highway gained altitude, culminating in a series of switchbacks climbing out of the canyon. A blue Scenic Overlook Ahead sign announced he arrived at the top, and Jack pulled into the parking area to catch a glimpse of the landscape below. Layers of hills dotted by a carpet of pine trees stretched for miles. Still struggling to forget his Boynton adventure, the view refreshed his troubled mind. With less than twenty miles to Flagstaff, he enjoyed a cigarette, transfixed by the beauty he viewed. On the way back to his car, he reached for his keys and heard a familiar voice.

"Hey, where you been?"

Jack turned and saw Pandora walking out of the woods.

"Good morning, Pandora. It's always a surprise to see you when I least expect it."

"I'm glad you finally decided to catch up with me."

"Yeah, I missed you, too," he announced in a flat response. "Need a ride?"

"I thought you'd never ask."

"Get in. How far you going this time? No, don't tell me, you're headed for friends in Flagstaff."

"Yeah, Flagstaff will do for now."

"I should have guessed."

For the moment, he seemed to accept the continuing saga of her unplanned appearances. He lacked the energy to pursue the Pandora puzzle, but curiosity nagged at his mind.

They drove along the two-lane highway, and Jack finally glanced at his now familiar hitchhiker. "I'll bet you're going to call this encounter another coincidence."

"Nope, third time's a charm, and I live a charmed life. Besides, you know there's no such thing as a coincidence."

Jack didn't smile. His mood grew dark and bitterly lashed out, "I guess there really are no accidents either — just unexpected murders."

"I know it's frustrating, but the more you dwell on the hit-and-run, the harder it will be to understand the clues about her death."

Wrapped up in his thoughts, he failed to catch Pandora's reference to Taylor. Instead, his mind focused on the lack of answers in the year-old case. Taylor's killer consumed all of Jack's attention and not Pandora's babbling.

"I know one thing for sure," he blurted. "I have the power to chat with ghosts, but not enough psychic energy to talk with Taylor."

Pandora ignored the driver's words and said, "Perhaps you're trying too hard when obvious messages exist everywhere."

"Right, Western Union sends me telegrams every day," he snapped. "This dilemma is not a parlor game, lady."

Pandora said nothing. The two rode in silence until they turned north on I-17 and drove the last few miles to Flagstaff. Jack exited the interstate and maneuvered onto local streets. A host of stoplights and rush hour traffic added to the congestion. His car inched its way toward the center of town and the Hotel Monte Vista. Pandora turned on the radio without asking, and David Cook's song "Light On" drifted into the front seat. Pandora started singing, intermittently humming a few bars when the words escaped her.

"Just try to keep my spirits up when there's no point to grieving." She sang, hummed a few bars and mouthed, "Try to leave a light on when I'm gone — something to rely on to get home — try to leave a light on when I'm gone."

Jack had no patience for such foolery. He could not tolerate the music or Pandora's voice and abruptly turned off the radio.

"I really don't like songs warbled by love-sick men who lost their lovers. Can't they find other things to sing about?" he grumbled.

"You know, if you pay more attention to the lyrics, you'll discover the words can change your life. Just a thought," she added. "By the way, can you let me out at the next corner?"

"Sure thing." Jack pulled to the curb and said, "Coincidence aside, this will probably be the last time I see you, right?"

"Who knows, anything's possible. I'm sort of habit-forming."

"Yeah, I know," he muttered. His tires squealed as he pulled away.

Chapter Twenty-Two

Jack found a parking space on San Francisco Street and stood in front of the huge brick edifice. The Monte Vista Hotel, built in 1927, earned a reputation for being haunted soon after it opened. Although over time, even the ghosts failed to attract tourists. Eight trains an hour passed in front of the building, making sleep impossible. As the town spread away from the railroad tracks, modern accommodations sprang up closer to the university and quiet neighborhoods, successfully drawing tourists away from the busy downtown area.

The current owners tried to revitalize the hotel by creating customized theme rooms around the persona of movie greats who once stayed there. The effort permitted the "Monte," as locals called it, to enjoy a resurgence of activity.

In the early 1950s, Hollywood studios established their headquarters at the hotel when they filmed westerns in Oak Creek Canyon. Now, memorabilia from Jane Russell, John Wayne, Gary Cooper, Bing Crosby and Spencer Tracy filled every available space. The Debbie Reynolds room, for example, greeted guests with various shades of shocking, bright pink and loud, crimson furniture. The gaudy room's décor attacked the senses, but became a unique conversation piece for those who could tolerate the furnishings — a great story for guests to share when they returned home. Jack rejected staying in this room because it reminded him more of a festival than a place to complete his assignment.

Overall, the funky, historic hotel appealed to Jack's sense of imagination. He stashed his suitcase in one of the "haunted rooms" and searched for a restaurant. He found The Cottage Place a few blocks from the hotel. It had been a vintage home, converted into a restaurant in the 1980s. The owners had refurbished "the old house on the corner" and turned it into a charming, homey eatery.

Jack ordered a gin martini and the tequila lime jumbo shrimp appetizer, followed by chicken piccata. He topped off the meal with a snifter of Grand Marnier and coffee.

Nostalgically, Jack recalled the quiet, romantic dinners, once an enjoyable pattern, shared with Taylor. To protect their anonymity, the couple often searched for small "mom and pop" restaurants like this one in out-of-the-way locations. When Jack finished his coffee, he thought, *Taylor would have enjoyed sharing this dinner with me tonight.*

On the way back to his hotel, he stopped at the Wine Loft on San Francisco Street to sample their selection of sweet after-dinner drinks. The hotel clerk suggested this diversion, and it didn't disappoint him. He made a note to include this establishment as a sidebar for his article about the "Monte spirits."

Jack returned to his room and reviewed the notes he made about various ghosts who called Monte their home. According to one story, the spirits of two prostitutes delighted in haunting male guests who stayed in his rented room. Flagstaff once had a red-light district across the tracks from the hotel, and a randy hotel guest invited two "ladies of the evening" to join him for a few hours of group interaction. The women accepted, anticipating a night filled with fun and profit. However, by morning police discovered the dead bodies of the ladies on the street below and the hotel guest missing.

Over the years, men who stayed in this room experienced disconcerting nights. The ghost registry claimed these guests woke up in the middle of the night and felt a woman's cold hand cover their mouth and then another hand grasp their throat. Pinned to the bed, a second female ghost would tease and torment the hotel guest in a form of erotic torture. Intrigued by the tale, Jack wanted to experience this phenomenon and add such an episode to his article.

Jack settled in for the night, but sounds from the saloon below and the passing trains challenged his ability to sleep. In time, he submitted to fatigue and experienced a series of fitful nightmares. Like many of his recent dreams, disconnected conversations failed to follow logical threads, but kept the writer fascinated. For example, in one dream episode, Jack interviewed the two prostitutes as he sat in bed.

"I don't understand why you ladies chose to spend the night with your 'john' in the hotel rather than going to your place of business across the tracks."

"You don't get it," said Sheila, a tall red-haired woman dressed in a flimsy negligee. "If we worked in our crib, we'd have to pay a percentage to the local police — split the profit with them. This invitation became a side job, and we'd keep all the money."

"The police got a cut of what you made?"

The second lady, a bleached-blonde dressed in a black corset and garter belt named Roxy, added, "Jack, none of us ladies who turn tricks in the red-light district could function without the law's protection. It's part of the business."

"You're not so naive to think the authorities looked the other way, are you?" Sheila added.

"I actually never thought about it."

"Look, honey," said Roxy, "even in a small town like Flagstaff, everyone had to make a living. The pimp, the cops and even the judges got a piece of the action."

"Did the action apply to booze, as well?" he asked.

"C'mon. Were you born yesterday? The Prohibition Law passed in 1919, and the cops didn't pay attention to the bootleg business here in Flagstaff or raid the Monte until 1931. You figure it out."

"I didn't know," said Jack. "I heard rumors the lounge downstairs distributed whiskey and beer to northern Arizona through its back door, but it never dawned on me the hooch business thrived at the Monte for so long."

"It did until the gentile folks in town got religion," Roxy said.

"Out here in Arizona, the mob didn't run booze, locals did." added Sheila.

When awake, Jack thought the dream seemed absurd. He remembered taking notes as his two gorgeous interviewees sprawled across his bed, occasionally adjusting their sheer, fluffy gowns in feigned modesty. In the dream, Jack tried to ignore their alluring attire and focus on the story. Awake, he could now visualize the conversation as if it really happened.

"You both claim public officials in small towns like Flagstaff could be bought back then, right?"

Sheila sat up, pulled her gown over an exposed breast and said, "What do you mean back then? Are you some kind of Puritan dunce? It's un-American not to buy-off officials, ain't it?"

Jack woke with a start. A group of college students on San Francisco Street had broken into a boisterous song, rattling him out of his dreamscape. He stared into the dark shadows dancing about the room as the flickering neon sign outside sputtered off and on. He realized the two ladies had not actually been present for the interview. However, the vivid images of the two spirits offered a moment of clarity.

Unable to sleep, he jumped out of bed and put on a pair of jeans and a sweatshirt. Jack grabbed his *one free cocktail* coupon from the top of his dresser and headed downstairs to the bar. He studied the surroundings through different eyes.

The bartender brought Jack a beer and informed him of last call.

Reading the man's name tag, Jack asked, "Say, Ron, can I ask you a question?"

"Sure, fire away."

"How much crap do you guys get from the liquor commission or the cops for operating this bar?"

"This is a college town, mister. We have ...," he hesitated, trying to find the most politically correct words, "what you'd call a mutual understanding with the police. We guarantee the college kids don't jump in their cars like idiots or leave here drunk. The cops don't want to deal with accidents caused by drunken kids, particularly when they have to explain those tragedies to parents who spend a lot of money sending their kids to NAU."

"So, you monitor college-aged drinking, and in return ... what?"

"If we do our job, they don't have to do theirs. Get my drift?"

"You're saying officials don't take bribes like they used to in the old days, but they look the other way when someone violates a minor rule."

"You got it. It's the old, *I'll-scratch-your-back-and-you-scratch-mine* mentality."

"So you cover for each other?"

"Yup."

"And nobody goes crazy if a few liquor laws are broken?"

"You got it. We're a mutual admiration society. Being hard-ass about everything is bad for business, public relations and political longevity. We don't give the puritanical crusaders anything to turn into a cause."

"The public's never the wiser and do-gooders spend their time in church or planning civic projects. They don't have to waste energy monitoring the bars," Jack added.

"Right, mister. And whenever something out of the ordinary happens, we work together to put a lid on it."

"You mean, cover it up?"

"Call it what you want, but that's the way it works in this town and in every other place across America. You can bet on it."

Jack downed the last gulp of beer, left a five-dollar tip and said, "Thanks for the civics lesson, Ron. I've been educated twice tonight."

Exhausted, the writer headed for his room and fell into bed without removing his clothes. In the morning, he awoke, located a coffee shop with an Internet link and opened his laptop. The keys clicked fervently as he described several intriguing tales about the Hotel Monte Vista from an historical perspective. His lighthearted article featured stories about the paranormal characters who still roamed Monte's guest rooms.

Jack enjoyed expanding on the notations he located in the hotel's ghost registry. One in particular fascinated him. Apparently, several guests recorded a number of encounters with the "meat man's ghost" who haunted a room on the second floor. They reported smelling fresh meat drying in the closet. Jack inspected the closet for himself and caught a faint whiff of cooked bacon. He smiled and attributed the odor to the kitchen on the first floor.

In spite of the discovery, his article contained tales of the other unique ghosts, sightings of poltergeists and bizarre aberrations — enough to intrigue his avid readers. His humorous approach created descriptions causing even him to laugh.

The Western Trails article, with its additional sidebars about Flagstaff's unique shops and popular night spots, painted an inviting image of this northern Arizona town and its location on historic Route 66. He e-mailed the story to Phil and relaxed. He spent the remainder of the evening following the college crowd around in their traditional pub crawl.

Jack shot pool and challenged various rivals to play for beers. Fatigue and an excessive amount of alcohol caused him to lose the ability to concentrate. Close to midnight, a smartass college kid with a big mouth took him for a hundred dollars. Instead of "teaching the punk a lesson," he heard the seductive whisper of sleep beckon him to bed. The loss of money didn't matter because he enjoyed the *guy thing* and liked the return to his competitive, macho side, even for one night. He had finally stepped outside of his grief, albeit momentarily, and enjoyed something close to feeling normal again.

Sleep came quickly, and Jack rested soundly until 3 a.m. when his excessive consumption urged him to use the bathroom. He returned to bed and started dreaming again. This time he lay on his back watching puffy clouds meander slowly across a sapphire-colored sky. He closed his eyes, and when they opened again, Taylor's image smiled at him. She leaned down and kissed him.

"How did you get here?" he asked.

"Darling, I am everywhere. You can find me in everything you do."

"I miss you so much!"

"I know, and I miss your touch as well," the dream image replied.

Jack reached up to caress her face, but couldn't make contact. "Taylor, I can talk with spirits, but I was unable to contact you in Boynton Canyon. I don't understand."

"It's okay. I am communicating with you now."

"Then tell me who killed you. I want to punish him."

"Remember, Sarah told you the car hit me from behind, and I never saw it coming."

"I know, but I thought you could help."

"Pay attention to other messages. They will help you find the answer."

"Now you sound like Pandora."

The clouds evaporated, and Taylor's image disappeared. Jack called out, "Taylor, don't go, don't go. I love you, Taylor ...."

He woke abruptly to an empty room. Night had transitioned into morning. Taylor's visit and the two prostitutes — just dreams. Jack shook the sleep from his brain, stripped off his nasty-smelling clothes and jumped in the shower.

Before checking out, the hotel clerk urged Jack to enjoy breakfast at the highly touted La Bellavia Restaurant. "If you can eat all of their signature three-pancake breakfast, the waitstaff will take your picture and post it on the bulletin board"

He barely finished one, but opened his laptop and added another story to his list of Flagstaff sidebars.

Stuffed and uncomfortable, Jack took a short walk on the Northern Arizona University campus. The start of Spring break left the campus deserted, permitting him to walk the area alone. He stopped at the student union and purchased a sweatshirt, then headed back to the hotel. The quiet morning gave him time to reflect on his recent dreams. He wondered how long such dreams would fill his nights. He set this unproductive thinking aside, loaded his car and drove out of town.

Chapter Twenty-Three

He headed east toward New Mexico. In seven hours, Jack planned to arrive at the La Fonda Inn in time for dinner. Santa Fe, known for its gastronomic delights and fine arts galleries, filled him with delightful anticipation. Given its illustrious reputation, he eagerly looked forward to spending several days in Santa Fe's historic downtown. This leg of his trip would invite his senses to feast on everything in the city from quality food to intriguing ghost stories.

The trip progressed smoothly, but thirty miles west of Winslow, Arizona, he saw signs beckoning tourists to visit the meteor crater. With time to spare, Jack felt the urge to indulge his curiosity and stop at the unusual phenomenon. He left the interstate and followed the narrow asphalt road to the natural marvel. *Perhaps the site will inspire future stories*, he reasoned.

As a small child, Jack recalled being frightened by falling meteors. He believed they were aliens from outer space. At the age of six, he couldn't differentiate between "meat eaters" from space and "meteors from space." He desperately wanted to avoid bloodthirsty aliens from remote galaxies who wanted to take him home for dinner. He'd hide in his closet whenever a falling star streaked across the night sky. But, when his first grade teacher clarified the misunderstanding, the budding learner became fascinated by the mysteries of space and the unknown wonders lurking in the wide expanse "out there."

He read about the Arizona crater in school, but now took the opportunity to see it in person. The ten-minute drive placed him at the welcome center perched on the edge of a deep crater stretching almost fifteen hundred feet across. Its immense size and grandeur astounded him.

Jack watched the explanatory movie documenting the site's history and various explorations conducted over the years. He walked outside to observe the actual evidence of the meteor's assault. Overwhelmed, he sat in awe of the gigantic scar left in the flat desert landscape. For more than an hour, the writer-turned-tourist studied the sight and pondered his place in the universe. Then, his mood turned philosophical. *When you see this, what happened to Taylor and I may not be significant in the big picture of things. Instead of fighting reality, I need to learn to deal with it.*

On his drive back to the highway, reason began to dominate his mind. *On earth, life and death routinely occur every day. I need to find an acceptable balance and stay in touch with my needs,* he thought. *It's the only way I will ever find happiness again.*

The empty road snaked through the desert landscape and filled Jack with loneliness. To fight the mood, he flipped on the radio. Jack Reed and The Velvet Underground belted out the song "Beginning To See The Light." The speakers rattled, and his fingers drummed the song's beat on the steering wheel. The isolated road permitted Jack to focus on the song's lyrics and the words finally began to make sense. Jack slowed his vehicle to a crawl. "Oh, my god," he shouted. "I'm beginning to see the light — the song is about me. Figure out what the words mean, Jack."

He pulled his car to the side of the road and attempted to control his excitement. *What did Pandora say?* He tried to remember her words. *'Lyrics reveal meaning.'* Jack got out of his vehicle and walked into the desert to clarify his new insight.

Blathering, he said, "You're either losing it, or it's beginning to make sense." In frustration, he turned around and headed back to the car. *What the hell happened to me in the last couple of days? I may be going crazy.*

He placed his hands on the hood and felt the warmth from the vehicle's engine. He stared at his reflection in the front window. *It seems strange, almost impossible,* he thought. *But, if I assume I actually heard voices from beyond and the song lyrics send me messages, perhaps I **am** beginning to see the light.*

"What did the lyrics say?" he spoke to the car. His mind remembered the words: *People work hard and still never get it right.* "The words tell me not to work too hard to find Taylor's killer. I need to slow down to understand the clues," he spoke aloud to the desert wind. He turned to speak to his reflection in the car's window. "I can only solve the mystery if I take time and use reason." *Relax, man, and get it right.*

His mind raced. Spirits had channeled messages to help him deal with grief, and now song lyrics offered clues to solve the murder. *You've been too busy feeling sorry for yourself and missed everything.* "Think, Jack," he said aloud. "Pandora told me to watch for the signs. Taylor talked about understanding messages. 'Let the world speak to you,' she said. 'Listen to the voices.'" He kicked at the gravel by the side of the road. "What a fool I've been — see the light, of course."

He climbed into his car and continued back to the interstate. He checked the time and calculated his side trip had frittered away valuable driving hours. But, he didn't regret the delay. He passed Winslow at 3 p.m. and realized the drive had only covered sixty miles since he left Flagstaff. Jack knew he wouldn't arrive in Santa Fe until late in the evening and decided not to push it. He cancelled his reservation at the La Fonda Hotel and elected to spend the night in Gallup, New Mexico. An overnight there would leave him refreshed for a short drive in the morning and put him in Santa Fe by lunch, another opportunity for a great meal.

Chapter Twenty-Four

Road construction delayed Jack's progress even more. He congratulated himself for the decision to stay in Gallup. *You can't write a good ghost story if you're fatigued.* Roadside signs began to appear along the interstate inviting travelers to stay at the historic La Secreta in downtown Gallup. Captivated by the possibility of more encounters with spirits, Jack headed for the inn.

Nostalgic memorabilia dripping with western authenticity filled the lobby. The night clerk told the traveler of the hotel's resident ghosts, and Jack decided to stay. After being assigned a room on the second floor, he located the restaurant and enjoyed a light evening meal. *The food doesn't come close to what Santa Fe will offer, but I'll appreciate it even more tomorrow.*

Jack recalled he had not seen Pandora all day. He had grown accustomed to listening to her sanguine comments, and for some unexplained reason, missed her chatter. He wanted to share the insights he discovered today with a person who might understand. *But, the woman has a life of her own,* he thought. *I'm not the center of her universe.*

Jack relaxed in his room and read a few pages of a western novel purchased in the gift shop. He had not read a book in over a year and enjoyed the pleasant diversion. However, tired eyes soon lulled him to sleep.

In the middle of the night, the sound of an argument awakened him. Loud voices filled his room. Jack sat up and said, "Who's there?" No response, yet the angry shouting match continued as if the combatants stood at the end of his bed.

Jack snapped on the table lamp. Still alone, the voices grew louder and exploded in his room with venomous, hateful words.

"You bitch! You slept with my best friend. You're just a whore!" a man's voice yelled.

"I don't care anymore," a woman responded. "I get lonely waiting for you to come home. I've got needs, too, you know!"

Jack noticed the words sounded slurred and garbled. He could tell they had been drinking. *But where are the voices coming from?*

Jack looked around for the source and said, "Who's talking? Show yourself."

The argument continued.

"After all I've done for you. Then you go and cheat on me," the male voice yelled again. "I ought to smack you."

Jack heard the woman cry. Through broken sobs she wailed, "You're so involved with your goddamn job. You never have time for me." More crying muffled her words.

Jack finally looked up toward the ceiling. The voices spilled out of the heating vent. The old hotel had not upgraded its ventilation system, and all the rooms on the same floor shared a common vent. The conduit magnified sounds, acting like a megaphone.

"Look, bitch," the man went on. "I have to support my ex-wife and three kids, and now you. The divorce cost me big bucks, and you want a lot of shit I can't afford."

"I hate you. I hate you," the woman yelled through her tears. Jack heard a glass shatter followed by the sound of a slap, more weeping and then silence.

He stood on a chair with his ear cocked to the vent and strained to listen. Stressful questions raced through his head. *Was the woman in trouble? Is she being beaten by a thug of a husband? Do I need to intervene or call the cops?*

Determined to be a Good Samaritan, he slipped on his pants and walked stealthily down the hall, listening for sounds at each door. *If I need to step in and break up a fight*, he screwed up his courage, *I'll do it.*

Jack located the sound of loud voices pouring through the closed door of room 226 and stood outside in silence. With only the width of a wooden panel separating him from the couple, the would-be hero listened more intently. He felt like a peeping Tom at the bedroom door, but heard the two resume their argument.

"I don't love you anymore," she said. "You're never around."

"What the fuck do you expect? I have to work all the time to support you." The man grumbled again about working double shifts to pay the bills and paying child support. A long silence seemed to end the ruckus, but the man exploded again. "Then, when I'm working my ass off, you screw my best friend. Why?"

"I had to get even with you for sleeping with those strippers and whores. How do you feel now, shithead?" The talk stopped abruptly, followed by the sound of bodies tussling. Jack prepared to knock on the door, but changed his mind when the woman's voice yelled, "Go ahead and hit me again if you've got the balls. I'll have you arrested, and they'll fire your ass."

The room grew quiet, and Jack put his ear to the door, but heard nothing. He stood barefoot, shivering in the hall and shook his head. He assumed excessive alcohol and fatigue finally disabled both of them. Satisfied the lover's quarrel had ended, and overcome by the cold air, he tiptoed back to his room, climbed into bed and fell asleep.

The high drama kept him from returning to a peaceful slumber. Jack tossed and turned for the remainder of the night. A montage of disconnected dreams tumbled through his head. Finally, the misty gray of pre-dawn replaced the black licorice night and woke him. Completely exhausted, Jack opened one eye, turned away from sunlight seeping through a crack in the curtains and snuggled deep into his bed. He felt exhausted.

Oblivious to time, Jack awoke to the sound of the same voices he heard the previous night. Even in his bleary, drowsy state, the writer heard the male voice utter a phrase that immediately snapped him awake. Unable to determine if the words came from a dream or flowed out of the vent, Jack vigorously shook his head to clear away the last cobwebs of sleep.

Did I hear that correctly? Did the guy just say, "Look, bitch, don't fuck with me again. I've already run over one woman, and I can easily take out another?"

Jack bolted out of bed, stumbling with grogginess, but determined to clear his senses and hear more. Overcome by a severe headache, he fell back into bed. He tried to recreate the words he heard. Then, an almost irrational thought seized his mind. *That voice — the same one I heard last night, the one behind door 226, admitted he killed a woman. He confessed to running over a woman with his car. Could he be Taylor's murderer? I get it.*

With some difficulty, Jack heaved his body out of bed again, stood on a chair and strained to hear more dialogue. "Say something else about the woman you ran over, you son-of-a-bitch," he whispered. *Say anything to let me know I heard a real voice, not one of my weird dreams.* Out of desperation, he spoke into the vent, "Hello, can anyone hear me?" No response.

Impatient, Jack's mind jumped to a wishful conclusion. *This can't be a coincidence. Even Pandora told me as much. I know I heard the voice of Taylor's killer.*

"Wait, Jack," he spoke into the slats in the vent. "This is crazy stuff, and I'm really tired." He remained standing on his chair, transfixed by the possibility of hearing another sound. He held his breath, like a caged bird sensing the presence of a cat. "How do I find the truth?" he spoke aloud again.

Anxiety and hope raced through his mind. Convinced he heard a confession, Jack started to pace, trying to decide what to do. He felt confined by his room and had to get out. He splashed cold water on his face, brushed his teeth and slipped into his jeans. He pulled on his new NAU sweatshirt, put on his loafers and headed downstairs.

He spotted the desk clerk, a woman in her early fifties, with atrocious-looking dyed hair piled on her head like a stack of moldy hay. She wore half-framed glasses tethered by a chain around her neck and remained focused on matching credit card receipts with checkout forms.

"Excuse me," Jack interrupted, "I need some information, please?" His high-pitched voice and shrill demand annoyed the woman.

She looked over her glasses and placed an index finger to her lips as a signal for him to be quiet while she counted.

Infuriated, he stomped around the lobby like a spoiled child. "Such insolence," he muttered. The woman remained aloof, ignored Jack's tantrum and continued her audit. Obviously agitated, Jack paced in front of the desk, his body language showing contempt. He let out a deep guttural sound causing the woman to glance over her glasses again.

"I'll be right with you, sir," she spoke tersely. She returned to her task and shook her head.

Jack approached the desk. "Please, I need to know one piece of information. Can I interrupt long enough to ask you one quick question?"

The woman sent him a look of disdain. Her face flushed, eyes reduced to tiny slits. Crimson blotches appeared above her starched, tightly buttoned collar and crawled up her neck. "Please exercise some courtesy, young man. Can't you see I'm busy?"

Jack pressed his lips together and silently glared at her. His movements let her know he had no intention of behaving.

With a huff, she put down her papers and placed a pen in the pile to hold her place. She frowned at him, and with a tisk of her tongue asked in a haughty tone, "What?"

Jack blurted his question. "Who stayed in room 226 last night? I need to know the name."

"Absolutely not, sir. We have a confidentiality policy at this hotel."

"But, you don't understand. The man in the room could have been involved in a hit-and-run accident ... a murderer who killed my wife!"

"Are you with the police department, sir? Do you have a badge or some credentials to show me?"

"No, but I heard him admit he ran over some woman!"

"Are you sure it wasn't a bad dream?"

"No, no, I was awake. I have to know his identity and talk to him."

"I'm sorry. Unless you have some official authorization, I cannot, in good conscience, violate my ethical responsibility to protect the identity of our guests. Besides, they probably checked out already."

Frustrated by her bean-counter mentality, Jack exploded, "Listen, woman, this is bullshit! I have a chance to solve a murder, and you have the audacity to play god and protect people's privacy?"

"Sir, you must calm down, or I'll be forced to call security."

"Hell, call security. Call the manager. Yes, I demand to speak to the manager," Jack shouted.

"Excuse me, sir," she said in an authoritative voice. "I am the manager, and your behavior has crossed the line." The deliberate, slow intonation re-established her authority and self-importance. "Either calm down or I'll have you forcibly ejected from the premises. It will be my pleasure to have you arrested." She reached for the telephone.

Not wanting to be derailed from his quest, Jack said, "Okay, okay. I quit. I'll leave on my own. No need to strong-arm me, lady." He backed away from the desk with his hands raised.

Still irritated, he tried to think of another way to discover the couple's identity. He walked upstairs, past his room, and headed down the hall. He knocked on the door to room 226. Slightly ajar, it opened with a gentle push. "Hello, anybody here?"

He walked into a deserted room. The maid had not yet cleaned it, and he had some time to himself. The Gestapo manager spoke the truth; they had already checked out. Jack inspected the room and looked in the bathroom. Wet towels littered the floor and tissues covered the counter. *Both of them must be slobs.*

VOICES

The bed, a disheveled mess with the bottom sheet torn away from the mattress, gave witness to the couple's fretful night. Jack glanced up at the heat vent and shook his head.

He found an empty bottle of Jack Daniels on the table next to the television and shards of broken glass on the floor. He sat in a chair and glanced around. His eyes searched for any clue to betray their identity.

His spotted a pad of paper sitting at an angle next to the telephone by the bed. He picked up the hotel notepad and saw the faint outline of a name, address and phone number on the top page. Jack took the pad back to his room, located a number 2 pencil and played Sherlock Holmes. *Jack Weston, private detective*, he thought. *I can't believe this old movie trick may work.* He lightly rubbed the graphite across the page in short strokes. Soon he could make out the words written on the previous page. White marks left from the indentations spelled: *Jim Swanson, Plaza Hotel, Las Vegas, N.M.* Further down, the numbers *(505) 429* ... became visible. The remaining digits were unreadable.

Jack turned on his laptop and searched for the Plaza Hotel in Las Vegas, New Mexico. He called and asked to speak to Jim Swanson. In a few minutes, the receptionist clicked back on and asked, "Excuse me, sir, when did Mr. Swanson check into the hotel?"

"I don't know, miss. By your question, I assume he isn't a guest and doesn't work for you."

"That's correct, sir. We do not have a Jim Swanson staying here or a reservation for him."

"Do you have any rooms available? I'd like to stay at the Plaza tonight."

Jack made the reservation and checked Google maps to determine time and distance to Las Vegas. He looked at his watch, almost 8 a.m. He'd have breakfast at a fast-food joint and cover the two-hundred-sixty miles in just over four hours. The drive would put him at the Plaza shortly after noon. Then he'd begin the search for James Swanson and his connection to the couple in 226. Motivated by renewed energy, Jack forgot about his headache and pushed on to Las Vegas.

Part Three: Making the Pieces Fit

There are no extra pieces in the universe.
Everyone is here because he or she has a place to fill,
and every piece must fit itself into the big jigsaw puzzle.

*— **Deepak Chopra***

Chapter Twenty-Five

Jack swung his car back onto the interstate and set the cruise control. He didn't want to lose more time chatting with the New Mexico Highway Patrol. Jack decided to abandon his scheduled stop in Santa Fe and pursue the man he suspected of killing Taylor. He planned to substitute a possible Plaza Hotel ghost story for the one he anticipated writing in Santa Fe. He counted on Phil's approval. *This hunt takes precedence over gourmet food or any ghost stories I can find in Santa Fe.*

For the next hour, Jack's mind re-played the words he heard the voice speak. *Real or imagined? Don't know, but I can't take a chance and let this lead evaporate.* Compelled to investigate the link between the voice's words and Taylor's death, he thought about Pandora. *Was his stay at the La Secreta Inn meant to be? Did the hotel reveal the "secret identity" of the murderer? Too bizarre to waste time analyzing it now. Just go after it.*

Jack had been so consumed with the voice he forgot to refuel before leaving Gallup. A glance at the gauge showed the car needed gas before he could reach Albuquerque. He randomly chose an off-ramp outside of Grants, New Mexico, and pulled into a truck stop. After fueling his vehicle, he paid inside and purchased a bottle of water for the final leg of the trip. When Jack returned to his car, he found Pandora leaning against his vehicle.

"Hi, Jack." She greeted him with a smile and said, "I recognized your car and thought you might like some company."

"Well, my little mystery lady, I assumed I'd seen the last of you. Apparently not."

"Jack, didn't I tell you I'd be there whenever you needed me?"

"You mentioned it a couple of times, but since I haven't seen you in days, I thought you might be stalking someone else by now."

"Remember, I'm a guardian angel," she smiled.

"Okay, Ms. Angel, jump in."

Initially, Jack chose to ignore this appearance. He decided delving into the conundrum would distract from his primary mission: finding the identity of the voice. The Pandora dilemma could wait. She didn't matter.

They rode without talking for several miles. Jack occasionally glanced at Pandora, who had pulled a sweater over her shoulders and fallen asleep. *With the exception of those horrid dreadlocks, Pandora has a sweet face. With a hot, soapy shower, a new hairstyle and some makeup, Miss Pandora would be presentable in most circles.*

The longer she slept and the further he drove, the more difficult it became to dismiss her continuous invasion of his space. He mentally reviewed her appearances and it frustrated him. *This is the fourth time I've picked her up. What's with that? Random occurrences, coincidence or some mystical message? No, that's crazy shit? Stop it, Jack.*

He shook a Camel out of its pack and grabbed it with his lips. With his left hand on the steering wheel, he found some matches in the console. Using the thumb and forefinger of his right hand, he deftly exposed one match from its cardboard container, bent it over, closed the cover and lit the match against the striking surface.

At the exact moment, Pandora opened her eyes and bolted upright. She seemed startled by the flame so close to her face and raised a hand to shield it. She quickly regained her composure, but still seemed flustered. She tried to minimize her reaction and forced a smile. "Have you been watching me sleep or concentrating on the road?"

Jack exhaled a cloud of smoke surrounding his grin. "I didn't think guardian angels ever slept."

"How long have I been out?" asked Pandora, without responding to his tease.

"About a half-hour."

She stretched her arms, yawned and turned to watch the desert landscape whiz by. "Tell me about your past couple of days," she finally asked.

Strange woman to figure out, he thought. *But, I wonder what she'll think of my new insight.*

"I heard the voices of more ghosts in my dreams. Then, a bartender in Flagstaff reminded me anyone can be bought — money talks — the American way of life."

"A bit jaded, isn't it?" Pandora said.

"Maybe, but greed keeps the system running. I forgot that simple truth."

Pandora changed the subject. "Listen to any good music lately?"

Perplexed, Jack looked at her and said, "Yeah, as a matter of fact, I did. Why do you ask?"

"There's a strong connection between what people think and the music they hear."

Jack continued. "You don't say. Surprisingly, one of the songs made sense to me."

"Tell me about it."

The driver looked at his wide-eyed companion and tried to determine if she was playing a mind game or seriously wanted to know his thoughts.

"Okay, if songs offer messages, you'll understand what I discovered yesterday." After sharing his epiphany about "Beginning to See the Light," Jack turned to Pandora and asked, "What do you think? Am I losing it, or tuned in?"

"My advice: heed the message and get it right."

"There's something else, Pandora."

"What?"

"Last night I heard the voice of Taylor's killer, and I'm on a mission to track him down." Jack explained the events of his encounter.

"So, if the voice you heard admitted killing Taylor, you're now on the trail of a *live* human, not a dead one."

Jack stared at his passenger and studied her sincerity. "Why do you continually step into my life, Pandora?"

"It doesn't matter. Our paths cross because of fate. I'm a good listener and give you great feedback. Guess you're lucky."

"Okay, mystery woman, I'll accept your lame answer for now, but we need to talk more about this."

"In time, we may." They drove into Albuquerque, and Pandora reached for the radio. "Do you mind?"

"No, fine ...."

The Evermore song "Light Surrounding You" filled the vehicle. Pandora listened to the tune for a while and then, as it had become her pattern, sang along. "I want you to know that I see the light surrounding you, so don't be afraid of something new." As with most other songs they listened to, she lost track of words and started humming the melody.

Jack listened to the lyrics. Pandora swayed to the rhythm and ignored him. Finally, he turned off the radio and stared at her in earnest.

"I've been thinking about what you said about song lyrics. What's so special about the words?"

"It's no big mystery. Music is a personal thing. The lyrics have special meaning for different people. So, figure out what the words say to you. Nothing more to explain."

Irritated by her response, Jack pondered his own question. *What do the words really mean? What message do I need to figure out?*

Jack felt confused, and a stress headache began to march across his forehead. He rubbed the back of his neck and turned his head toward Pandora to ask for more explanation, but she had already slumped down and fallen asleep again.

They reached Albuquerque and headed north. In spite of fatigue, lack of sleep and anxiety, Jack made a commitment to cover the remaining distance between Albuquerque and Las Vegas to rendezvous with James Swanson and the mysterious voice.

In less than an hour, Pandora sat up, stretched and announced, "Jack, I want to stop in Santa Fe. You can let me off at the next exit. I'll thumb a ride into town."

"You sure? I can take you into the city."

"No, thanks. You're too kind. I know you've got important business at the Plaza Hotel. I'll just hitchhike."

Jack let her out and continued his trek. As he drove over Glorieta Pass, his mind returned to his conversations with Pandora. *When did I first mention Taylor's death? How did she know? I told her I was headed for Las Vegas, but I don't remember saying anything about the Plaza Hotel? Did she guess?*

He shook his head and said aloud, "I can't take time to wonder about her any more. I have to find the voice." He checked the odometer and calculated he'd arrive in Las Vegas in less than an hour. *First things first: locate Jim Swanson, He's my only hope.*

Chapter Twenty-Six

Jack reached Las Vegas shortly after noon and followed the posted signs to the Plaza Hotel. The street opened into a Spanish-style town square, reminiscent of the nostalgic trappings of frontier history. Las Vegas had not been on Jack's original list of cities to visit, and he knew nothing about the town or its past. He'd have to dig around to find material for his next travel article.

Jack parked across from the hotel and registered. The desk clerk suggested he stay in room 310 if he wanted to encounter haunted spirits. Guests claimed the ghost of the former owner, Byron T. Mills, appeared there some nights. After inspecting the room, Jack contacted Phil to report his new location.

"Where have you been for the last two days?" Phil shouted into the phone.

"Sorry, Phil," offered Jack. "I got sidetracked and fell into a big rabbit hole."

"What the hell are you talking about? Don't get cute with me just because you're writing Pulitzer Prize stuff."

"Sorry, a personal joke. Lighten up, boss."

"When will you be sending me your Santa Fe story?"

"It's the reason I called. I'm not in Santa Fe. I moved on to Las Vegas."

"What the hell are you doing in Vegas? Don't tell me you had the urge to gamble."

"No, Phil, wrong Las Vegas. I'm at the Plaza Hotel in Las Vegas, New Mexico. I discovered another haunted hotel while chasing down a voice."

"A voice? Okay, have you been smoking something with the rabbit friend of yours?"

"No, no, the rabbit and I had dinner with Alice, but I'm all right."

"I warned you about going off the deep end, Jack. Do you need medical help?"

"Relax, I'm joking. It's a long story, and I can't talk about it now. Have patience, and I promise to send another article from here."

"Okay, but I need your commitment to check in more frequently so I can keep the vultures off my back. Remember, your assignment stretched the traditional boundaries of our magazine."

"Yeah, I remember and appreciate the opportunity. However, I have also tracked down information about Taylor's death and need to pursue it."

"Damn it, Jack. I didn't send you out of Phoenix to play detective. You're supposed to use your time away to heal and not dig into the past."

"I couldn't help it, Phil, the past found me. Besides, the voices I've heard from the other side have guided me, cleared my thinking about Taylor's murder. I'll tell you more about it when I get back. Too much to share on the phone. I don't want you to think I'm crazy and fire me."

"Too late, my friend, I'm already uncomfortable with what you're doing. You sure you're okay?"

"Yes, Phil, trust me. I am stronger today than I have been in months."

Jack hung up and strolled into the plaza square to become more familiar with the town. He thought about his editor's loyalty and concern. *Nice to have a friend like Phil.*

Jack explored the historical setting and began to take notes for his next article. One of the last Spanish colonies established in the United States, Las Vegas had been settled in 1835 by Mexicans. The town consisted of several buildings surrounded by low, adobe walls enclosing a rectangular plaza. For years, the city thrived as a shelter on the Santa Fe Trail. Las Vegas had been the only town along the route to protect merchants and travelers from the Apaches who preyed on isolated wagons filled with trade goods.

Jack located the local newspaper office, the Las Vegas *Optic,* and talked with the editor. After they exchanged initial pleasantries, Jack expressed a desire to learn more about the community. Joshua Moore, the editor, offered the writer a wealth of historical stories.

"During the Mexican-American War, Gen. Stephen Kearney declared all of New Mexico an American possession as he marched through this area. The arrival of the railroad in 1879 divided the place into two separate towns. The train brought in settlers and doubled the population to nearly fifteen hundred residents."

"What happened then?" Jack asked.

"Americans and Europeans, mostly whites, constructed buildings on the east side of the Gallinas River while the original Spanish and Indian settlers remained on this side. The decision created an intense economic, political and social rivalry between the two Las Vegas communities."

"Early trouble?"

"Yup, strained relations among the inhabitants continued for decades. Racial tensions caused havoc between the two feuding populations. The two cities finally came together in 1970, long after Las Vegas lost its strategic importance."

"I read Las Vegas had a reputation as a tough frontier town. True?"

"Absolutely, a local writer named Ralph Emerson Twitchell perpetuated the legend." The editor handed Jack a brochure with Twitchell's picture on the front cover. Jack opened the flier and read: *Without exception, there is no town which harbored a more disreputable gang of desperadoes and outlaws than Las Vegas, New Mexico.*

"What's your favorite story about the town, Josh?"

"I've got several, but a couple will give you a taste of the old days."

Jack took out his notebook and recorded the details.

"Doc Holiday and his lady friend, Big-nose Kate, top the list of the two most notorious residents who ever lived in Vegas. A vigilante committee wanted to hang Doc for killing a local hero in a gunfight, and the couple had to vamoose in the middle of the night. They headed for Tombstone, and you know the rest of his tale."

"I sure do."

"Then," Joshua continued, "the story involving Pat Garrett and Billy the Kid spiced up the town's reputation. Garrett captured the Kid and dragged Billy across the plaza in chains and shackles, putting on a public display to shame him."

"How did the locals feel?"

"They liked the Kid more than Garrett and watched the show, rooting for the Kid the whole time. Billy escaped and continued his crime spree until Garrett shot him dead at Fort Sumner, New Mexico. Garrett wanted to prove he was the better man, so he sent the Kid's trigger finger back to the editor of the Las Vegas *Optic*. The newspaper preserved it in an alcohol-filled jar, displayed for all to see in the newspaper's front window."

"Where's the jar?" asked Jack.

"Can't say, nobody's pointing a finger."

Jack smiled.

"Ya know, once the railroad arrived, the town became more civilized. But still, after 1880, the local vigilantes tried to tame the town by killing, murdering or hanging at least twenty-nine people."

"I didn't realize Las Vegas had been so violent, sort of a Wild West cauldron."

"Las Vegas developed a tough reputation. It's the only town in New Mexico to ever hang a woman, but even the lynching got botched by a new sheriff."

"Really? Sounds like a story I need to include in my article. Tell me."

"According to most accounts, Paula Angel's lover jilted her. Then, she arranged to meet with him privately for one last goodbye, and during their embrace, Paula buried a bowie knife in his stomach, killing him instantly. After a quick trial, the court condemned her to die. The judge's exact words said she had to be *'hanged by the neck until she was dead.'* He specified her execution had to occur in public *'between the hours of ten a.m. and four p.m.'* at a suitable place. The judge, a secret member of the vigilantes, wanted to send a message: Las Vegas was civilized."

"Pretty ruthless way to convey his intent, wasn't it?"

"No matter. It's the way they did things back then. Anyway, on the day of her hanging, people from miles around came to watch the spectacle."

"Better than television back in the 1800s," Jack quipped.

"The sheriff drove her in a wagon, along with a recently constructed coffin, to a cottonwood tree on the outskirts of old town. He slipped the noose around her neck and drove away. He must have been nervous, because in his haste, the law officer neglected to tie Paula's hands behind her back. To his horror and gasps of the spectators, she struggled to hold onto the noose, fighting to stay alive."

"Really," Jack interjected.

"It gets worse," Joshua grinned. "The crowd rushed forward, cut Paula down and begged the sheriff to set her free. They claimed she had been hanged and lived. If hung again, they pleaded, her spirit would haunt the city and its residents forever."

"Great, another ghost story I can write," Jack commented.

"But, the sheriff refused to listen to their cries for mercy. He claimed she had not been hanged *'until dead'* between the hours of *'ten and four.'* He told the crowd the time had not passed, and she was not dead yet. Therefore, they'd do it again. The second attempt worked. To this day, some people say they still see her ghost wandering the hills around Las Vegas."

The editor watched Jack write his final notes and asked, "Do you believe in ghosts, Mr. Weston?"

"Damn right, I do. I've had more than my share of run-ins with them."

On his walk back to the inn, Jack congratulated himself for his good fortune. Joshua's stories would add flavor to the article he planned to write. He felt certain Phil and the editorial staff at *Western Trails* would be pleased. The article could easily be written and still give him time to attend to his personal business.

He consumed a late lunch at the Landmark Grill located in the hotel. The menu, filled with a variety of southwest dishes, made Jack's palate tingle. However, he ate light, ordering the Greek salad and a cup of a spicy green chili stew, enough to satisfy his immediate hunger. The Landmark's dinner menu convinced him to return to savor more of the restaurant's delightful food later in the evening. He also reasoned the more time he spent at the hotel, the greater his chance of meeting James Swanson.

When the waitress delivered Jack's lunch order, he probed for information about the man. "Excuse me, Francine, I'm staying here for the night, but I would like to locate an old acquaintance. Do you know a man named James Swanson?"

"Nope, the name doesn't sound familiar, but I'll ask the kitchen staff if they know him."

She soon returned shaking her head. "Nobody recognizes the name. Can I get you a phone directory so you can find his number?"

"Sure, thanks."

James Swanson's name could not be found listed in Las Vegas or any other town in the area. When the waitress came back with the check, she asked, "Find him?" Jack shook his head. "Well, the bar opens at 4 p.m. If he ever comes in for a drink, they'll know him."

"Thanks for the tip. I'll drop by later." Jack returned to his room and became aware of his personal hygiene needs. After a day in the car, his unpleasant smell begged him to shower and shave. He spent the remainder of the afternoon relaxing in his room.

By early evening, Jack sat at the bar and ordered a Rusty Nail. Jen, the bartender, brought him a bowl of pretzels and remained to chat with her new customer.

"Just passing through?" she asked.

"Depends if I can find a former classmate, a fellow named James Swanson."

"Why are you looking for Jimmy?"

"You know James Swanson?"

"You bet. He comes in here every other night or so."

"Any idea how I can get in touch with him?"

"Nope. He lives somewhere outside of town. Moved here a few months ago."

"No phone?"

"He's got a cell phone, but never gave me the number. Jimmy's retired, you know."

"I didn't know James retired." Jack tried to maintain the charade and hoped the woman believed his story.

"Yep, he only finished one dollhouse last year ... can't focus much anymore."

Jack pressed Jen for more information. "He makes dollhouses?" Jack had no clue about how dollhouses connected with the voice and tried to hide his confusion.

"He's one of the most renowned dollhouse makers in the country. You should have known what your *old* friend did for a living," she added.

Her response made him feel uneasy. *Had he blown his story?*

Jack maintained eye contact with Jen and tried to recover from the gaff. "I know James from way back in the old days ... high school. Then, making wooden toys had been a hobby. I haven't seen him in years."

She pressed her lips together, gave her customer a hard look and scratched her head. After a moment, Jen relaxed and promised to call him if James came in for a drink. Jack told her he'd be in room 310 writing an article for a magazine.

"Oh, are you doing an article on old man Mill's ghost?" She quickly added, "For what magazine?"

"*Western Trails*," Jack said, handing the bartender his business card. "I'll bring you a complimentary copy," he offered in an attempt to reinforce his credentials. "Jen, it's very important I talk with James. So, if he comes in, please let me know."

If he shows up, I'll call your room or cell," … looking at the card … "Mr. Weston," she said, and placed it by the cash register.

Jack downed the last of his drink and placed a twenty-dollar bill in the bartender's palm. "This is for your trouble, Jen. I really need to see him."

"You got it, boss!" she responded and slipped the crisp picture of Andrew Jackson down the front of her blouse for safekeeping.

Money always speaks louder than friendship, he thought.

Jack stepped across the lobby and anticipated tasting more of the Landmark's authentic southwest food. With mouthwatering enthusiasm, he chose the Blue Corn Enchilada dish. The chef stuffed homemade blue corn tortillas with chicken, cheese and spicy green chili sauce — the same filling he savored at lunch. Two bottles of his favorite beer and several glasses of water barely quenched the fire attacking his delicate taste buds. Perspiring, Jack told the waiter the meal had been the tastiest dish he'd eaten in months.

After dinner, he peeked into the Byron Mills Saloon and caught Jen's eye. She shook her head to let him know James Swanson had not arrived. He acknowledged her gesture with a wave and went upstairs to write.

Chapter Twenty-Seven

The story of Las Vegas flowed onto his computer screen with ease. Jack's words captured the richness of the town's historical setting and the hotel's charm. The current owners had remodeled the aging Plaza and carefully refurbished each room to its former Victorian splendor. They also expanded the hotel to an adjoining building. The construction added several bedrooms, a large meeting space and a quaint gift shop. Jack believed tales of the city's historic rascals, coupled with vivid description of the hotel's amenities, would motivate curious readers to explore this southwestern gem. Jack returned to the bar around 9 p.m. to chat with Jen. James Swanson failed to appear. Around midnight, Jack feared he may have reached a dead end and had no idea what to do next.

His pursuit of the voice depended on making contact with James Swanson. He needed to be patient, a quality not easily embraced by a man driven by anger. Jack anticipated a quiet night's sleep and walked upstairs to his room. He put the key in the door and smelled a faint scent of lilac perfume. *That's strange*, he thought. Then he remembered lilac fragrance had been an integral part of the Byron T. Mills' ghost legend. *Is Mills walking around the hotel tonight?* He stepped into his room and whispered, "Bring it on, Mills. I've been with ghosts who wouldn't think of sporting such a sissy smell."

Jack continued talking out loud, "You know, I shouldn't even be in this hotel tonight. I promised my editor I'd do a story about ghosts back in Santa Fe. So, you'd better make my visit worthwhile, or I'll make you look bad." Jack waited for Mills to show a sign of his presence, but a familiar silence filled the room.

He couldn't determine if his last drink made him feel cocky about interactions with ghosts, but he wanted to confront Byron Mills' spirit to show he wasn't afraid. The unknown voices of spirits no longer astounded him, and Jack counted on Mills to make an appearance.

"You know, Byron, if I can be so familiar," he said, "when you lose everything in life, fear and amusement no longer motivates the detached observer. So, bring it on. Give me your best shot. But, do me one favor, huh? Make James Swanson appear."

The silence in the room caused Jack to sigh. He prepared for bed and felt disappointed. *A few days ago I enjoyed talking with ghosts, and now it's old stuff. Nothing special about it anymore. To bed, I need to finish the article tomorrow and keep my masters in L. A. happy.*

Jack slept soundly for several hours, but close to 3 a.m., the aroma of cigar smoke woke him. Eyes still shut, he sniffed the air and remembered his experiment with Faith. He tolerated cigarette smoke, but since Prescott, detested the heavy smell of cigars. Half asleep, he dragged himself out of bed, raised the window and opened the door to the hallway. The chill made Jack wonder if the hotel's heating system had broken.

He lowered the window, but left it cracked to let in fresh air. Snow had fallen all evening, and a layer of white powder had already accumulated on the ledge. The cold wind caused him to shiver, jump back into bed and bury his body under the soft, warm covers. Jack pushed the disturbance out of his mind and, within minutes, drifted back to sleep. However, another dream soon invaded his slumber.

At breakfast the next morning, he recorded the vivid details of his night vision. Jack felt a hand shake him awake. He opened his eyes to observe a man sitting on the edge of the bed surrounded by billows of heavy cigar smoke. He sat up and looked into the eyes of a man dressed in a vintage, turn-of-the-century suit. The man tilted his head back, exhaled a puff of smoke and laughed.

Jack pushed his body against the headboard, rubbed his eyes and stared at his visitor. "Don't tell me, let me guess. You're Byron T. Mills, right?" Jack asked in the dream.

"Very perceptive, sir. The ghost of Byron Mills at your service." The man nodded politely and tipped his hat.

"Legend says you only show up in this room to haunt female guests."

"You're really an impudent young man, aren't you? I knew you planned to write an article about my hotel, and I needed to make sure your readers know the truth. I want to defend my hotel's reputation."

"Since when do ghosts care about media coverage?"

"Oh, it always helps to keep the legend alive, even if you aren't," Mills' ghost smirked.

"Okay, Byron, I don't have a pad and pen to take notes, but I'll remember the gist of this conversation in the morning, after I'm fully awake."

"Good," the ghost answered and shifted his weight on the soft bed.

"From what I read about the Plaza," Jack slipped into his interview mode, "you bought the place shortly after it was built in 1886."

"Correct, a great investment. Brisk business in Las Vegas and 'The Belle of the Southwest,' as we used to call the Plaza, sat in the heart of everything. I made a lot of money."

"If that's the case, why did you decide to dismantle it and sell off all the furniture?"

"Times changed, and I wanted to do other things — leave town, travel, invest in California and start another business."

"Not a good reason to sell it off piece by piece."

"I agree, but those pesky vigilantes grabbed control of the east side and took the fun out of this town." He puffed on his cigar and reflected on what seemed to be a painful past. "They wanted to kill the Old West and civilize it. The vigilantes forced most of the riffraff, scallywags and hoodlums to move over here, old Las Vegas, and they terrorized the Plaza. It wasn't much fun to manage a hotel anymore — gun fights, bullet holes, saloon brawls, you know."

"Why didn't you sell it outright?"

"During difficult economic times, it's hard to get anyone to buy a hotel. I decided to sell it off a piece at a time and eventually demolish the building."

"What changed your mind?"

"I guess," he paused, "I got sentimental about the place. I couldn't bring myself to sell or destroy this gem."

Jack interrupted, "You became an old softy. I thought good entrepreneurs separate emotion from business."

"Right you are, young man. I fell in love with the place and never left it."

"You still haunt the hotel because you love it?"

"Correct! And, I also have a lot of fun spooking little old ladies who stay here. I get a kick out of it. I may be dead, but still enjoy a good joke." He laughed at the memory of his pranks.

"I didn't know people who died had a choice to hang around and stay among the living or, for that matter, had a sense of humor."

"If your life is filled with ambivalence, and you die with unfinished business, you can choose to stick around for a while and work things out. How long it takes is meaningless. Ghosts have no sense of time — days, months or years. Time, my boy, is an obscure notion created by living humans. The concept permits you to maintain a false sense of control. Time does not actually exist."

Jack ignored a philosophical discussion and returned to his guest's original reason for haunting the hotel. "What problems do you need to work out as a ghost?"

"It's all about conveying the message to others," he paused. "I sensed you were open to my message, and I decided to come into your dreams."

"Okay," Jack laughed, "what message do you want to tell me?"

"It's the secret of being successful in business and life. No matter if you run a hotel or write for a magazine, you must always, always manage your business with your head and not your heart — separate emotions from actions. It's the essential message."

"What do you mean? Most people believe success comes by finding a balance between the two."

"Not always. Let's take you, for example. You're a writer who lost his wife in a terrible accident. You know she was murdered, but can't prove it."

"How did you know about her death?" Jack hesitated. "Never mind, your answer will only confuse me. Make your point, Mills."

"Emotion has hampered your investigation. You miss important clues because your heart interferes with your head."

"Now you sound like the hitchhiker I met."

"Right, even Pandora couldn't help you concentrate."

"This dream's getting weird … as if the whole thing isn't already. I have no idea how you know Pandora, and I'm not going down that path, either. After all, this is only a dream." Jack sat in silence for a moment and then asked, "What advice can you offer to help me separate emotion from logic?"

Mills took another puff on his cigar, straightened up and said, "I'm here tonight to tell you how to do it."

"Go on."

"Jack, you've got to understand you can never be with Taylor again. Stop feeling sorry for yourself. Accept reality. You've spent too much time grieving. It's over. Get used to it. Understand?"

"Yes …," Jack hesitated. "I know you're right. It's been over a year since I lost her."

"Use your energy to solve the crime, Mr. Weston. Take care of business and your heart will heal itself. Think like the man who killed Taylor. Find the motive for the delay in the case. Use your reporter's instincts and ask good questions."

"I can't; it's too complicated. I only have bits and pieces."

"Nonsense. You've got much more than you realize. For the past couple weeks, lots of voices have given you clues. But, damn it, you don't listen."

"What are you saying?"

"Pay attention, you pitiful bag of emotional crap. Stop feeling and start thinking. You'll be able to figure it out."

Jack woke to the sound of the wind whistling through the partially opened window. He scrambled out of bed and felt a cold blast of air filling the room. He peered through the curtains to see a major spring storm raging outside and twelve inches of heavy, wet snow covering the plaza. He heard the distinct sound of spinning tires from a lone car struggling to navigate the slick streets.

Jack shivered, shook his body awake and said, "What a crazy dream." *After two nights in this place, it's having a strange effect on me.*

On his way past the front desk, the clerk informed him the storm had forced the closure of the interstate as far north as Raton Pass and south to Glorieta Pass. The storm snowed in Las Vegas and travelers had to wait until the roads could be plowed. At best, the highways would not be cleared until morning. *Good,* he thought, *it gives Swanson another day to show up.*

At breakfast, he sipped his third cup of coffee and made a commitment to approach Taylor's death in a more businesslike manner. Mills made sense. He could now understand the logic and made a commitment to hear the next messages with reason rather than emotion.

144

Chapter Twenty-Eight

Stranded by the storm, Jack spent the day writing and then used the Internet to research the meaning of dreams. Mills' message provided a personal point of view, and his *Western Trails* article about the town and the ghost of its former owner evolved into an exquisite story. Late in the morning, Jack e-mailed the polished article and added the legend of Byron Mills to the mix of characters who once roamed the streets of Las Vegas. Within an hour, Phil enthusiastically responded with more accolades and guaranteed the magazine would cover his expenses.

Jack used his snowbound day to read and answer e-mails from friends he had abandoned during his self-imposed isolation. He posted clever messages on Facebook and scanned previously unopened Internet jokes. Jack also thought about Byron Mills' visit and pondered strategies to replace self-pity with reason.

When the bar opened, Jack enjoyed a beer and chatted with Jen. She assured him the storm caused locals to develop cabin fever and Swanson, along with most of her regulars, would be out in force tonight. "Beer and talk cures claustrophobia."

Jack returned to his room, clicked on the television, kicked off his shoes and stretched out. He must have dozed off because the telephone startled him. "Hi, this is Jen. Mr. Swanson just walked in and ordered a beer."

Jack glanced at the clock and realized he'd been asleep for two hours. "I'll be right down." After splashing water on his face, he hastily dressed in slacks and a sweater and headed for the bar.

He walked into the saloon and spotted Jen. She nodded toward the far end of the bar where an older, gray-haired man sat cradling a half-empty glass. Swanson wore a plaid lumberjack shirt and baggy Dockers. Black suspenders permitted oversized pants to hang loosely around his middle and provided enough room to accommodate a large beer belly. Jack observed the man steady his beer with both hands. The glass shook as he consumed a mouthful of the golden liquid.

"This seat taken?" Jack asked, pointing to the stool next to Swanson.

"Sit down, mister. It's a free country. Enjoy an adult beverage with me."

Jack introduced himself.

"My name is James Swanson. Pleased to meet you."

"I think you're the man I'm looking for — hear you make dollhouses."

"I used to be the best dollhouse maker in the United States, but not anymore." He held out a hand, and Jack noticed a visible shaking. Swanson used his free hand to hold the other one in place. "See this?" he said. "I don't know if I gripped those tiny tools so long it caused the shaking, or if it's the onset of something like Parkinson's. It's damn shitty because now I have to hold my beer with both hands."

Jen threw a towel at James and chortled, "It's from drinking too much booze."

"Hush up, woman. I've been drinking all my life and won't have some barmaid lecture me about my favorite habit," he snapped back.

"You mean, I'll have to put up with you as a regular for a while?"

"Only if you treat me with more respect and stop talking crap! This ain't the only bar in town, ya' know."

"Yeah, but I'm the friendliest. How about another beer? I can offer you a refill …."

"I won't complain."

Jack interrupted the jousting and paid for Swanson's next drink.

"Thanks, appreciate it," Swanson said. "So, who told you about my dollhouses?"

"I heard people talking about your craft when I stayed in Gallup. I'm interested in those unique skills. They told me I'd find you here in Las Vegas."

"You know," James paused to take a swallow, "you're the second fellow this week who asked me about my work." Turning to the bartender, he shouted, "See, Jen, a man with my reputation tries to retire, enjoy a few drinks and pleasant conversation, but still people come out of the woodwork to find him."

"Yeah, yeah, yeah," she waved a hand at him. "If you're so famous, make sure to pay your bar tab by the end of the night, or I'll have to tell the reporters about your bad habits."

Jack knew he had the right man, but didn't want to raise suspicion about his quest. "I'm a travel writer for *Western Trails Magazine*," he said and handed James a business card. "Tell me about your former occupation. I'm always looking for a human interest story to add to my articles."

"As a kid, my grandpa taught me how to use carving tools and a jigsaw. He and I made a little dollhouse for my sister, and it got me hooked. Later, I started my own business and designed bigger toy houses. I even crafted all of the miniature furnishings. Word got out, and I began doing custom work for big shots and rich bastards who didn't mind paying top price for my modest hobby."

"You must have developed a pretty good reputation," Jack responded.

"Yup. Once my son built me a website, I couldn't keep up with the orders."

"Feel pretty good about your work, don't you?"

"Damn right! I won't brag, mind you," James said, as he drained the remainder of the glass, "but I'd say I used to be the best custom dollhouse maker in the country."

"Another beer?" Jack asked.

"Sure, partner. If you buy and write about me, I'd do anything to spread the Swanson dollhouse legend. You ought to go on the Internet and search for my name:

www.swansondollhouses.com. You can see pictures of the great work I do … rather, did."

"Your hobby fascinates me, Mr. Swanson. I promise to include you in a future story. I don't think I've ever met a man with your particular talent."

"Yeah, people still know about me and try to talk me into making them a custom model. But," he said, holding one shaking arm in the air, "they don't know about my hands, my disability. I have to send them away."

"James, you said another guy came looking for you this week?" Jack steered the conversation back to Swanson's knowledge of *the voice*.

"Yup. A big, burly guy came into the bar and asked me to build a dollhouse for his kids. He showed up with a mousy-looking woman, probably his wife, who stood behind him and said nothing. I never did get her name. Pretty strange since it's usually the woman who orders my work."

"Interesting," Jack noted.

"She didn't look too happy about it and spent most of her time in the gift shop next door. The guy said he'd been divorced and wanted to send the dollhouse to his kids in Arizona."

"Arizona? I'm from there myself. Perhaps I know him. Did he give you a name?"

"He did. Let me think what it was." Jack held his breath as Swanson scratched his head to recall a name he heard only once a few days earlier.

"Let's see, his face reminded me of Sean Connery, you know, the young James Bond type, but he had a mean son-of-a-bitch sneer — big body like Steven Seagal, scary enough to make me feel uncomfortable. But, I memorized his name because I associate clients with movie and TV stars. It's a good trick when you run a business like mine. Was it Stan Barker? … Scott Baker? … No, I hired Scott to cut out wooden pieces for my dollhouses a few years back."

Swanson's hesitation frustrated Jack, who encouraged the confused man with animated facial and hand gestures. A casual observer would have mistaken the writer for a novice mime. "Take your time, James. I guess it may be a long shot whether I know him or not. You want another beer?"

"You bet! Jen," he shouted, "set `em up again for the two of us. By the way, do you remember the guy from Arizona who wanted me to make his kid a dollhouse? What the hell was his name?"

"I thought it was Steve something," she answered.

"Yeah, Steve something. Like the movie star, Seagal" James smiled with satisfaction. That's how I remembered him.

"Steve? ... Hmm, ... you know, James," Jack intervened. "I really feel I might know him. Try to remember his last name."

"Yeah, yeah, I can get it. Give me a minute. Now it's a matter of pride. I know all of my customers, even the ones who don't order my houses." As soon as the last words popped out of his mouth, Swanson smiled and slapped Jack on the arm. "It's Baxter. ... His name is Steve Baxter!" he said triumphantly.

"Steve Baxter," Jack repeated and studied his memory bank to match a face with the name.

"Do you know him? Steve Baxter," James repeated.

"No, I don't think so," Jack hesitated. "But, perhaps ...," his voice trailed off.

Swanson tried to be helpful and added, "I can tell you something else about him. They live in Glendale, but he works in the north part of the valley — Cave Hills, Fountain Ridge, Desert something ...."

"Desert Valley?"

"Right, it's where Baxter works."

"Really? Desert Valley. You learn a lot about people, don't you?"

"Yup, I'm kind of a friendly cuss. Over the years, I've mastered the secret of knowing exactly what my customers want by being a good listener. My houses had to find a good home and be loved. I'm like a miniature architect. The more I know about folks, the better I can meet their needs," Swanson smiled.

"How long did you two talk?"

"Not long. Once he learned I wasn't in the dollhouse business anymore, he and the woman hightailed it outta here … said he wanted to cover more miles before they stopped for the night."

Jack leaned forward. "Did he say where they were going?"

"Yup. Something about a conference up in Colorado, not sure where though."

"Well," Jack hesitated, hoping to extract an additional bit of information to find the voice, "I should know the man because I live in Desert Valley, too, and it's a small town."

"You live in Desert Valley?" Swanson said.

Jack looked at James and nodded.

"Ain't that a nice coincidence? Well, mister, if you do, it should be pretty easy to find him."

"Why, James?"

"All you have to do is go down to the police station and ask. He's a cop."

The last three words made Jack's stomach flip and cave in like someone sucker punched him in the gut. He swallowed hard. A sick feeling seeped throughout his entire body.

"A cop? Are you sure?"

"Absolutely, that's what he said."

Jack began to perspire and turned pale. The words, *a cop,* resonated in his brain. Adrenalin shot through his veins as blind anger smothered him like a heavy woolen blanket. Sick to his stomach and reeling with emotion, Jack looked at Swanson and then Jen.

"Excuse me, I need to get something important from my car. Thanks, Mr. Swanson. Jen, I'll be back to pay my tab."

Jack rushed out of the hotel and dashed across the street into the plaza where he vomited behind a tall elm tree near his parked car.

Chapter Twenty-Nine

His stomach churned and caused more gag reflexes. He bent over several times and vacated the remnants in his supper. Jack wandered the plaza, trudging through the heavy falling snow. The link between Steve Baxter and the investigation flashed through his head. He looked up at a streetlight to check the descending flakes and yelled into the empty plaza. "Okay, I get it! I'm beginning to see the light!" Jack's emotional rollercoaster plunged and rocked between confusion and sickness. His feelings raced between rage and exasperation. Bursts of uncontrolled anger shattered his thinking.

Jack shouted into the snowy night, "He's a cop! He's a damn cop." He took a deep breath and whispered the words, "A cop killed Taylor. Now I know why the Desert Valley police force covered for him."

He stumbled around in the mounds of snow. *What did the bartender in Flagstaff say? 'It's sort of a mutual admiration society.'* Jack slipped on a patch of ice and tumbled into the snow. He lay there, sprawled on his back, and looked into the crystal filled night sky. "A cop runs over Taylor, kills her, and they cover it up because it's bad for ... business, public relations?"

They sat on the investigation and let the cop go free. "God, I'm so angry!" he shouted into the cold, crisp air. He lay still and tried to calm down. He watched the steam from his breath rise and evaporate in the cold air.

It's up to me to catch him. Use logic, man. What's in Colorado for a cop? Swanson said he's headed for a conference. What conference? Reason seized Jack's brain. He stood up, ignored his snow-covered body and raced across the plaza. He burst into the lobby and ran up the three flights of stairs to his room.

In a matter of seconds, an Internet search for law enforcement conferences in Colorado provided the answer. He read the announcement on his monitor:

*The National Law Enforcement Technology Center, in
collaboration with the Northern Regional Lab Group of
Colorado, will sponsor a five-day seminar at Colorado State
University in Fort Collins, Colorado.*

The seminar included training in proper DNA sample collection, victim's advocate support and seminars for issues related to crimes against persons. The conference invited the members of all law enforcement agencies in Wyoming, Utah, New Mexico and Arizona to attend. The dates listed on the screen indicated the conference started two days ago. *Baxter's still in Fort Collins,* he thought. *I have to get out of here as soon as they clear the damn roads.*

Jack clicked off the computer and sat in silence. He took a deep breath and visualized Baxter, his wife's killer, sitting in a hotel less than five hundred miles away. *I'll find the bastard and kill him. Sean Connery's face and Steven Seagal's body — not much to go on.*

The Internet site for the Desert Valley Police Department did not include employee photographs. Perhaps, he can get more information from Swanson. He ran downstairs and found the bar closed. He asked the desk clerk if James Swanson went home. The night clerk shrugged and said he didn't know the man.

Temporarily discouraged, Jack paced the lobby. *How will I locate him at Colorado State University? Don't know … just have to poke around until I do. Once I get to the conference, I'll still have a couple of days to find him.*

Jack spent a restless night and lapsed into short periods of sleep. His agitation and unresolved anger kept him on edge. Fatigued when he awoke, Jack thought, *at least Mills didn't rub my nose in it and knew enough to stay away.*

Before checking out and paying his bar bill, the desk clerk informed Jack highway crews had worked all night to clear the interstate. Even though the interstate in New Mexico remained snow packed and icy, once he got over Raton Pass and into Colorado, the roads turned clear and dry. With the good news, Jack packed and left.

Under normal conditions, the drive from Las Vegas over Raton Pass takes two hours; however, with traffic limited to one lane, vehicles crawled to the top. The delay increased his anxiety. He feared the conference would continue to slip away, and he'd lose the opportunity to find Steve Baxter.

The snow-covered ruts finally led to Raton's summit, and he breathed a sigh of relief. The promise of dry highways in Colorado, some twenty miles down the other side, buoyed his spirits.

Jack began to negotiate his icy trek down the mountain toward the Colorado flatlands when he spotted a bundled blonde hunched over by the road. *Oh, no, it's her again,* he thought.

In spite of hair caked with snow and a soaked, down-filled jacket pulled around her face, Jack easily recognized Pandora's familiar, small frame.

He found a clear spot and opened the door. Shivering and unable to speak, Pandora entered the vehicle accompanied by a cold blast of air. It quickly mixed with the warmth of the car's heater. For a brief moment, a faint aroma of roses filled his nostrils, but the scent dissipated as soon as he pulled back into traffic. Jack looked at the pathetic body in the passenger's seat trembling with cold. Pent up anger spilled over, and he dumped it on Pandora. Her appearances could no longer be considered an accident or coincidental.

"Okay, I'm done. No more games, lady. Who the hell are you, and why are you following me?"

Still freezing, Pandora looked at Jack and held up an index finger. "J-Ju ... st a m-min ... ute, J-Jack," she stuttered, her body convulsing from the cold.

The car began its decent down Raton Pass, and Jack frequently applied the brake to maintain a safe distance between his car and the vehicles swerving on the ice in front of him. Caught in the immediate tension of driving at speeds compromised by the pull of gravity, Jack focused on the road and temporarily ignored the hitchhiker.

The highway twisted and turned down the pass. Almost unnoticed, the San Juan Mountains dramatically appeared in the distance, offering a spectacular view in the morning sun. Snow-covered peaks glistened like white diamonds and sparkled with brilliance against the deep blue sky. The magenta color of the mountains and a cloudless sky welcomed the two travelers to Colorado.

"Wow! Aren't those mountains gorgeous?" a more comfortable Pandora said and pointed out the front window for Jack's benefit. "Such an incredible sight. I'll miss them."

Jack took a quick glance at the view and said, "They're beautiful. Taylor would have loved seeing this, but you, don't try to avoid my questions."

"I'm sure she would have," Pandora said. "How have you been, Jack?"

"Stop! Enough of your polite chitchat," he snapped. "I don't believe our past meetings happened by accident. I think you've been stalking me."

"Not exactly."

"What the hell does *not exactly* mean?"

"It means I was sent to help you, Jack, that's all."

"Who sent you to help me? … Did Phil send you?"

"Not exactly."

"Here we go again with the not exactly shit." He gulped in an exasperated breath. "Will you please stop playing games and tell me what this is about?"

"Okay, but you may not follow my explanation."

"Try me. I've still got a long drive, and this time, I won't let you out of the car until you tell me the whole story. Got it?"

"Oh, so now it's a kidnapping," she said in a teasing tone. "You know, crossing state lines …." She grinned, but Jack didn't react. She pressed her lips together, smacked them and acquiesced. "Okay, I'll answer all of your questions. Just let me do it in my own way."

"Shoot, I'm not going anywhere ... and neither are you."

"I've sort of been your emotional guide."

"Emotional guide? Bullshit. It doesn't make sense."

"Please listen without judgment, and I'll explain. Can you promise to listen and not interrupt?"

"Yes, yes, get on with it."

"And suspend your disbelief until I finish?"

Jack nodded. A line of cars were backed up at the bottom of the pass, and he had to refocus on driving. He signaled Pandora to wait until the vehicles started moving again.

Chapter Thirty

"Okay, go ahead — time to explain." Jack exhaled and looked at his passenger.

"I knew about your terrible loss and understood this trip would offer an opportunity to regain control of your life," she began.

"How did you know?"

She cut off his question and touched his arm. "Jack, you promised to listen and not interrupt until I finish."

"Right, I'm sorry … continue."

"Think back to the lessons you learned when you heard the voices in your dreams. Do you remember what they said? You know, those ghosts." She paused and waited for him to respond.

Jack recalled his dream conversations with Faith, Harvey, Mills and the two prostitutes. "Yeah, but they were only dreams."

"Yes, but powerful ones. Do you remember what they taught you?"

"Get rid of depression, be persistent, seek justice, and don't trust the system."

"Right. Precise summary."

"Oh, yeah, and a couple of nights ago, Byron Mills coached me on how to balance emotion and logic. But, I realize the subconscious mind plays out problems in dreams." He paused and added, "How did you know I dreamt about Mills?"

"No interruptions, Jack!"

"Okay, okay, I'll listen … go ahead."

"Prior to your stay at the La Secreta Inn, your experiences primed you to become a better listener. Your dreams gave you practice in hearing messages. You could make sense of the voice you heard in Gallup because the spirits trained you."

Jack's head snapped up, and gave Pandora a questioning glance. "But …."

She held an index finger to her lips, reminding Jack to remain quiet. "Do you understand how centered you have become? You no longer flounder in self-pity. And, except for an occasional angry outburst caused by things you don't understand, you seem to be in control of your feelings."

"Yeah, you're right."

"Shh," she whispered, "there's more."

"Think about it, Jack. You have spent so much time wrapped up in yourself, you haven't paid attention to all the signs — messages the universe sent. You've ignored the obvious."

"What signs?" an exasperated Jack interjected.

"Recall the music we've shared in our travels together? Back in Prescott, I encouraged you to listen to the lyrics and determine how the message fits your life."

"What message? Music's mostly a diversion," he said.

"Let me help you. We talked about the meaning of the lyrics to "Blinded by the Light.""

"Oh, yeah, I remember now. On the way to Jerome, we rocked to "Light My Fire," then, David Cook's "Light On" … and Evermore's "Light Surrounding You.""

"Jack, I'll give you credit for being an intelligent man, but sometimes, you're really dense. Thankfully, you're beginning to see the light."

"Yeah, I told you about …." His voice trailed off as he silently analyzed her words.

Pandora continued. "What do these songs tell you?"

Jack shook his head, puzzled by her challenge. "I don't know," the confused driver blurted out. "What does any of this have to do with Taylor's murder?"

"I can't say anymore. I'm not allowed. Go with it, Jack. Use your brain and figure it out."

"None of it makes sense." He paused and then jumped on her words. "What do you mean *not allowed*? Who do you work for? Who won't allow you to share things with me?"

"It's not important," she turned away. "You'll understand when you're ready."

He slowly put her words together and mumbled, "You believe the songs contain clues, huh?"

Pandora ignored him, sat quietly and looked out into the vacant plains surrounding the interstate. Snow had accumulated along the thin lath fences placed in strategic locations next to the road. The piles looked like squat snowmen protecting the highway from an icy, powdery invasion.

Consumed with Pandora's conundrum, Jack broke the silence again. "I remembered I heard one song I hated," he volunteered. "I listened to Pink Floyd's tune "Fearless" on the ride back to Sedona from Boynton Canyon."

"What were you doing before you heard the song?"

"I hiked Boynton and tried to communicate with Taylor, but couldn't."

"But, you did. Think about the words."

Jack hummed the melody and repeated some of the lyrics.

Again, he gave Pandora an astonished look. She smiled and nodded. She moved her index finger in small circles urging him to continue.

"And as I rise above the tree line and the clouds, I look down," His voice choked with emotion but he continued, "hearing the sound of the things you've said today ...."

Pandora cocked her head and paused so Jack could revel in his own discovery.

"Oh, my god, she did communicate with me. Taylor talked to me through the song. I get it, I get it. I finally get it!" Tears dropped out of his eyes and flowed down his crimson cheeks like small rivers. "She let me know she's all right," he managed between sobs. "She let me know I don't have to worry about her."

Pandora took a deep breath and turned away, pretending to count more snow barriers guarding the highway. When Jack stopped weeping, he looked at his mysterious passenger, took in a breath and exhaled a deep sigh.

"You still haven't answered my first question," he said, wiping the tears with the sleeve of his coat. "Who are you, and who sent you to help me?"

"Please, be satisfied with what I said: I am Pandora, and I came to bring you hope. Why can't you accept my answer?"

"Not good enough, lady. Talk to me."

"You probably won't believe me, so don't try to figure it out. You've got a lot more important things to do than knowing who I am."

"Not okay. Don't avoid my question again. I need to know," he said.

Pandora struggled to find an appropriate way to explain. At last, she took another deep breath and began. "Jack, hope is an emotion ... a feeling ... a conscious place with no form or physical substance. Nobody ever captured the feeling of hope on a canvas or with a camera."

Jack gave his passenger a puzzled look. "Stop the mumbo-jumbo shit. Speak to me in plain English."

She disregarded his outburst. "I told you earlier I came to help you heal and make sense of your life. My assignment was to bring you hope. I think I succeeded."

"The voices in my dreams and the *human* voice I heard in New Mexico gave me hope," he said. "Hope so I can find Taylor's killer. But you didn't have anything to do with that, or did you?"

Without waiting for Pandora to respond, he continued. "And, what's this crap about an assignment? Who assigned you to do anything for me?" Jack didn't pause. His thoughts rattled off like the final stages of corn popping on the stove. When he finished the inquisition, he gave his passenger a hard stare.

She disregarded his outburst and said, "Imagine I'm another *voice* you've heard. I've tried to guide your thinking and soothe your heart. For the most part, you listened to me because you see me as a person sitting in your car ... not a ghost in your dreams.

"What?"

"Please listen," she said. "You didn't hear or understand my message, so I had to find you again and again until you got it. I was forced to break through the thick, irrational layer of human emotion blocking your mind."

"What do you mean *human?*" Jack fixated on the word. "Who sent you? How did you know where to find me? How did you know I'd pick you up all those times?" Jack rattled on.

Pandora absorbed his staccato and silently stared at Jack. Finally, she announced, "I know you won't understand or accept my answer."

His anxious, moist eyes begged her to speak. In a low whisper, he asked again, "Don't avoid my most important question: Pandora, who sent you?"

"My dear, Mr. Weston, I am Pandora, a myth. I am not real. I'm a thought, a feeling sent to heal your pain. Nothing more."

"What?" the incredulous driver said. He reached over and touched her arm. "You are flesh and blood — as real as I am. Don't fuck around with me, anymore."

"Reality occurs in the mind of the beholder. It's true, I have been real to you, but I am not real in this world."

"Damn it, woman, can't you give me a straight answer? Now you want me to believe you're from another time and place?"

"Sort of …."

"No, no, no, … no more bullshit. I'm not going down that path again. Just tell me who sent you?"

Pandora hesitated. Her silence seemed endless as he waited for an answer. After a long moment, she looked out the window and softly said, "Taylor."

"What did you say? Speak up, woman," he barked.

She turned in his direction, looked into his angry eyes and quietly said, "Taylor sent me."

No time elapsed between her words and his reaction, "Bullshit! A lie. Don't mess with me, woman! I need to know the truth."

Agitated and unable to find the words, Jack needed time to think of a different approach. He broke the tension and said, "I have to stop for gas and hit the head, but when I come back, I expect a better answer. No more of this hocus-pocus gibberish, got it?"

Pandora sat motionless and looked away. Within minutes, he spied an exit ramp and followed it to a gas station. He got out and set the gas pump to automatically fill the tank.

"I need to use the bathroom. But, you have a lot more explaining to do, young lady, so don't go anywhere. I'll be right back."

Pandora watched Jack walk into the building. Before entering, he turned to make sure she remained in the car. Through the front window, she waved at him, smiled and silently mouthed the words, "Bye, Jack."

He didn't notice.

#####

A thorough search of the premises and a brief interrogation of other drivers failed to locate anyone who had seen Pandora. She had disappeared. Later, Jack reasoned, *she probably got another ride because I was on her case. I'll see her again.*

He drove further north and reconstructed his experiences with the mysterious woman. *Was she real or my imagination? She had to be real. I heard her voice. I talked with her. I touched her.*

Jack's mind wandered to their last conversation. *It's mean-spirited to say Taylor sent her. Who does she think she is? Damn her for joking about Taylor.*

The longer Jack drove, the more he pondered what happened. *Where did she go? People who claim to be spirits don't evaporate, or do they? Ghosts aren't real, either, but I've had my share of encounters with them over the past week, haven't I?*

Chapter Thirty-One

Exhausted by the cold and stressed by her difficult assignment, Pandora located the hidden entrance, slipped in and looked for a place to sleep. Abandoned by its owners in 1907, the Manitou Grand Caverns had been all but forgotten by the modern world. Originally developed to compete with the Cave of the Winds as a tourist attraction, nobody remembered the actual reason why the Manitou Caverns closed. However, local legend suggested the cave and its interior caverns were sealed due to an unusual number of paranormal incidents interfering with the workers. The frightened owners dynamited the entrance and concentrated on developing Cave of the Winds.

Pandora found an isolated space between labyrinths of overhanging stalactites and slept for a long time. When she awoke, the light from a fire, flickering on the walls of an adjoining chamber, frightened her. Since childhood, flames always scared her, but Pandora relaxed as soon as she recognized her surroundings. She reviewed her encounters with Jack Weston and let out a tired sigh. *I've done this for nineteen years, and he turned out to be my most difficult case. Isn't it supposed to get easier with practice?*

Pandora remembered the time when she first became a spirit. Her parents left her safely sleeping and went to a holiday party down the block. Unexpectedly, a fire started and ravaged the young girl's home. Flames engulfed the house, and she fell unconscious on the floor near her bedroom door. The five-year-old girl panicked and cried for help. No one responded.

A guardian angel watched the child's plight. Overwhelmed with compassion, he snatched her away before she experienced death. His moment of personal weakness changed her future. The angel presented the child to the gatekeeper only to discover his intervention was premature.

The girl had been destined to survive the fire and live with pain, marked by hideous scars.

"What have you done? You violated our code," the gatekeeper shouted.

"I'm sorry, sir. I couldn't stand to watch the child suffer," the angel replied.

"It's not your place to judge such things. The book indicates her pain and suffering would inspire hope in others. Your action robbed humanity of a precious gift."

"I didn't know. I couldn't help myself. I played guardian angel too well. Sir, can you do anything to make up for my mistake?"

"Bring the girl to me, and I'll chat with her."

The guardian presented the bewildered child to the gatekeeper. He looked at her pure innocence, and his demeanor softened. Her smile and soft blue eyes stirred emotions he had long forgotten. The girl's angelic face and curly blonde hair accentuated her bright, attentive eyes now filled with wonder. She glowed in his presence.

"I understand the reason for your folly," he murmured in soft tones. He looked down at the girl and said, "You're probably confused about all of this, aren't you?"

"Yes, where are we? I remember the fire and crying for help, and now I'm here."

"You won't understand any of this, but you have reached the entrance to the next life. Unfortunately, you've arrived much too early. Your work among humans is not finished."

The young child looked confused and didn't know what to say. She stared quietly at the gatekeeper and waited. He looked into the book, thought for a moment, and then smiled. "I've got a wonderful solution."

"Please share," the angel said.

"The book indicates she had been scheduled to remain on earth in human form for another twenty years and then cross into the next dimension."

"Oh, in human years, twenty isn't a long span of what *they* call time," the guardian replied.

"Precisely," the gatekeeper said. "It's why I can devise an alternative plan so she can fulfill her destiny."

He looked down at the girl and said, "Child, your experience was supposed to inspire others, to help them find hope. I am going to turn you into a spirit to walk among humans and perform this important task. You will be assigned this duty for the next twenty human years. What do you think?"

The girl thought for a moment and asked, "Do you mean I'll be like a fairy princess or something?"

The gatekeeper chuckled, "Not really a fairy, but you will become the spirit of hope and fulfill your fate."

"Oh," she said. "Sounds like fun. You mean I get to talk to kids my own age and help them?"

"Precisely."

"Okay, I'll do it. I'll be Mary Roberts, fairy spirit."

"I'm sorry, dear. You can't use your human name for this assignment. Mary Roberts, the human, is gone."

Still not understanding the gatekeeper, the perplexed child looked at him and asked, "Well, what shall I be called?"

"Let me think," the gatekeeper grinned. "You remind me of a spirit I helped in another place and time. I'll call you Pandora. She was also sent to earth to bring hope to humans. Pandora became a symbolic silver lining behind every dark cloud."

"Pandora, Pandora, Pandora," the girl said several times. "I like it. Pandora is a fun name."

Nineteen years later, Pandora lay in a corner of the Manitou Grand Caverns reflecting on the assignment she accepted long ago. Her fear of fire remained the only recollection of her past life.

Pandora, in her role of a child-like fairy, guided other small children with her presence. Not always seen by adults, she often became a child's make-believe friend. Magical in nature, her actions helped youngsters avoid dangers or make decisions sending them safely through life.

She matured into a physical being, and her spirit transformed with those she helped. In adolescence, she struggled through puberty and young adulthood. Her actions modeled ways to assist her human counterparts. Then, as a mature adult, Pandora's spirit changed into more human-like behaviors. Even though Pandora lacked human substance, her spirit became susceptible to fatigue and required frequent renewal in the magic of the Manitou Cave.

Now, at twenty-four human years, her spirit felt weighed down by the emotions she had accumulated through her various adult assignments, especially with Jack. She longed for the time when she could cross over to a new life. *I can't do this much longer,* she thought. *I'm glad my time here is almost over.*

The sound of laughter distracted her thoughts. She knew the noise came from one of the cavern's cathedral-like rooms. She rubbed the sleep from her eyes, stretched and searched for its source. Behind an ancient pipe organ sat the familiar face of a man who wore wire-rimmed glasses and a down vest. Carl's friendly smile radiated through the misty light of the cave. Pandora felt warm and safe in his presence. She walked quietly into the cavern and studied every detail as if for the last time. Carl continued to joke with another spirit messenger like herself, who had arrived the day before she did. The two looked up and acknowledged her presence.

"Hello, Pandora. How's my favorite spirit?"

"I'm tired, Carl. This was a tough one. Lots of baggage to unload before he even got a clue."

"Did you succeed?"

"Yeah, but it took all my energy and persistence. I'm getting too old for this sort of thing."

"You're one of our best," he said. "But, I know you'll soon be making the transition. For now, however, rest in the sanctuary, recharge your energy, and get ready for your next mission."

"I feel a lot better being with you. I only have a few more human interventions and look forward to moving on."

VOICES

Carl handed Pandora a wrapped package and, out of habit, reviewed the familiar protocols. "Here are your things. Shower and play in Rainbow Falls. The longer you remain in the warm water, the more rejuvenated you'll feel. I promise."

"Thanks, Carl," she said. "I always recover from my assignments when I come here."

He pointed to an entrance leading to another chamber in the cavern. She took the plastic bag from Carl and headed toward the sound of the splashing water. The narrow pathway opened into a space lined with glowing mineral chips providing light for the room. The sight of the sparkling onyx and quartz crystals afforded a magnificent setting for the energy-filled shower pouring out from an underground stream near the cave's ceiling. The thunderous sound of the cascading waterfall begged Pandora to play in its warm liquid.

She removed her blouse and fiesta skirt, slipped on a robe and left the old clothes neatly folded on a bench. She walked to a preparation area, picked up a pair of scissors and cut her dreadlocks as close to her scalp as possible. Then, she stepped into the warm pool and stood under the rushing water. To her delight, the natural thermal springs offered a soothing massage. Pandora washed the remnants of her hair three times to loosen the final stubborn tufts of her dreadlocks. She stepped out of the pool, slipped on a soft terrycloth robe and towel-dried her short hair. She gazed at her image in the pool and shook her head. "I've finally washed out that terrible hairstyle. But, if Jack can figure out his life, it was worth the discomfort."

She dropped her robe and prepared to dress in the new set of clothes. Pandora glanced into the pool again and looked at her tiny frame. *I could be mistaken for a small boy or a young girl,* she thought. *I wonder what I'll look like the next time.* Her petite features became an asset in her line of work. She shrugged and said, "Oh well, the best it's going to get for now."

She opened Carl's package and slipped on a pair of old, tight-fitting blue jeans, a maroon Stanford University sweatshirt, a set of rugged, well-worn hiking boots, a John

167

Deer baseball cap and a down-filled winter coat. Checking her image in the water again, she laughed at the new Pandora.

She retraced her steps and found Carl playing rock songs on the organ. A small group of spirit travelers clapped along with the music. Others swayed to the rhythm or danced about the room. Pandora had not experienced such fun in weeks, and she could feel the joy returning to her soul.

Two spirits laughed and ran wildly into the room, interrupting the frivolity. One of them chuckled as he said, "Did you see the surprised look on the woman's face? She almost fell over when she saw your cloudy image on the picture she took?"

"Yeah, really funny," the other one added a hearty laugh. "Her entire family almost abandoned the tour when she showed them a picture of a *real* ghost."

The spirits slapped each other on the back with uncontrollable zeal.

Carl chastised the two for their rude prank. "Boys, the secret passage between this cave and the tourist side protects our sanctuary from the human world. Their side is off limits. Do you understand?"

"Yes, sir," they mumbled.

"Our on-going security depends on it. Your mischief may cause some nosey, precocious human children to ramp up their courage and invade our refuge."

"We were only having fun with them," one of the two spirits said.

"It's not okay. If they discover us, we'll lose this renewal site."

"We're sorry," they said in unison.

"From now on, confine your play to our side of the caves and leave the lantern tour to the human visitors."

"Okay, okay," the taller of the two said. "We promise we'll be good."

The two giggled like small children and chased each other into another dark opening embedded in the rock walls.

"Young ones," Carl said as he watched the two disappear. "They have so much pent up energy in their human form but know so little."

"Oh, Carl, don't be so hard on them. Isn't it wonderful how a small amount of amusement can change their attitude?"

"You're right, Pandora. If more humans took time to enjoy life and play like children, there'd be much less stress in the world. More importantly, they wouldn't need us."

"I remember when I used to tease people," she said. "I had such fun."

"Your behavior became quite a handful for us, as well."

"I apologize, Carl, but most humans don't like to play. They're too serious."

"They don't laugh enough and fear change or the unknown," Carl added. "It's the reason they die so young."

"Yes, I'm lucky. I discovered joy the first time out." She smiled and gave Carl a hug.

"It's always nice to have you drop by our little refuge, Pandora. Stop in before you make your transition so I can say goodbye."

"Thanks, Carl. I really love your energy." She gave Carl another hug and announced, "I'm okay, all rested and ready to hit the road. I'll say my last goodbye in a few months."

"I'll look forward to your return, Pandora. You've earned the transition."

In less than an hour, Pandora stood shivering on U.S. Highway 24 with her thumb extended, waiting for a ride. She knew this particular assignment would end in Niles, Illinois, a Chicago suburb close to O'Hare Airport. Boarding a plane, she'd fly to Seattle, Washington, and locate the next person she was assigned to help. Then, she'd be on the road, hitchhiking to Vancouver to meet another one. She looked forward to connecting with humans one last time before returning to the cave to meet with the gatekeeper again.

A 1999 Dodge pickup pulled to the side of the road about twenty yards ahead of the hitchhiker. Pandora ran to the truck and peered into the open passenger window.

"How ya' doing, Mac?" she asked.

"How do you know my name is Mac?" the voice from inside questioned.

"Just a coincidence," she said. "When I hitchhike across the country and get rides from truckers, I call them Mac ... sort of an ice breaker. You know, like waitresses who call all their customers honey."

"Oh, okay. Well, get in. How far are you going?"

"Limon, for now."

"Me, too." He pulled into traffic and mingled with the other vehicles headed east.

Chapter Thirty-Two

Jack drove another hour toward his destination. He wracked his brain trying to sort out the meaning of his *Pandora experience*, as he labeled it. Each bizarre encounter had added to his confusion and now another stress-induced headache pounded in his forehead. *Perhaps lunch and a beer might reduce my tension.* He located an Applebee's and the hostess escorted him to a table. He asked for a glass of water, swallowed two Tylenol, and ordered a hamburger, fries and a Bud.

He turned on his laptop and searched for the lyrics to the tunes he heard on the trip. Then, he opened his notebook and recorded the details of Taylor's death from a different perspective. His writing now focused on the words spoken by ghosts combined with song lyrics, especially those he listened to when Pandora rode with him as a passenger. *If I can figure out what all this means, It may help solve Taylor's murder.*

Jack wrote: *What does light have to do with the case?*

Blinded by the light … another runner in the night. *The words must refer to Taylor*, he thought. *She was running in the night. But, what light blinded her?*

He hummed the melody and wrote more lyrics: *The time to hesitate is through … no time to wallow in the mire* …. He softly sang, "Come on, baby, light my fire … come on, baby, light my fire." I get it. *She's telling me to stop grieving. But what does "come on, light my fire" mean? How do I light the night on fire?*

Jack wrote a line from another song: *Try to leave a light on when I'm gone. I understand this one*, he thought. *Sarah told me Taylor didn't see the car hit her. Sad to leave, she wants me to keep a light on after she's gone. But what kind of light? A porch light? A hall light? A candle? What?*

Another line confused him. He wrote it in large letters on his page. *Cos, I see the light surrounding you.* "I see the light surrounding you. What kind of light surrounds her or surrounds me?" he asked aloud.

When he had written all the words and lyrics that seemed to fit, Jack drew a line across his notepad and wrote information about Steve Baxter:

1. *Cop for the Desert Valley Police Department.*

2. *Married, drinks heavily, and beats his wife.*

3. *Department may have been covering for him. But why?*

4. *Why was Steve driving on those back roads? ... On duty? Off duty? Drinking? Lost?*

He underlined the last set of questions, looked at his scribbling, shook his head and closed the notebook. *I have no clue about this cop. How do I learn more about him?*

"Damn," Jack whispered, "all I've got is a lot of stuff about song lyrics and a name. How does it fit together? If my P.I. can believe any of it, she'll be able to make sense of this whole adventure. If she doesn't, I'll have to check into a nut house."

Then his mood lightened, and he tried to be humorous. *Maybe she can get it right, be or I can get lucky, find the bastard and beat the shit out of him.* Armed with a new determination, he finished lunch and continued his drive to Fort Collins.

Chapter Thirty-Three

Jack arrived in the city around 4 p.m. and checked into the Armstrong Hotel on College Avenue. The 1932 historic hotel intrigued him. Located a few blocks from Colorado State University, it also sat in the center of the Old Town district. He could easily walk to campus and explore the heart of the city, as well. Jack asked for a room facing College Avenue, and the desk clerk selected 202, a large, vintage room with a queen-sized bed and oak floors. Its huge picture window gave Jack a view of the main drag and most of downtown.

Early the next morning, Jack walked to the university and located the law enforcement conference registration desk at the university's student union. He approached a woman who sifted through a pile of unclaimed name tags and asked if his old friend, Steve Baxter, had registered. The clerk obliged and searched for Baxter's name on her computer. She informed him Baxter had picked up his registration packet a couple of days ago, but she had no idea which sessions he had chosen to attend.

Jack asked the woman how attendees communicated with each other during the conference. She suggested he leave a written message with his phone number tacked to the community bulletin board near the registration desk. She directed him to the pin board strategically located in the center of the hallway. He noticed various messages already taped or stapled to the front of it.

Jack composed a pointed note designed to evoke an immediate response. It said: *Blinded by the light gives one clear insight, especially when the accident happened at night! I know you did it. Call "Jack" at (623) 342-5987.* He taped the note shut, posted it in the Arizona section of the board and wrote "To Steve Baxter" in oversized, bold letters.

Jack examined the conference's list of events and noticed a general session had been scheduled for the large auditorium in twenty minutes. Participants drifted through the doors as

Jack approached the room. The featured speaker, the head of the FBI, would pack the place. Jack reasoned Steve Baxter might attend this event. He walked into the auditorium and counted six entrances. *It's a longshot, but I'll stand in front of the main double doors and read participant's name tags as they enter. I may get lucky.* Jack watched the attendees file past him until the crowd thinned to a few late arrivals. His approach proved unproductive.

Jack grew tired of his futile search and returned to the hotel. After a short nap, he asked the desk clerk for directions to a casual place where locals go for dinner. Jack found The Crown Pub within easy walking distance of the Armstrong. He entered the establishment and immediately sensed the warm, friendly ambiance. People of all ages packed the place. The college crowd mingled with businessmen and older patrons. The hum of pleasant conversation and laughter rippled through the air, adding to the agreeable atmosphere. Jack found a seat at the bar and scanned the interior.

The owners had decorated the bar to resemble an upscale English tavern. Rich walnut panels lined the walls with a bar running the length of the room's north side. Couples and small groups occupied most of the wooden tables, enjoying drinks or food. Jack studied the large selection of beers on tap in front of him and admired the extensive selection of single malt scotch bottles perched on mirrored shelves behind the bar. He congratulated himself for finding a quality restaurant with a vibrant local patronage.

Michael, one of the two owners, had been tending bar for the overflow crowd and interrupted his observations. The bartender placed a cardboard coaster in front of him and said, "Good evening. What can I get for you?"

"I'll have a Rusty Nail before dinner."

Michael smiled. "I haven't served a Rusty Nail since we hosted a book signing here for an Arizona author."

"I'm from Arizona, too. I like Rusty Nails — a pleasant before dinner cocktail, sort of like a scotch-manhattan."

Michael returned with the drink and said, "I'm Michael, and you are …?"

"My name is Jack Weston. I'm a writer myself, but not novels. I work for *Western Trails Magazine.*"

"Where do you live in Arizona?"

"Desert Valley."

"Oh, our author friend lives in Glendale. Is it close to Desert Valley?"

"Yeah, about thirty miles west."

"What brings you to Fort Collins? Are you doing a story about the city?"

"No, I'm looking for someone attending the law conference at Colorado State."

"What's his name? Maybe he's been in for a drink or dinner."

"He's a police officer named Steve Baxter. Do you know him?"

Michael scrunched his face and searched his memory. He shook his head, looked down the bar and shouted, "Hey, Jeff, do you know an Arizona cop named Steve Baxter?"

Jeff, the Crown's co-owner, walked toward the two men and said, "Steve Baxter. The name doesn't ring a bell. What does he look like?"

"Big guy … sort of looks like Steven Seagal with a Sean Connery face, but I never met him.

Jeff grinned and said, "Couldn't miss a guy who looked like him."

Jack smiled and added, "I need to interview him for a story." He handed Jeff one of his cards.

"If he comes in, we'll call you. By your description, he should be easy to spot."

Jeff put the card in his pocket and walked to the other end of the bar to finish washing glasses. Michael headed toward a customer seated at one of the tables, leaving Jack alone to sip his drink and study the menu.

"Excuse me, bartender, sir, sir …," a woman, sitting at the bar directly in front of Jeff, begged to get his attention. The running water in the sink prevented him from hearing her pleas.

Finally, he looked up from his task and noticed. He turned off the water and responded, "It's Jeff. What can I do for you?"

"Jeff, did I hear the man at the end of the bar ask for Steve Baxter?"

"I think so. Do you know him?"

"Yes, I do," she nodded. "Who's the man?" she said, pointing toward Jack.

Jeff reached into his pocket and pulled out the business card. The woman took it, walked to the end of the bar and tapped Jack on the shoulder. Startled, he jumped.

"Pardon me, sir. I didn't mean to surprise you, but I understand you're looking for Steve Baxter. Are you a friend of his?"

Jack recovered and said, "Sorry, you didn't scare me. My mind had drifted to other things." He studied her face for a moment and decided to be honest. "No, I'm definitely not a friend, but I am looking for Steve Baxter. It's a matter of personal business."

His terse response did not faze the woman. She pulled out the bar stool and asked, "May I sit down?"

"Of course."

"If Steve's not a friend, and you don't know him, why are you trying to find the man?"

"It's personal, Ms. …?"

"Oh, excuse my rudeness. My name is Racy Lanne," she said, offering Jack her hand. "I already know you're Jack Weston. Jeff showed me your card."

"Pleased to meet you," he smiled. His gaze followed the lines of her body from head to toe. She had a beautiful face with piercing blue eyes and long, silky red hair flowing down her back. She must have been in her late twenties, but displayed a mature attitude far exceeding her age. She projected an air of self-confidence, and it impressed him.

"Okay, before we talk about Steve Baxter," Jack smiled at her, "you need to tell me about your unique name."

"Oh, that. ... It's always a nice story, but I never get tired of telling people about my parents' sense of humor."

Jack shifted in his chair and faced her with an anticipatory grin.

"You see, my parents' last name is Lanne. Mom and Dad have been devoted stockcar fans since their teens, long before they ever got married. At one of those races, they conceived me in the back seat of a hot Chevy coup, and when it came time to name me, the choice was obvious. They called me Racy ... Racy Lanne. Nobody ever forgets me or the story."

The icebreaker tale lowered Jack's defenses. Her presence and easy-going manner captivated his attention. "I'm sure I won't forget it, either," he smiled and touched her arm. The physical move surprised him since he had not touched another woman in over a year — other than Pandora, and who could tell if she had been real.

Racy, the human, didn't flinch at his contact, instead she studied his eyes and smiled.

To get past the awkward moment, Jack picked up his drink and took a sip. "How do you know Steve Baxter?" he asked.

His question squelched her pleasant façade. She snapped, "He's the son-of-a-bitch who got me fired."

Her response surprised Jack. He recognized the two shared something in common: They both hated Steve Baxter.

"Pretty blunt. Tell me how he got you fired?"

"I hope you're not a friend or relative because I always make it a point to let people know how much I despise him."

"No, no, I don't even know the man. But, wow! Tell me what happened to you."

"I used to work as a dispatcher for the Desert Valley Police Department," she began. "Baxter got me fired because I questioned his travel log. I know he changed it on purpose. When I discovered he tampered with the record and lied about it, I blew the whistle on him."

Jack stared into Racy's eyes and tried to find relevance to her story. It didn't make sense, but he said, "Yes, continue."

"It's against department policy to change your daily log. But a few days after I told my supervisor about the changes Baxter made, I received a written reprimand. They put a copy in my file and told me I'd be fired if my attitude didn't improve."

Jack let more of the story seep into his brain, but it failed to make a connection to Taylor's death.

Then, with a slight glow appearing on her face, she added, "Attitude? What attitude?" She threw her hands in the air. "I did my job. I followed department policy and couldn't figure out what pissed them off. By the end of the month, the department let me go for incompetence and insubordination. I spent almost all of last year working crappy jobs until I landed with the Glendale Police Department. I had to come here and attend this law conference to get trained."

Jack shook his head. "Terrible way to treat people."

"Right, and if you ask me, it's all bullshit."

Questions now swirled in Jack's head. *By coincidence,* Jack thought, *this woman, a stranger, might know essential information about Baxter. She seems real, and unlike the quirky Pandora, this lady gives me straight answers. Was this meeting an accident or another part of a plan? You're getting paranoid, Jack. Figure out what she knows.*

"I feel fortunate meeting you like this. I'd like to talk with you more about how you got fired. Do you have time and feel comfortable sharing it with me?"

"Sure. Buy me another glass of wine, and I'll tell you everything I know."

"Good," Jack said and signaled Jeff to bring another round of drinks for Racy and himself. "I live in Desert Valley, too, and Steve may have known about an accident involving my deceased wife. Finding someone who worked with Baxter, a thousand miles from Arizona, seems unlikely, but a lot of strange things have happened to me over the past couple of weeks."

"I don't believe in coincidences," she said. "Small world, us meeting like this, but meant to be, I guess."

"Then let me buy you dinner, and we can talk more."

"Fine, let's eat here. The menu looks great."

Jack and Racy moved to a table along the wall and sat side-by-side to better hear each other talk. They ordered from The Crown Pub's extensive menu. She requested the house specialty, the King's Chicken Curry, and he ordered another Crown favorite, the London Broil. Jack selected draft beers from the local Belgium Brewery, and the two began a more detailed conversation.

"Can I ask you a question about Baxter's travel log?" Jack inquired.

"Sure, go ahead."

"Why do you think he changed it?"

"Sometimes officers need extra cash and volunteer to take a double shift. Steve normally worked days from 7 a.m. to 5 p.m., Saturday through Wednesday. But on that particular Wednesday, he volunteered to take an overtime shift scheduled from 9 p.m. to 7 a.m. the next morning. With such long hours, officers who work a double usually get tired in the early morning hours. So, at the end of their shift, they stay awake by spending the last few hours driving around in low crime areas. They keep under the radar to avoid making mistakes. On Wednesday evening, I heard his chatter on the radio. He complained about how hard it was to stay alert and focused."

"Wait a minute. You're telling me after working from Saturday through Wednesday, Baxter picked up an extra shift lasting all night? That means he only had four hours of rest between his two shifts?"

"Right. If he even took any down time, I know he didn't sleep. We don't have sleeping facilities at the station."

"And because fatigue set in," Jack started putting the details together, "he drove into a remote area of the county to avoid trouble."

"Yes, but everyone does that. It's common practice."

Jack pondered her words, waiting for Racy to share more.

"I know he just drove around in the boonies and got lost," Racy added.

"Why do you say ... lost?"

"He checked in with me about 5 a.m., joked he found some back country roads requiring supervision. He told me he drove so far out in the desert the GPS lost its signal. I heard him hitting it and cursing."

"You're saying Baxter didn't know where he was and drove around to kill time?"

"Yes. But when he turned in his travel log, those lost miles never showed up — like he didn't drive any of the places he told me about on the radio. It confused me, so I reported the incident to my superior and got fired for it."

Stunned by the simplicity of Racy's information, Jack made an immediate connection between Baxter's movements and Taylor's death. Astonished by the clarity of his discovery, he took a deep breath and slowly let it out. He stared at his dinner companion and said nothing. However, the lyrics of a song screamed in his ears: I'm beginning to see the light.

"Racy, I have one more question, and I want you to take your time before answering it. Please, it's very important. If it fits, I'll tell you about my connection to Steve Baxter."

"Okay, what else do you want to know?"

"Do you remember the exact date Baxter did his double shift and adjusted his travel log?"

"Let me think. It's been a while ...."

"Perhaps last February?" Jack asked.

"Yeah, right. It happened sometime around the middle of the month because I got fired in early March."

"How about February 16th?" Jack offered and held his breath again.

"Bingo! The exact day — a couple of days after Valentines Day. I remember now."

Jack slammed his fists on the table so hard it scared Racy. "I'm sorry, but I need to take a break for a minute," he said.

"Don't go away. I'll be right back, and I promise I'll tell you how our stories mesh."

He headed toward the bathroom and turned around to see a confused, worried look on her face. "Please wait until I collect my thoughts. Please ... stay there. I promise I'll explain everything when I return. Just give me a minute."

Jack passed the bathroom and stepped onto the Crown's back patio. Employees stood in the crisp spring air enjoying a brief smoke break. They stared at the animated, angry intruder and stopped talking. Jack reached into his shirt pocket and pulled out two dollars. "Anyone got a cigarette I can buy?" The dishwasher accepted the money, handed Jack one and lit it for him. Jack inhaled deeply and blew out a lungful of smoke. He paced into the alley behind the restaurant and kicked over a garbage can. He vainly attempted to replace his intense anger with logic, but it didn't work. The rage finally subsided and reason returned. "Damn, the pieces fit. It all fits. Now, how do I prove it?"

He took several deep breaths and remembered his attractive dinner guest. He discarded the half-finished cigarette, stepped on the remnants and returned to Racy. "I'm sorry I got so angry. Your story solved the mystery I have been plagued with for the past year."

She looked at him quizzically and asked, "Mystery about what?"

Emotion choked him as the story of Taylor's death, months of stalled police action and personal grief occupied most of his last year. He tiptoed around his personal struggles with depression and ignored details of the road trip. He credited Phil and Dr. Aberdeen with saving his life.

When the story of Jack's year-long odyssey ended, Racy uttered a heartfelt response, "Oh, my god. I felt sorry for myself for getting fired, but you ... you lost your wife and almost stopped living." She looked into his tearful eyes, leaned over and hugged him. "Oh, you poor soul."

The gesture pushed him over the edge and streams of tears coursed down his face. He wept openly and let his tension spill into the cloth napkin covering his face. Racy sat quietly patting his arm and rubbing his back as she comforted the distraught man.

After a few minutes, Jack took a deep breath, wiped his face again and looked at Racy.

"Let's get out of here. I need some air."

Chapter Thirty-Four

Jack paid the check and the pair abandoned an unfinished dinner. The cool spring air encouraged Racy to put her arm around Jack for warmth and support. Silently, they meandered through the streets of Old Town and finally stood in front of Jay's Bistro. Shivering from the cold, Jack suggested they stop for a nightcap.

Jay's Bistro, an intimate, upscale restaurant, offered customers an ambiance of class accentuated by elegant décor. Jack and Racy found a quiet booth in the softly lit bar. A table along the wall gave the couple a secluded place to talk.

Jack ordered drinks as the couple sat side-by-side on the soft leather bench. For a few moments of brief silence, they pondered the impact of their random connection. "I'm flabbergasted by the coincidence of meeting you tonight," Jack said. "Nothing would have made sense without our talk."

"Stranger things have happened in life. Besides, I believe things are meant to be."

"Well, coincidence or fate, thank you for helping make the pieces fit. Now it all makes sense."

She nodded and said, "You're welcome." Then added, "Baxter may have been tired, or fell asleep while driving, and killed Taylor by accident. He probably panicked and tried to hide the crime by altering his log. Manslaughter against a police officer would have sent him to jail."

"His actions give us a motive, but why would the whole investigation team protect him?"

"I don't know. Perhaps the new guys in forensics did a sloppy job and messed up the evidence. Maybe some of it got lost. It happens," she said.

"It's possible, but they may have fired you to get rid of the one person they couldn't control. They discredited you and eliminated a potential witness. If the department tried to protect one of their own, Steve's log had to disappear in the shuffle."

"Really frustrating," Racy said. "Baxter may be the guy who killed your wife, but if the police won't cooperate, you will never prove it."

"I can't believe the entire force is corrupt."

"No, Jack, I know a lot of honest cops and detectives on the Desert Valley police force. They're hard-working, solid, ethical officers."

"I have no idea what's going on, but I hired a private eye in Arizona to investigate. She'll go after it with some of this new information. In the meantime, I need to locate Baxter and look him in the eye. I want to see what Taylor's killer looks like and let him know I'm onto him."

"It may be impossible here in Colorado. We've just finished four days of seminars. Today, participants took off to attend workshops at various field sites around the region. They've headed to Denver, Cheyenne and Colorado Springs for hands-on training. Who knows where Baxter went."

"Well, I've done all I can in Colorado. Tomorrow, I'll drive back to Arizona and meet with my private eye."

"Sorry, Jack, but at least you and I connected."

"I'm glad we did. A friend of mine reminded me there are no accidents. What were the chances of running into you at the Crown Pub? Aside from being a former Desert Valley police dispatcher, I know nothing about you."

His statement shifted the conversation from unpleasant business to the more enjoyable exchange between a man and a woman who just met. The next hour of talk covered the usual topics couples share on a first date. After their third drink, the sexual energy between the two intensified. At some point during the evening, Racy placed her arm on Jack's back and gently rubbed it. Occasionally, her fingers twirled the long hairs on the back of his neck, reminding Jack of Taylor's touch.

The couple sat close, and frequent brushes with each other's arm or leg occurred throughout their animated conversation. Racy's perfume, a jasmine-scented Channel No. 5, aroused Jack's senses and made the dialogue flow more easily. They shared stories and giddily reacted to each other's tales. Their light chitchat continued for another hour.

When Racy returned from a bathroom break, Jack noticed the sensual sway in her walk, and it stirred a long dormant feeling. He stood up to let her into the booth and felt the warmth of her body press against his. The buzz in his head and mounting sexual desire warned him he had consumed too much alcohol on an empty stomach.

"We'd better go, Racy. Where are you staying?"

"I have a room at the Best Western right across from the university. It's about six blocks down College Avenue, almost a straight shot from here."

"Okay, I'll walk you home."

Jack paid for the drinks and helped Racy put on her coat. He gently pulled her hair from beneath the confines of the coat's restraining fabric — another intimate gesture. As they stepped into the cold air, Jack turned to Racy, put his arms around her and kissed her on the lips. She kissed him back. They lingered in the moment, enfolded in an embrace. They looked into each other's eyes with a sense of expectancy.

"It's been a long time since I kissed a woman. It felt good. Thank you," he said.

"My pleasure, Mr. Weston," she said, slurring her words. "As a police official, it is my duty to serve and protect, especially if I enjoy the assignment."

He put his arm around her, grinned and said, "So, I'm your assignment, eh?"

"Yep. I think you need someone to help you make it back to a normal life. You've spent too much time trying to figure out the past. It's time to deal with a real, live, flesh-and-blood woman, again."

"I assume you're talking about yourself, Ms. Racy?"

"This former dispatcher is at your service, sir." She tried to stand at attention and salute, but excessive alcohol challenged her equilibrium. Jack grabbed her around the waist to steady her, and the couple wove their way down the sidewalk arm in arm.

The distance to the Best Western may have overwhelmed the inebriated couple. Exhausted by the time they reached the entrance to the Armstrong Hotel, Jack stopped and kissed her again. This time the embrace lasted longer and with greater intensity. He brushed the tip of his tongue against her lips which parted in an intimate acceptance. He hugged her and looked up at the hotel sign.

The booze and the cold slowed his thinking. Mesmerized by the beautiful woman in his arms, Jack responded to his sensual needs.

"Let's get out of the cold. This is my hotel. Come upstairs, and let me show you … my antique …," he slurred.

"You call it an antique. You're not so old," she giggled. At first, he didn't understand her implication, but smiled when he did.

"Yeah, guys often give unique names to their *attached* friend."

In his room, fully clothed, they stretched out on his vintage bed and embraced. Jack felt her warm arms surround him. Unexpectedly, his emotions crashed, and he withdrew from her. Racy sensed the shift in his mood and looked into his eyes. Tears soaked the pillow under Jack's head. Racy pressed her body against his, held him and stroked his hair.

Torn between physical lust and waves of sadness, Jack felt adrift in conflicting emotions. Racy's breasts and inviting hips pressed against him and begged for attention. However, his heart filled with sorrow and grief for Taylor. He felt a sexual craving for her, yet his body protested, as if he owed a loyalty to his deceased wife. Distracted by his feelings, Jack's erection disappeared. He lay on his back and wept uncontrollably.

Racy helped Jack undress, and she disrobed as well. They slipped under the covers and lay together in each other's arms.

Jack looked at Racy with pleading eyes and said, "Please, Racy, I can't do this. I want to make love with you, but my body won't cooperate."

She stroked his face in a comforting gesture and said nothing.

"Too much has happened tonight, and I can't get past my loss."

"It's okay, Jack. I understand. We can make love another time. Our embrace will do for now."

"I'm so sorry, Racy. It's not you. It's me. I feel guilty about this." Jack raised his body and balanced on one arm. "I want you to know I think you're a very sexy, beautiful woman. Only, I'm not ready to give you my heart."

"Please, don't worry about it. Let me hold you for awhile." She pulled Jack into the softness of her breasts and felt his wet tears moisten her skin. They both fell asleep, wrapped in each other's embrace.

Sometime during the night, she left. When he woke, Jack found a note sitting on the dresser.

Jack, I really like you and want to see you again in Arizona. I live in Glendale. Call me when you get back. My number is (623) 945-2359. If I can help you solve Taylor's murder or provide any more information, please call. Fondly, Racy.

Jack reached for a couple of Tylenol to address his hangover. Emotionally, he still smarted from his unexpected bout of impotence. "What happened to me last night?" he asked the rumpled bed. "I can't go back in time to save Taylor, and I can't live in the present to enjoy the company of an attractive woman. I'm really fucked up."

He vaguely remembered his conversation with Racy, but couldn't recall many of the details. A wave of guilt smothered his ego. "I'm in bed with a beautiful woman and can't get it up? I guess it's true what they say — this will happen to every man now and then — but, it never happened when I made love with Taylor."

His guilty self-talk moved Jack to the shower. He remembered how sensual Racy's body felt and how wonderful she smelled. He dried off and noticed the memory of Racy stimulated a response in his body. He looked down at a growing erection and said, "Sure, now you show up — too late. But, next time, you'd better be ready, my favorite antique."

Jack promised there would be a next time. She turned him on, and now he had to rescue his bruised ego. Even though he failed to perform, it made him realize he successfully overcame a huge barrier. After more than a year, he finally entertained thoughts about making love with another woman, a realization that would help him move on with life.

In spite of this insight, his mind returned to the goal of finding justice for Taylor. Solving her murder took priority over fostering another relationship. He packed, checked out of the hotel and pointed his car toward Arizona. Possible answers waited a thousand miles away.

Chapter Thirty-Five

The fifteen-hour drive brought Jack back to his Desert Valley home shortly after midnight. Although the radio provided constant companionship throughout the journey, none of the songs played lyrics to offer greater insights about Taylor.

Exhausted, Jack slept late. After downing a cup of coffee the next morning, he sorted through the mail and planned his next move. His extended absence created feelings of nostalgia for his house and former lifestyle. He meandered on a tour of his home, lingering over the photographs Michelle snapped before the wedding. This time, he felt more sadness than agony about losing Taylor. *The trip helped me turn a corner. I'm now on a mission to solve this thing.*

More resolved than ever, he diligently handled mundane chores requiring immediate attention and made two essential telephone calls. The first to Phil Slocum informed the editor he had returned to the valley.

"Jack, nice to hear from you, again. Your articles continue to be superb. Everyone here in L.A. agrees it's the best writing you've ever submitted."

"Thanks, Phil. You could say I got the stories from the horse's mouth."

"I know. If I read between the lines, I can almost hear the voices of ghosts speaking to you and dictating their stories."

"Let's just say I've discovered the secret of communicating with the other side. Now I have too many voices in my head."

"Whatever it takes, Jack. Keep listening because your articles are brilliant. What do you plan to write next?"

"Not really sure, but I'd like to do an article about the secret messages in songs or perhaps one about how to find truth in unusual places. I'll work out the details."

"You know, old friend, I think those stories could work, but they're not your style. Readers expect something else from you. So, I'd caution not to go down unfamiliar paths when you've found a formula that works. Besides, you need to remember *Western Trails* is a travel magazine and won't print any paranormal stuff for its own sake. It strays too far from our mission."

"Well, then, you guys will have to put me on sabbatical again because I'm a bit distracted."

"I know, but don't wait too long. In another month, we'll be looking for an article from you for the summer travel edition. I hope you can tap into those voices of yours and create something else to print."

"Thanks for being honest, Phil. I'll see what I can do."

Jack hung up and searched for the phone number to make the second, more important call.

"Hello, Sarah McShay speaking."

"Hi, Sarah, it's Jack Weston. I just got back from an incredible road trip, and I need to talk with you. I caught a huge break in the case." He paused. "I know who killed Taylor, and I need you to prove it."

"Great news, Jack. What do you have?"

"Too much to share on the phone. We need to have a face-to-face because some of it's … well, sort of unbelievable. You may not buy it."

Jack arranged to meet Sarah at Zendejas Restaurant around 4 p.m. He arrived early and felt his stomach twist into knots. He fought a growing nausea and broke into a sweat. The memory of this place, where he and Taylor met, tugged at his emotions. However, he knew he had to get past those feelings. Michelle saw Jack enter and came from behind the bar to give him a warm hug. Nanette followed and welcomed him with a smile.

"Jack, how are you doing?"

"Fine, Nanette. It's good to be able to walk in here, again."

"We've really missed you," Michelle said.

His sick sensation disappeared. "Thanks. It's been a tough ride, but I've turned the corner, and I'm ready to move ahead."

"Great to have you back," Nanette added.

"Thanks. I've always enjoyed this place, but the memories kept me away."

"We understand. Let me buy you a beer to celebrate," Nanette offered.

"Great, I'll have a Bud. I'd like to sit on the patio. I'm expecting someone to join me."

He located a table, swallowed hard and let out a deep breath. He made it back to *their* place without a problem. The visit provided Jack with a litmus test to see if he achieved more balance. He had. Now Jack reasoned his meeting with the P.I. would let Taylor know he still searched for justice.

Sarah arrived and greeted Jack with an outstretched hand. She ordered a beer and, after a bit of small talk, asked, "You said you know who killed Taylor."

Jack told her about the confession he heard through the heating duct and his pursuit of the voice to the Plaza Hotel where he discovered Baxter's identity. He recounted his trip to Fort Collins and the accidental meeting with Racy Lanne.

"It's an amazing story," she said. As usual, Sarah fiddled with her hair and had trouble sitting still. Ironically, Jack missed watching the detective's antics and smiled at her. However, his lighthearted thought quickly vanished when her response crushed his murder theory.

"It's not enough — all coincidental information. You have a complaint from a disgruntled employee, this Racy chick, who was fired. Baxter could have been driving anywhere and not even close to where Taylor died. There's no driving log or any other evidence to suggest he was at the hit-and-run scene. We have no case."

She tried to straighten her hair again, failed, then whipped her legs under her body and hunched down on them. "Gotta have more evidence to nail him," she said. "None of this will stand up in court."

Temporarily deflated, Jack failed to understand why Sarah couldn't follow the logical connection between the voice he heard, Racy's story and Baxter's altered travel log. "It's so clear to me. Why can't you see it like I do?"

"You're trying too hard, and it's obscured your thinking. Here's the problem. You only heard a voice and angry words spoken in an argument. The voice did not admit killing Taylor — only said things spoken in the heat of the moment."

Jack shook his head and tried to discount her explanation.

She continued. "To complicate matters, you never saw the man who said those things. You heard a voice. In court, it would be your word against his, and you'd lose."

"Okay, I can't prove it was Baxter. I only know the man who spent the night down the hall from me in room 226 headed for a dollhouse maker in Las Vegas. I found Swanson, who told me he met Baxter. Isn't it enough proof?"

"Nope, you never saw Baxter in room 226. You have no proof he wrote the note on the pad you found. Someone else could have been a guest in the hotel the night before, wrote on the pad, and the maid didn't replace it. Baxter's meeting with Swanson could have been another coincidence."

"Well, what about Racy Lanne's story?"

"How much do you know about her?" Sarah fidgeted in her chair again and pressed her point. "She could be a wacko and have a history as a troublemaker or a person who thrives on high drama." Sarah paused and rearranged her legs as she churned out logical responses to refute every point of Jack's theory. "A person doesn't get fired for one reprimand. You have to go through due process before getting canned. If it happened like she said, the woman would have filed a complaint with the state. Did she?"

"I don't know, but I've spent some time with her. She's a nice person."

"Right," Sarah said. "You two ordered dinner, a couple drinks, a few hours of talk, and then ended up in bed. Sounds more like a one-night stand, my friend. You know nothing about her integrity, do you?"

"I guess not." Jack solemnly stared into his beer glass.

"Do you have anything else?"

Jack looked at the private investigator and wondered if he should risk sharing his experience with Pandora. If the P.I. had trouble with the physical clues, she'd really think he had lost it. He shook his head and turned away.

Sarah closed her notebook, finished her beer and prepared to leave. She took another swipe at her unruly shock of hair and rose from the table. Her abrupt demeanor told him this meeting had been a waste of time.

Out of desperation, Jack stopped her. "Sarah, I do have something else, but I'm not sure you'll believe it." He took a deep breath and waited.

Jack's sincerity captured Sarah's attention, and she hesitated. "I'll listen to whatever you've got, if it helps, or not."

"Fair enough," he said.

Michelle brought out two more pints of Budweiser, and Sarah opened her notebook. With a quick swallow of beer, Jack began. "Do you believe it's possible to talk with spirits?"

"You mean like channeling ghosts and stuff?"

"Yeah."

"I haven't thought about it. I think hysteria drives some people to believe in such things. It opens them to scam artists who play the con and extort money from an easy mark. Some people are gullible enough to attempt to unload their guilt and apologize to a dead relative through a séance for a price." She paused and said, "Well, Jack, to be honest, probably not."

Skepticism filled the space between them. Jack looked dejected.

"Please don't tell me ghosts convinced you Baxter killed Taylor," she said, closing her notebook again.

"No, no, Sarah. Please hear me out. It's nothing like you think. But, something strange did happen out there, and it doesn't make sense."

The critical look on Sarah's face confirmed she didn't believe him. In desperation, he tried a different approach.

"I'm going to share something with you I can't explain or understand. Listen and withhold judgment until I'm finished.

If you think I'm crazy, you can leave, and I promise I won't bother you again. Okay?"

"All right, Jack. You gotta know, if it's nonsense, we're done."

"Agreed. See what you make of this."

Jack told Sarah about his frequent encounters with Pandora and her sudden disappearance. Sarah heard Jack's story of communicating with the voices in his dreams. Anxiously, he watched Sarah shake her head in disbelief.

In spite of the tale's incredulity, he pressed on, "Pandora claimed Taylor sent her to help me."

Sarah folded her hands on the table and stared into the parking lot, an unaccustomed calm gesture for the hyper woman. With a blank stare, she listened to Jack ramble about Pandora's spirit. He noticed her body language and said, "You're not buying any of this, are you?"

"Nope, not a bit. I can't believe some hippie-chick, who claimed to be a spirit and, coincidentally, found you on the road from time to time, convinced you she was a messenger from the other side ... sent by Taylor, no less. You've waded into deep water. Want my advice? Go see Doc Aberdeen. You need more help."

Jack felt deflated, and an awkward silence enveloped the two.

"But, to tell you the truth, I've run into crazier things than this," the detective finally admitted. "I'll go along with you for a few more minutes. She impatiently drummed her fingers on the table. "Get to the point. Did this spirit-chick tell you anything I can use for hard evidence?"

Jack looked at his companion and scratched his head. "I've made some notes. Perhaps there's something here to help."

Jack unfolded the piece of paper he saved from his lunch stop in Denver: the song lyrics, his questions and a few thoughts Jack recalled from his exchanges with Pandora — all on one page, like a puzzle for Sarah to solve.

Now in her element, Sarah studied the list, withdrew a yellow marker from her notebook and highlighted specific items.

"Okay, Jack," she said, "I'll work the mystery for a bit. Let's assume Pandora gave you a real message." Sarah pointed to something on the page. "You didn't understand what she tried to say because you may have been too close to it."

For the first time in their conversation, Jack felt as if the sleuth understood his plea.

"You asked good questions when you analyzed your experience. A light in the night offers the biggest clue. What light does she mean?" Sarah pondered out loud.

"Does it make any sense to you?" Jack pressed.

Sarah stared at the page for a long time. Then, she fumbled through her notebook until she found a page covered with hand-drawn sketches. She studied the drawings and looked back at the song lyrics. Sarah sat back, ran her hands through her hair several times, and finally smiled at him.

Glued to the detective's facial gyrations, Jack could no longer remain a quiet observer. "What? What have you discovered?"

Sarah put the pages down and flashed a serious look. "Let's say this Pandora knew something we didn't. For whatever reason, she couldn't tell you — nope, the message had to be in some kind of code for you to figure out." Sarah paused and added, "Bet it's an unspoken agreement with all those fairy-types." She smiled at her cleverness.

Jack ignored the attempted humor and tried to comprehend. Confused, he asked, "A code? Can you break it? What does the message say?"

"Pandora provided a breakthrough to connect Baxter with the murder, and you couldn't see the light." She grinned at him and enjoyed another private joke.

"Okay, Sarah. Knock it off. Talk to me."

She laughed. Her voice grew somber and quietly said, "Remember, I told you Taylor's autopsy found abrasions, cuts and glass embedded in her shoulder."

"Yes."

"The coroner couldn't figure out how those cuts got there — blamed them on glass in the road. But, if you connect those cuts to all the nonsense about a *light,* it makes perfect sense. Light appears over and over again in all the songs. It's the one consistent clue and solves the puzzle," she shouted.

Still bewildered, Jack shrugged and tried to follow her thinking. He gave Sarah an exasperated look and threw up his hands in frustration. "What!"

"Jack! Blinded by the light … surrounded by the light … light my fire … leave a light on when I'm gone. … You get it, Jack?"

"No."

"Look, Taylor's hit-and-run killer struck her from behind. She never saw or heard a car. The force of the impact tossed her over the hood of the vehicle, and she landed on the road where she died.

Sarah's reconstruction of the accident gnawed at Jack's stomach, but his attention remained fixed on her words. "So, …."

"Here's the message Pandora shared, the message we missed during the investigation. When she flipped over the car, her shoulder broke a light, but not just any light. It was a spotlight like the one attached to the door of a police squad car. The light they use to shine on suspects. It surrounds them! It lights their fire!"

"Oh, my god, how simple, how obvious!" yelled Jack as he jumped out of his chair and kissed Sarah on the forehead.

Surprised, the detective blushed, but continued. "The force of Taylor's body clipped Baxter's spotlight when she flew over the hood at an angle, and it broke. Shards of glass from his light became embedded in her shoulder. The lab report indicated Taylor picked up the glass when her body skidded on the road. But, they were wrong."

"Why couldn't the crime lab identify the source of the glass fragments? Are they part of a cover-up?"

"I'm not sure. You moved her body and messed up the entire crime scene. By the time the lab guys got there, you had disturbed everything."

"I'm sorry, but I couldn't help myself. I didn't know. I was in shock."

"Understandable. But now I know what I'm looking for. I'll try to find the hard evidence to make the case work for us."

"How do you plan to prove the glass came from Baxter's squad car light?" Jack asked.

"Okay, okay, here's the plan. I'll start by learning more about Baxter's driving record at the Division of Motor Vehicles."

"Why waste your time?"

"The information may tell me more about him and his driving patterns."

"How will you connect Baxter to Taylor's death?"

"I'll set up an informal golf date with a friend of mine who works in Desert Valley's vehicle maintenance department. Frank will tell me if Steve had his squad car repaired around the time of the hit-and-run."

"You'll learn this by playing golf?"

"Yeah, it will be less suspicious. Then, I'll visit the crime scene. It may be a long shot, but I might find some stray glass shards in the road and match them with the light on a police squad car. It's been a year and not many people drive out there. So, I may get lucky."

"Let me know if you find anything to confirm Pandora's clues," Jack said.

"I will. In the meantime, you check out Racy Lanne's background to see if she had an axe to grind or if she's a victim, too."

"Sounds like a good plan to me."

Sarah shook her head in disbelief. "This has got to be a first. Some paranormal chick solves a crime. If it's true, I'll need to schedule an appointment with my friendly psychic."

Jack smiled at her insight. The pair finished their beers and agreed to meet again when they had more answers.

Chapter Thirty-Six

Sarah had been a P.I. for three years before Jack hired her. She had a solid reputation and earned a decent living. Her success relied on the extensive social and professional network she developed while serving on the police force. Former co-workers respected her diligence and work ethic. Above all, she always spoke the truth and everyone trusted her. She had been blackballed in an ego struggle with her superior, and many former peers wanted her to make it as a private eye.

When Frank Peterson picked up the phone and responded to Sarah's invitation, he suspected the sleuth an ulterior motive, but agreed nonetheless. He missed her exuberance and positive energy.

"Frank, how about a quick round of golf? I'll spot you a shot per hole."

"I don't know, Sarah. The last time we played, you took me to the cleaners. I lost twenty-five bucks. I thought all the sharks out there played pool."

"Sorry, Frank, my daddy taught me how to swim on the greens."

"Okay, Sarah. If I get one shot a hole, and we limit the bets to the longest drive and fewest putts, I think I can get away without spending my grandson's college fund."

"You drive a hard bargain, but you're on. I'll make the reservation for Tuesday at 10 a.m. Meet you at The Legend at Arrowhead golf course. I'll buy lunch after the front nine."

"Of course, you will. By then, you'll have enough money to buy a three-course dinner and a bottle of fine wine. I'll count on your generosity to invite me to share it with you."

They chuckled and hung up.

Sarah arrived a half-hour early to hit a bucket of balls before Frank showed. She purchased his greens fee and reserved an electric cart for the two of them. *It's money well-spent*, she thought. *I love combining business and pleasure.*

Frank snickered when he realized Sarah had pre-purchased everything. He figured he'd probably lose enough on each hole to make up for her investment.

Nothing in this world comes free, he thought. *She'll pump me for information and do it with a smile.* The two golfers recognized the real game, but pretended otherwise — the mark of close friends. Outwardly, their friendship seemed to be a mismatch — Frank, the old salt with thirty years on the force, matched with an impudent "young Turk" who spit in the face of authority. Their affinity had been forged by a common display of irreverence for authority and strong sense of independence.

Frank arrived shortly before tee-time, which gave him an opportunity to tease Sarah and hit a few practice putts before the starter called their names. The light, mid-week crowd permitted them to play as a twosome, a perfect opportunity for uninterrupted talk. The two split the first few holes and bolstered Frank's sense of confidence. According to their agreement, he cut one stroke off every hole and enjoyed a five dollar advantage as they approached the ninth hole. The unskilled foursome playing ahead of them developed an attraction to the water hazard and spent additional time drowning golf balls. The delay gave Sarah a chance to quiz Frank about Baxter. His temporary financial advantage softened him to her inquiry.

"Frank, do you know Officer Steve Baxter?" she asked.

"Yeah, seen him around and serviced his squad car a couple of times."

"Do you recall the last time he brought his car in for more than the usual oil change or regular maintenance?"

"Let me think. It must have been a year ago. Steve told me he and his boy were playing baseball, and the kid smacked a line drive that broke one of his spotlights."

"Did you log it in your book?"

"Nah, those kinds of things happen when you take your squad car home. So, I changed out the light and replaced the broken cover. No big deal."

"It happened around the middle of February last year?"

"Yeah, why do you ask?"

"Oh, nothing important. I'm investigating a hunch about an unreported accident."

"Look, Sarah, I don't want to get the guy in trouble," Frank said. "I like him. He's always been nice to me — does a good job on patrol. I pitch in and help out the good guys when they need something extra." Back peddling, Frank added, "I don't think this kind of piddle-ass crap should be reported. He had an accident during off hours, plain and simple. A decent cop shouldn't catch hell for a problem he has with city property — not on my watch."

"I understand, Frank. It's cool. You've always helped us get out of jams. I know your heart's in the right place. The force could always count on you to cover their ass."

"Exactly. When Frank Peterson retires, I want all of you young squirts to remember me and what I did to made your lives better."

"You bet, Frank, we'll put up a statue," she smirked. "But right now, I want to watch your incredible slice, because it's going to pay for a full tank of gas tonight. You're up!"

Sarah bought Frank lunch in the clubhouse. By the eighteenth green, Frank had lost enough strokes for Sarah to fill her gas tank twice. His rusty play and fatigue, pitted against her skills, made the difference. Frank sank his last putt and turned to Sarah, "Is Steve Baxter involved in some kind of a civilian dispute?"

"You guessed it. A client hired me to check out a concern about an accident involving Baxter's vehicle — nothing more."

"So, let's see if I understand what happened today. You beat the hell out of me, pumped me for information and now get paid by the civilian who hired you?"

"That's about it. Ain't life a bitch?"

"Okay, sister, you owe me. Next time we play, I'll take two strokes a hole, if you don't mind."

"Of course, Frank, you gave me a lot today. Let's do this again next week."

"Make it next month. I can't afford to play any sooner. But, I know we'll play again because it's always a pleasure being your personal snitch and getting whipped for it."

Sarah laughed and gave Frank a hug. "It's why I love you, Frank. You're such a good sport about it."

Chapter Thirty-Seven

The next day, the P.I. headed to Phoenix and the Arizona Motor Vehicle Division. She examined Steve Baxter's driving record and discovered he had accrued several moving violations as an adult. The year before Steve became a Desert Valley police officer, he worked for the Goodyear Police Department. In one year, he had been involved in two accidents and received another speeding citation during off-hours. She found another picture of Steve taken by a roadside camera, but professional courtesy permitted him to expunge the violation. Sarah surmised Goodyear fired him based on this record.

Going back to his early years as a driver, Sarah's search revealed Baxter also had his license suspended at the age of eighteen for drag racing and reckless endangerment. Sarah deduced her suspect loved driving fast and with no regard for posted speed limits.

The P.I. conducted a background search of Baxter's family and learned Steve's mother had a different last name. Court records revealed Cynthia Baxter divorced Fred Baxter when Steve turned sixteen. It must have been a messy split because the record also included a restraining order filed against Fred. A lengthy police report listed six interventions related to domestic violence. The last disturbance sent Fred to jail. Shortly after, Cynthia filed for divorce.

Sarah concluded Steve lived through some rocky times as an impressionable teenager and became an unwilling witness to the demise of his family. He transformed into a rebellious youth who replaced speed for lack of power. The loss of his license may have been the best thing to happen to the angry boy. *But, losing your license never eliminates the pain of watching your family fall apart, does it, Baxter?*

"Still angry, huh, Steve? How did you ever become a cop?" she said aloud in her isolated cubicle.

Sarah examined Mrs. Baxter's legal file and noted an interesting addendum. When Steve turned eighteen, Cynthia Baxter became Mrs. Sam Williamson. Sarah figured the second marriage must have added another stressor to the teenager's life.

How did the change affect your behavior, Steve? Why does the name Sam Williamson sound familiar? I recognize it, but in what context?

Finally, Sarah looked at Steve Baxter's personal file. She discovered the man married Pamela Sloan when he turned twenty-two. The couple had three children: Steve Jr., Brad and Millie. They lived in a modest three-bedroom house near downtown Peoria for almost a decade until the couple divorced three years ago. Pamela's divorce petition included the catchall phrase about *irreconcilable differences*. In the subsequent hearing, the judge ordered Steve to pay child support and alimony large enough to cover the house payment. Sarah wrote the words *irreconcilable differences* in her notebook, and added, *Now at age thirty-two, is Steve still dealing with unresolved issues? If so, probably unsuccessfully.*

One more document turned up in Sarah's search. A marriage license filed by Steve Baxter and Lynn Showers indicated the couple had been married for almost two years. They rented a townhouse off of 83rd Avenue and Bell Road, near the 101 bypass. The location offered Steve convenient access to his job in Desert Valley and his biological children. Sarah made a note to visit Steve's neighborhood to see if his acquaintances could expand on the image she began to create of Steve Baxter's personality.

Even though it had been a year since the hit-and-run, Sarah drove her car north to locate the crime scene. She wanted to get a firsthand look at the site. *If Officer Baxter liked to speed, he must have let it all out on those isolated country roads,* she thought. *Perhaps he had been tired, lost or careless. If Steve Baxter drove on the dark, deserted road where Taylor had been jogging, the combination of those conditions may have ended in disaster.*

Sarah turned off the last paved highway in Desert Valley and onto a series of dusty gravel roads. She got lost a couple of times and finally located the road leading to the accident scene. In the past year, Desert Valley showed evidence of rapid expansion. Billboards and signs posted in the fields advertised the future construction of a gated subdivision called Vista View. One billboard pictured custom houses ranging from $350,000 to $500,000. Another sign flaunted an artist's rendition of an expansive activity center, swimming pool and golf course with a "coming soon" banner taped across the pictures. The Desert Valley City Council must have collaborated with the developers because the city's utility department began installing light poles along the roadside. They looked like a series of functionless, metal sentinels waiting for an electrical connection. Sarah shook her head and said out loud, "When will this unchecked growth stop? People are destroying the entire desert."

About twenty yards short of the accident scene, Sarah noticed the road took a sharp turn to the left. She slowed down to maneuver her vehicle into the acute angle and immediately came upon the scene of the hit-and-run. "That's it," she shouted, "I see how it happened!"

Sarah's creative mind reconstructed the accident. *In the last two hours of his overtime shift, Officer Baxter chose to drive around in this unincorporated area of the county.* Sarah continued to imagine the scenario: *He's tired, lost and, like always, driving too fast. According to Racy's story, he checks his non-functioning GPS and has to use the vehicle's radio to communicate with other officers. He gets distracted and doesn't watch the road. Steve misses the sharp curve because it's too dark. Traveling at a high speed, his car probably fishtails to negotiate the curve at the exact spot where Taylor's running. She's listening to music on her iPod and doesn't hear the vehicle. The impact is immediate and deadly. Taylor flies over the hood of his squad car, scraps her shoulder on his spotlight, breaks it and lands on the road ... right about here.*

Sarah looked at a spot in the road where Taylor may have fallen. *Later, Jack finds her body, picks it up, and his movements mess up the area and obliterate most of the forensic evidence.*

If that's a possibility, Sarah thought, *the glass shards from Steve's spotlight should be right over ... there.* She walked back ten feet in the road and bent down to examine the surface. She slipped on a pair of rubber gloves and removed a small whiskbroom from her pocket. She crouched down on all fours, resembling a lizard more than a human being. At a particular spot, Sarah brushed accumulated sand and gravel from a three-foot area.

She stretched out flat on the road's surface, her face pressed against the gravel. Within seconds, she spotted her treasure and smiled. The sun reflected off shards of broken glass strewn in a consistent pattern at the edge of her swept circle. Sarah reached for an envelope and tweezers — standard equipment for detectives — and carefully placed the broken pieces of glass in the brown enclosure. "If these match with your broken light, Steve, we've got you," she whispered into the wind.

A shiver ran through her body. Sarah realized she may have just found the evidence to connect Steve Baxter to Taylor's hit-and-run death. *Why didn't the Desert Valley forensics team find these shards when they first investigated the scene?* she asked herself. The thought bothered the detective enough to listen to her gut. *Sloppy work?* she pondered. *Inexperience? Contaminated crime scene? Cover-up? I'm not sure which, but something tells me not to trust them.*

The P.I. chose to hold the evidence in her possession until she could make an appointment with a friend in the Phoenix FBI office. They would conduct an independent investigation of the glass shards. It may take more time, but, at least this evidence won't get *lost* in the custody of the Desert Valley Police Department.

Chapter Thirty-Eight

Frank told Steve about his golf game with Sarah. His loyal, fraternity-like mentality required him to give his uniformed brother a heads-up. Steve accepted the information with disinterest and shrugged it off, but internally, he seethed. *I can't believe it. After an entire year, some pipsqueak P.I. tries to poke a hole in my alibi. Not if I can help it.* Steve gunned his engine and the squad car squealed as he exited the parking lot.

Steve Baxter loved the authority attached to his job, and this setback got in the way of his self-image. Since joining the force, he brandished power to intimidate others. His badge and revolver gave him the muscle to do anything he chose. On patrol, he could write speeding tickets and watch drivers sweat, or issue warning citations and let them feel like they beat the system. He often used force to humble and squelch people's bravado and swagger. His greatest pleasure: putting down men in front of their female companions.

Today he only felt anger for the circumstances putting him in this predicament. Steve drove around for miles and ignored his responsibility as an officer. He needed time to settle down and clear his head. Life constantly dealt him a series of negative blows. As he drove, memories of his past reeled through his mind like so many bad clips on YouTube.

Steve hated his mother. He blamed her for the humiliation of his father's descent into alcoholism. She caused his father to turn violent. At sixteen, he refused to accept the divorce and felt guilty he couldn't find the secret formula, the ability to reunite his parents. Eventually, Steve's father abandoned him altogether, slipped into an alcoholic demise and died. Counselors and teachers dismissed Steve's anger and attributed his attitude to being an impressionable teenager, typical juvenile behavior. It would change as he matured, nothing more to worry about.

His mother remarried two years after the divorce. Her choice compounded his anger, and Steve believed it had been another part of her insensitivity. Although the man she married treated his mother with respect and lavished her with money and gifts, Steve disliked his new "dad" and never accepted him. Something phony about his slick demeanor betrayed a lack of moral fiber. Sam Williamson resembled one of those sweet-talking, slimy con artists who could glad-hand you with a plastered-on smile and secretly pick your pocket at the same time. Steve felt Sam acted like a filthy bug needing to be squashed.

But Sam Williamson's charm won his mother's affection and loyalty. A lawyer by trade, he epitomized all the nasty jokes about the legal profession: Sam could be comfortable swimming with sharks and survive — a professional courtesy. Sam loved telling the joke, but Steve hated his smug confidence.

Sam and Steve co-existed in a shaky truce charged with unspoken tension. Steve avoided his new stepfather and stayed out of family matters. At eighteen, he became a "streetwise hood" and explored life without adult supervision.

Even though Steve lost his license for reckless driving, Sam used his legal influence to rescue his ungrateful stepson and had him back on the streets within months. His act of political chicanery should have forged a respectful bond between the two, but the uneasy relationship continued. In time, they established a mutual understanding: Sam pursued his love affair with Cynthia, and Steve refrained from challenging Sam's presence. In turn, Sam paid Steve a hefty allowance to "get lost." By nineteen, Steve lived in a downtown Phoenix apartment with friends, and Sam paid the rent.

When Sam Williamson ran for state senate and won, Steve decided to cut the final ties with his mother. She had adopted the man's upper-class behaviors and became Sam's doting wife at important social events. Steve detested her false air of snobbery, and visits to the house became awkward. In time, she also welcomed a divorce from her angry son. Their mutual separation occurred without words.

Steve joined the army to get away. The two-year experience sculpted his body and turned him into a muscular hulk of a man. His training developed a physical and mental toughness, a necessary preparation for the police force. A non-life-threatening injury led to an early discharge, and he enrolled in the Phoenix Police Academy as a logical extension of his military training.

Initially, his relationship with his first wife, Pamela, had worked out nicely due to her patient, forgiving nature. Unfortunately, her co-dependent personality and a fear of Steve's angry rants led the marriage to a disastrous conclusion. The financial responsibilities of an ex-wife and three children added to Steve's smoldering hate.

Steve spent the next year barhopping, coaxing one woman after another into bed. Finally, he met Lynn, and she got pregnant. He decided to marry her because he wanted to settle down with a woman who could meet his demands. However, after a brief honeymoon, the man realized he had burdened himself with the image and personality of his mother. Now in his third year of marriage, Steve reverted to old habits and used her as a target to vent his unresolved feelings. He rained verbal and physical abuse on her whenever the mood struck or his alcohol-induced emotions surfaced.

Filled with a resentment impacting every aspect of his life, his future drastically changed after he had been dropped from the Goodyear Police Department. His supervisor gave him the option to resign or be fired. He chose the former rather than have another smudge on his record.

Out of work for several months, Sam intervened again and cashed in a political favor. He convinced the Desert Valley Police Department to hire his stepson. The city had a policy requiring all new employees to serve a twelve-month probationary period. When the accident occurred, Steve was within weeks of fulfilling the obligation. The hit-and-run occurred. It capped a long series of bad luck going back to when he turned sixteen.

#####

An hour before sunrise, Steve looked up from his faulty GPS and saw Taylor's body catapult over the hood of his vehicle. He knew he killed her. An unaccustomed panic gripped him. He jumped out of the car and ran back to her crumpled frame. He stood over her just as the last breath of air hissed from her lungs. He watched her body relax. He felt for a pulse — none. He shined a flashlight into her pupils. No sign of life. Steve scuffed his way back to the squad car so no visible trace of his footprints remained in the gravel roadbed.

Fear replaced reason as he sped away from the scene. He drove down one unknown road after another until, by chance, his vehicle found a paved highway leading toward the lights of a city in the distant horizon. He located an isolated parking lot behind a gas station and made the most important call of his life. He used one of the few pay phones left in the area.

"Hello, Sam, sorry to wake you at such an early hour, but I'm in real bad trouble."

"Steve, what the hell's the matter with you? Can't this wait until tomorrow?"

"No, damn it! It can't wait. It is tomorrow, and I need your help now."

"Okay, Steve, give me a chance to get out of bed and wake up. I can't help you when I'm half-asleep. Call me back in ten minutes, and we'll talk in private, away from your mother."

"Anything you say, Sam, but I have to work fast on this thing."

Steve impatiently watched the clock, and as the sun began to peek over the horizon, the distraught officer called Williamson a second time.

"Hello, Steve. What's the big problem?"

210

"Sam, this time I'm up shit creek. I hit and killed a jogger in the dark. I was still on patrol."

"What! Are you sure?"

"Of course, I am. I watched the chick die."

"God, Steve, of all the crazy things to happen right now, this is the worst. I'm up for re-election this fall, and Desert Valley's trying to pass the additional sales tax to expand its services, including the police force. If this story breaks, all of us can kiss our ass's goodbye."

"If you weren't so self-centered about your goddamn politics, you'd also figure out it's my problem, as well. I could get sent to prison for manslaughter, and it would end my career. The guys I put away would have a field day with me behind bars. I'd be dead meat."

Silence filled the phone line as the horror of the event continued to race through Steve's mind. Aware of the uncomfortable stillness, Steve blabbered into the phone, "Look, Sam, for mother's sake and *your* fucking political future, you've got to make this thing disappear. Please help me, Sam."

"Slow down, Steve. I can handle things from this end, but you've got to take care of some details. First, get your ass into a coffee shop and make sure people see you. Then, change your travel log and erase all records indicating you drove in the area. Next, find a self-service car wash and scrub your vehicle by hand ... twice. Pay attention to every spot she might have come in contact with, especially the wheel wells. When your shift ends, go straight home and wait for my call. And, for god's sake, don't talk to your mother. Understand all I said, Steve?"

"Yeah, got it and, Sam, thanks for saving my ass."

Chapter Thirty-Nine

Sam hung up and took a sip of coffee. He twirled the telephone cord around his finger and thought of all the times his stepson made Cynthia cry. *Such a self-centered jackass,* he thought. *I wish he'd go away and stay out of our lives. He's just trouble.*

Sam Williamson, the ultimate politician, had established a successful legal career in the Phoenix valley. He enjoyed a reputation for being someone who made things happen. His political skills developed though a combination of experience and good fortune. He forged his political power and created an extensive social network. Sam had the ability to help others and then cash in his "acts of kindness." He owned people and reminded them of their obligations to him. The reciprocal exchange of favors often crossed ethical and moral lines, but a consistent "ends justifying the means" philosophy benefitted everyone involved, especially Sam.

Shortly after marrying Cynthia, political organizers approached Sam and encouraged him to run for the state senate. Endorsed by a formidable political power, he pledged to work for the best interests of the party. Sam Williamson became a prominent state senator and soon developed the financial and social resources to become an influential player. All important legislation required Sam's approval before it became a law. In time, the party considered him a possible candidate for governor or the House of Representatives in Washington. However, Sam had no such aspirations because he thrived on the power to control a smaller, manageable environment. Such power brought him many opportunities to line his pockets and expand political currency.

When Steve's call woke him, Sam viewed it as nothing more than a minor political predicament — a need to slap a pesky mosquito. The problem required immediate attention, but would be resolved with minimal effort. The situation could be settled in a low-key manner and handled from a comfortable distance. Of course, several palms had to be greased and past markers called in. No problem.

When he considered the big picture, this accident didn't concern him. The future of Desert Valley and his own re-election necessitated the elimination of any scandal leaked to the media. He had to remain aloof and separate from his wife's reckless son. Others would handle the messy details.

Sam looked at his watch — 7:15 a.m. He envisioned John Thompson, the Desert Valley Chief of Police, sitting in his office drinking his first cup of coffee. Sam made the call.

"This is John Thompson. How can I help you?"

"Hello, bubba, Sam here!"

"Sam, good buddy, I haven't heard from you in awhile. How they hangin'?"

"Always in good shape, my friend. Say, John, we've got a situation only you can handle."

"What is it?"

"In an hour or so, your office will get a telephone call about a missing jogger. Only she's not missing. She's dead, killed in an accident."

John often heard such reports and handled this one without emotion. Nonchalantly, John asked, "Why is this accident my trouble, Sam?"

"Because it involves one of your officers, and if the facts get media coverage, it will flush the special election for you guys down the toilet."

"Got it. Won't let it happen. Loss of jobs and major cutbacks ... can't afford it. What do you want me to do?"

"When the call comes in, investigate the crime scene, but don't make it too formal. I'd like you to personally review the findings so nothing points back to the department. Finally, as a personal favor to me, you need to get Steve Baxter off the fucking streets and turn him into a desk jockey. Got it?"

"Sam, I know I owe you for the additional dollars you found for our budget last year. Those state discretionary funds did the trick. But, I tell you, this favor should square things between us, right?"

"You bet, but I'll count on you to make this thing go away for good and get buried before the election."

"You got it."

"And, losing any incriminating evidence may help. I hear such things happen sometimes in a forensics lockup."

"Don't worry about a thing, Sam. It's like the accident never occurred."

"Good and, John, when your son goes back to ASU next fall, I'm sure he'll appreciate the tuition waiver from an anonymous donor. Should help him with expenses."

"Thank you, Sam. I know my son has worked hard for that kind of break."

#####

John Thompson, a practical man, maintained a blind, steadfast loyalty to the people who got him elected and kept him in office. He had always been a good field soldier and never questioned assignments or requests from those up the ladder.

This morning, he reasoned no good would come from a meticulous investigation of a hit-and-run accident. It would be disastrous if they discovered a police officer had run down one of those health-nut joggers who dodge traffic at all hours of the night. *I'll never understand why they don't do their workouts in a health club like everyone else,* he thought. *Only loony bins run in the desert in the dark. Besides, finding the driver who ran over the woman won't bring her back to life.*

He stood up, poured himself a second cup of coffee and looked out his office window into miles of desert landscape.

A detailed investigation may attract a lot of negative publicity for Desert Valley, bad risk for the community's future. These kinds of accidents happen all the time. Baxter didn't hit her on purpose — didn't even know her — just a patrol officer fulfilling his obligation to the city. Someone happened to be in the wrong place at the wrong time. Yes, he thought, *it would be best for all concerned to make the problem go away. No harm, no foul.*

Bill Lamperes

A few days later, Thompson learned a low-level dispatcher had filed a complaint against Baxter for altering his travel log. John instructed his duty captain to put the woman in her place with a written reprimand and get rid of her as soon as possible. Such an irrational move by a goody two-shoes employee pressed his anger button. *If people don't know their place, their boundaries,* he thought, *they don't deserve to work for us.*

Chapter Forty

Jack mustered enough confidence to call Racy and ask her to dinner. He arranged to meet her at Cartwright's in Cave Creek at 7 p.m. Jack arrived early and waited in the bar. As he finished his first martini, Racy's unmistakable red hair heralded her arrival. She had it pulled back into a thick ponytail cascading over one shoulder. The hairstyle and the formfitting, knee-length black dress accentuated her alluring figure. Once her eyes adjusted to the restaurant's dim light, she spotted Jack, smiled and joined him at the bar.

"Thanks for calling. I wondered if you'd ever find the time after your Colorado drama."

Jack failed to understand she referred to his inability to locate Steve Baxter and not his personal embarrassment. "Yeah, I kinda let you down. I'm sorry."

She laughed and patted him on the shoulder, "Oh, that! Don't feel bad about our night together. I'm glad I could be there for you."

In spite of her assurance, Jack continued his apology. "Sorry, I couldn't think of anything except Taylor."

"I know. It's okay. The combination of emotional stress and alcohol can turn a man into Jell-O. It happens occasionally," she assured him.

"You need to know I didn't invite you here to try again. This time, I want to start over and get to know more about Racy, the person."

"Getting to know each other before going to bed? What a novel idea. It will be a new experience for me," Racy grinned and slapped him on the knee.

He smiled and asked what she wanted to drink. Cartwright's, a popular restaurant with the locals, usually had a waiting list, but the hostess promised the couple would be seated in another twenty minutes. The delay offered them time to linger in the bar and talk.

After taking a sip of a cosmopolitan, she asked, "Make any progress in connecting Baxter to the hit-and-run?"

"Yes, Sarah, my private investigator, talked with Frank, an employee from Desert Valley's vehicle maintenance division. He confirmed Baxter had a broken spotlight and fixed it shortly after the accident. She's hoping to find some hard evidence to connect the crime to Steve."

"What's next?"

"It's difficult to figure out who to trust. They may have fired you because you snitched on Steve, but we can't prove anything."

They sat quietly, sipping their drinks, each lost in thought until Racy asked, "Have you considered taking the case to the district attorney? Perhaps he can do something to help you."

"We thought about it, but if Sarah decides to do it, things could get messy for you."

"Me? I've got nothing to hide. I did my job and followed department policy. I never had anything against Baxter."

"I know, but you may get blamed for causing trouble."

"I've never been a troublemaker in any of my jobs. I know redheads have a reputation for being spunky fighters, and I'm no exception. So, let them bring it on."

Jack smiled at her feisty words and said, "Slow down, lady. We're supposed to be on a date."

Racy grinned and took another sip. "Yes, it's the main reason I accepted your invitation. Besides, I've been gone from the Desert Valley Police Department for over a year. I can't hurt anyone."

"Don't kid yourself. Your testimony could link Baxter to the scene. You've got to remember I heard Baxter admit he already ran over one woman and could do it again. If his mind works like that, your life may be in danger."

"It's beginning to sound like we're involved in some Hollywood spy movie."

"I'm just telling you to be careful."

The hostess interrupted, "Weston, party of two."

A table by the fireplace added to the romantic ambiance of the setting. As they sat down, Jack's body tensed for a moment, and he removed the single rose sitting in the vase on the table. He handed it to the hostess and responded to Racy's puzzled look. "It will give us a better view of the fire."

"How delightful. I'm dining with a classy man. I'm impressed."

"I told you I have to apologize for a lot. I fell asleep like a limp ragdoll in the presence of a beautiful woman, and, believe me, it's the first time it's ever happened to me."

"Stop it, Jack! Get over it. But, if your sensitive ego forces you to do so, I'll gladly be the recipient of all your make-up gifts."

The waiter arrived with menus, and the couple asked about his dinner recommendations. The restaurant, known for its exquisite all-natural beef, motivated Jack to order the New York strip steak, rare, prepared Oscar style. Racy surprised Jack by ordering a comfort food, chicken-fried meatloaf made with beef, elk and buffalo. They shared a Caesar salad for two and a bottle of exquisite California wine.

"You surprise me, Racy. I didn't know you were such a hearty eater," Jack teased.

"I grew up in Texas and learned to eat a good dinner every night."

The fire cast a warm glow on Racy's face, and Jack noticed how beautiful she looked in the soft, flickering light. In Colorado, he had been too distracted and focused on Steve Baxter to study her lovely features. However, tonight, as she sat across from him, Jack's eyes drank in her natural beauty. Strands of errant red hair enhanced her radiant smile. Her blue eyes sparkled in the glowing light and twinkled when she looked at him. Jack felt attracted to the woman he had met by chance on a cool Colorado evening. Now, in a more relaxed setting, his long-dormant emotions created an unexpected desire for her.

"I need to apologize once more. Not for my failure to perform, but for my bizarre reactions. I struggled so long with Taylor's death I became emotionally frozen."

"Thank you. I accept the apology."

She gazed into the man's eyes, and her look encouraged him to continue.

"Racy, I didn't think I could ever feel anything for another woman again. Then, you appeared. You need to know I'm quite attracted to you."

"I feel the same about you, Jack. Our non-lovemaking evening provided a pleasant start for a relationship."

"How so?"

All of the men in my past have been dominant and demanding. The guys I dated have been aggressive, and I often felt used, treated like their personal sex object."

"Not all men are aggressive, sexist pigs. It's too bad you haven't been with men who honor and respect women."

She smiled across the table and blushed, "Not until I held you all night at the Armstrong. I never had such an experience before."

Now Jack blushed. "You've got me trapped, lady. I don't know if I should argue I'm not the kind of weepy, soft-hearted guy, or tell you I'm soft and cuddly. You know, a man in touch with my feminine side."

She laughed and held her hand over her mouth to hide a giggle. "Why don't you try to be yourself, and we'll see how things go."

They both laughed and returned to their tasty entrées. The evening progressed, and Jack and Racy explored each other's family history, likes and dislikes, backgrounds and personalities. They frequently exchanged meaningful glances and touched hands as they shared favorite memories.

Jack learned Racy's family moved to Arizona from Texas, and she graduated from Mesa High School. She then enrolled at Grand Canyon University to become a legal secretary. When money ran out, Racy quit school and found a job with law enforcement. She wanted to become a victim's advocate;

the dispatch job with the Desert Valley Police Department would look good on her résumé and pay the bills so she could continue as a part-time student.

Jack discovered Racy got married when she turned twenty-two. It only lasted a year because her husband became a domineering, mean-spirited man. He smothered her emotions and belittled her dreams. When she realized he had monitored her phone calls and checked every credit card purchase, she confronted him. He turned violent and started physically abusing her. Within a year, she filed for a divorce. For the past couple of years, Racy had focused on completing her degree in criminology. Her studies consumed most of her life and left no time to pursue another romantic relationship.

"Before I met you," she said, "I didn't need to have a man in my life. I thought most men were Neanderthal beasts, who kept women to clean the cave or for sexual release."

"Someday you'll meet a man who will show you a gentle side."

"Oh, I think I have, but he may not be ready to accept my affection," she said, placing her hand on top of his.

Jack absorbed her words and felt a stirring in his body, followed by a quick pang of guilt. He looked at his dinner date and said, "I have to resolve Taylor's death before I can think about building a new relationship." More silence followed, and then he added, "But, if you exercise patience …," his voice trailed off.

Racy squeezed his hand and said, "I understand, Jack. I'm very patient in matters of the heart. But who knows how quickly things can change."

Jack leaned across the table and gently kissed her on the cheek. Lost in her scent, he touched her face with his hand and kissed her on the lips. It felt like velvet.

She smiled, sat back and looked into his eyes. "See, things are changing already. But, we can take our time. You have an issue to resolve, and I'm not going anywhere. I'd feel more comfortable if we didn't have unfinished business in our way."

Jack picked up her hand and surrounded it with both of his. He gently kissed her fingertips. "You're absolutely right. I have been consumed with my pain and anger long enough. You deserve all my attention."

The couple lingered over coffee and snifters of Grand Mariner. By 11 p.m., they were the last customers in the restaurant. The evening had been packed with stories and laughter and balanced by sorrowful insights from their long-forgotten childhood. Within the confines of the romantic restaurant, Racy and Jack had connected and became lost in time and place. Jack paid the check and waited at the front door for Racy to return from the bathroom.

When they stepped into the cool night air, Jack noticed three vehicles in the parking lot: his 2008 Honda Accord, her 1980 Ford Mustang and a Desert Valley police squad car with its lights flashing. An officer stood next to Jack's vehicle with a nightstick in his hand.

"You the owner of this car, mister?" the voice from the shadowed figure asked.

Jack seemed oblivious to the upcoming confrontation, but Racy immediately recognized the danger. She held Jack's arm and squeezed it so hard he winced in pain. Startled by her move, he looked at Racy and saw the fear. Before the officer spoke again, Racy whispered, "It's him. It's Steve."

Instantly Jack's demeanor changed. He could barely contain his anger. Gallons of adrenalin coursed through his body and triggered his fight response. Speechless by the physical presence of Taylor's killer, Jack gulped in short, rapid breaths. He swallowed hard, felt his heart race and tried to maintain control. He told himself: *stay cool, keep it together.* He couldn't ruin the case with a wild confrontation where words and actions could jeopardize the investigation.

The officer continued, "Give me your driver's license, registration and proof of insurance. Hand 'em over, bud."

Baxter didn't wait for Jack's response. As soon as he finished the practiced speech, his eyes moved from Jack's face to the woman holding his arm.

"It's you. What the fuck are you doing with him? Oh, now I get it. You two are trying to frame me, and you filled his head with a bunch of shit!"

Jack stepped forward, ready to deck the officer. However, Racy dug her nails in deeper and stopped his progress.

In a calm voice, she asked, "Pretty far from the Desert Valley city limits, aren't you, Steve?"

"A police officer never knows when he's going to run into people who violate the law," he snickered and slapped the nightstick against his palm to emphasize the whack sound of wood against flesh.

"What the hell are you talking about?" Jack contested, "We're not even in the car yet."

"For example," the officer droned on, "someone could be violating an Arizona law by driving a car with a broken taillight." He then swung the nightstick against the red plastic cover at the rear of Jack's vehicle, instantly shattering it and sending shards of plastic and a broken light bulb across the gravel.

Jack lunged forward in protest, but Racy's grip tightened. Seething, Jack looked into her pleading eyes and stopped. He took several deep breaths and exhaled. Slowly, he turned and aimed a furious look at the officer who played a masterful game of intimidation.

"You think this is going to make a difference? You can't scare me, Baxter," Jack said.

"Look, buddy, you're sticking your nose into things — things way beyond you. You've got nothing on me, so back off!" His intense eyes fixed on Jack. "Frank told me you tried to send your little private eye to dig up shit on me, but nothing. She got nothing. Not even the story from this lying bitch will help. The department fired her because she's trouble. She's a known liar."

Jack could no longer resist and blurted, "I heard you admit killing a woman!"

"You're dreaming, buddy. You can't prove a thing. In fact, the way you're rambling, I think you're drunk."

"You're full of shit, Baxter," Jack shouted.

"Don't try anything. I'm conducting an investigation and can arrest both of you for obstructing an officer."

"C'mon, Steve, you've got to be kidding," Racy intervened.

"Not kidding, just doing my job." He looked at Jack and added, "Mister, I think you're too drunk to drive home, especially in a vehicle with a broken taillight."

"Steve, get serious," Racy pleaded.

"I am serious, woman."

He turned to Jack with his hand on an unbuttoned gun holster and demanded, "You need to take a sobriety test, bud. Stand up straight and touch your nose with the index finger of each hand until I tell you to stop."

"That's more bullshit," shouted Jack.

He strained against Racy's hold, and she gave him a somber look. "Cooperate with him, Jack. It could get ugly, and Baxter will use his gun if he's even slightly pushed. He's got the law on his side."

Jack took in several deep breaths and exhaled slowly to regain control. In a moment, he looked at Steve. "Okay, give me your fucking test, Baxter."

Steve had Jack complete the nose-touching assessment, forced him to walk a straight line and recite the alphabet backwards. Baxter then made Jack blow into a breathalyzer. When the humiliation ended, Steve informed Jack his breath analysis exceeded the legal limit of alcohol consumption, and he couldn't drive. Jack needed to have someone take him home or call a cab. If he drove out of Cartwright's parking lot, Steve promised to make an immediate arrest.

To avoid more problems, Racy stepped between the two men and said, "I'll drive him home." She held Jack's hands and glared into Steve's eyes. The officer backed down.

Baxter got into his squad car and lowered the window. "Mister, just know things could get a lot worse, understand my drift? You live out in the boondocks. Never know what kind of things could happen to people who live out there

—passing strangers, burglars, danger lurking in the desert with no police protection."

Baxter sneered at the couple and drove away. Racy shivered and turned to Jack for a comforting hug. His anger receded as the sweet-smelling woman held him in a bear-like grip. Jack left his car at Cartwright's and let Racy drive him home.

Chapter Forty-One

The morning sunlight broke through the window and woke Jack from a pleasant slumber. He stretched, yawned and rolled over. His outstretched fingers lightly combed through Racy's soft scarlet hair. How marvelous she had been last night. *Sleeping with Racy, so very different from Taylor,* he thought. Making love with her had evolved into a soft, gentle, yet passionate time. No awkward moments tempered their passion. Their lovemaking had been comfortable and moved him to a new level of appreciation for the beautiful woman.

Jack remembered he unlocked the front door and took Racy in his arms. They relished a long kiss before walking upstairs, where they anxiously, but tenderly undressed each other and enjoyed the exquisite feeling of a naked embrace. The two lovers explored each other in a deliberate serenity of bliss.

Each kiss expressed the joy and wonder of discovery. The hour of passion transitioned into the welcome veil of sleep. They remained locked in each other's arms all night. For the moment, with their sexual tension and emotional needs fulfilled, the world seemed to relax.

Racy woke when she felt Jack's touch. She rolled over, opened her eyes and smiled at him, "What a wonderful night. Thank you for inviting me to stay," she said.

He smiled back and joked, "The least I could do. I didn't have enough money to tip the taxi driver."

"If that's what I get for a tip, I'll drive you anywhere."

"I guess the relationship has moved much faster than we planned," he said.

"It's amazing how fear can trigger deeper needs. "Are you okay with what happened?"

He kissed her hair and then her face. She sat up and let the sheet slip down her body. Racy pulled Jack's face to hers and kissed him. He responded with increased ardor. They spent the next hour locked in a passionate dance. Satiated by their lovemaking, the couple lay entwined and silently drifted into private thoughts.

Jack broke the spell by recalling their encounter with Baxter. "Steve's one crazy loose cannon, isn't he? I'm afraid we haven't seen the last of him."

"He frightens me because the badge gives him the authority to do anything."

"I know. He scared me, too," Jack said. I'm sorry he found us together. Now he's got to silence both of us."

"What an ugly thought, but you don't have to worry about me. I have a job with the Glendale Police Department, and my new friends all have guns. You, on the other hand, can't count on anybody for help. He could do what he wants out here, and nobody would know."

"You're right, Racy. I'll be careful, but, I think he's only using intimidation to get me to back off."

"Your P.I. must have pushed the right buttons because Steve came looking for you."

"I guess so. I'll give Sarah a call later. But for now," he said, "let's take a hot shower so I can wash your back and other essential locations. Then, I'll make you one of my world-famous cheese and vegetable omelets."

"You actually cook? I'm more impressed with every new thing I learn about you, Mr. Weston."

"You need to know women from all over the world have begged to stay overnight with me just so they could enjoy the gourmet breakfast I prepare for them in the morning."

Smiling broadly, she said, "Right, and if you ever run out of travel ideas for *Western Trails*, you can always become a fiction writer."

They laughed and headed for the shower.

Later that morning Jack placed a call to Sarah to inform her about his experience with Baxter. Sarah wasn't surprised about the officer's strong-arm tactics. "I hit pay dirt with Frank's information," Sarah said. She revealed the details of her crime scene search and finding the glass shards.

"If he suspects anything, he may be scared," Jack said.

"Just a word of caution, desperate people can be dangerous. Watch out for him."

"You can bet on it. I'll be very careful from now on. And, Sarah, the same goes for you."

"Don't worry about me, Jack. I'm too wiry to be intimidated by a big cop," she said. "And here's something else to add more drama. My investigation uncovered another interesting fact about Baxter."

"What's that?"

"I think I know why the Desert Valley police may have sat on the investigation. But, I don't want to talk about it on the phone. I'll turn all my evidence over to the FBI next week and let them go after it."

"Good. I hope they can figure it out and lock up the bastard."

"Let me do the legwork. I've got the glass shards from Steve's spotlight in my office and will personally take them to the FBI next Wednesday."

"Okay, I'll wait to hear from you."

"And, Jack, please lay low and be extremely careful."

"Oh, don't worry, he successfully scared the crap out of me last night. Racy and I will be cautious."

"When did you and Racy become an item? No, don't tell me, I have enough puzzles to figure out."

Jack hung up and looked at Racy. "You know what they say ...."

She looked at him quizzically, "What?"

"There's always safety in numbers. After I get my car from Cartwright's, I think you need to stay here for the rest of the weekend. We can go out for a light dinner tonight."

"Jack Weston, you have such a charming way about you. Of course, for our *mutual protection* and safety, I think we should spend the weekend together. Do you have a guestroom I could use?"

"Oh, my dear lady, I have much nicer accommodations than the cold, lonely guestroom."

They exchanged a smile and prepared to rescue Jack's car. They drove to Racy's apartment to pick up clothes and other necessities she'd need for another overnight. After a quick dinner, they returned to the protective walls of Jack's desert castle and got comfortable.

Chapter Forty-Two

Wednesday came and went with no news from Sarah. She couldn't be reached by phone or e-mail. An uneasy tension filled Jack's mind. Baxter's anticipated "next move" failed to materialize. Each night, Racy parked her vehicle in Jack's garage to keep it hidden. Feeling paranoid and fearful, Jack drove Racy to her job in downtown Glendale each morning and then spent the day in the library researching topics for his next article. However, the anxiety of the unknown distracted his concentration, and he often sat in front of a blank computer screen.

On Friday evening, Jack and Racy stopped at Zendejas Grill for dinner. Michelle and Nanette delighted in learning more about the new woman in Jack's life. More importantly, they enjoyed seeing Jack laugh again. After dinner, the couple sat at the bar talking with Michelle. The two women chatted about growing up in Montana.

Jack glanced at the televisions mounted above the bar and caught a glimpse of Sarah's face. "Michelle, Michelle, please turn up the sound."

A grim-faced newscaster read the story of how a private investigator named Sarah McShay had been found dead in her office, the apparent victim of suicide from a self-inflicted gunshot wound.

Stunned, Jack jumped off his barstool and shouted, "No, no, he killed Sarah. I can't believe it."

"Jack, we don't know all the facts," Racy said. "Let's go to the Glendale Police Department. I'll find out who's handling the case, and we'll get the straight story."

"Sorry, Michelle, we've got to go. This is so upsetting."
They arrived at the Glendale Police Department and sprinted up the stairs to the detective offices. Racy located Detective Mike Fuller's office at the rear of the building.

"Hello, Racy, what brings you in this evening?"

"Mike, this is Jack Weston. He hired Sarah McShay to work on a case. She found some incriminating evidence and now she's dead. We suspect foul play."

"Jack," he nodded at Racy's guest and motioned for both of them to sit down. "Racy, I don't usually share information about an on-going investigation, especially with civilians, but since you work for the department, I'll make an exception."

"Good. What proof do you have she actually killed herself?" Jack blurted.

"This morning, we found her body sitting at her desk with the gun still in her hand. She took one bullet to the heart and died instantly."

"No, it doesn't make sense," Jack said. "I talked to her last weekend, and she told me she found evidence to break open my case. She spoke with such enthusiasm about it, like she had just won big money on a game show. She told me how much she loved solving puzzles like this."

"Jack, did you know she was gay?" Fuller asked.

"I had my suspicions, but what's it got do with her death?"

"We know people try to kill themselves when they're depressed. Her mom told us Sarah and her partner had a fight and broke off their five-year relationship. Her partner moved out of town with another woman. We suspect Sarah was distraught over the loss."

"Losing a relationship wouldn't have pushed the Sarah I know over the edge," Jack said.

"We found a suicide note typed on her computer screen."

"Her computer screen," Jack shouted. "When I sat in her office, the computer was covered with a thick layer of dust. I don't think she ever used the damn thing."

"I know it's unusual to leave a suicide note on a computer, and only the key pad had been cleaned. We're also puzzled by the fact two shots had been fired.

"Two shots," Jack said.

"Yeah, one bullet turned up in the wall, like she changed her mind or something. Can't tell for sure."

"How strange," Racy commented.

"Right, the case still has some loopholes. The evidence doesn't add up," Fuller responded. "We need to study the forensics reports when they come back."

"Any sign of a struggle?" asked Racy.

"At first, we thought she had been robbed because the place was a mess. Her office had been trashed and files strewn all over the floor. Then, we noticed the dried sandwiches and unfinished soup in filthy bowls — the place reeked. We figured it was all part of her lifestyle."

"I agree. She never impressed me as someone who prided herself on cleanliness," Jack added.

"Let me suggest another scenario, Mike," Racy suggested. "What if someone she knew visited her office, and they talked about a case. The visitor may have sat in the chair right in front of her. When he stood up to end their conversation, the killer could have reached across the desk and shot her point blank."

"Exactly," chimed an excited Jack. "He staged the suicide scene, typed the note on the computer, and wiped the keyboard to get rid of his prints. Then, he placed the gun in her hand and fired it at the wall to leave gun powder residue on her fingers."

"Your story paints a wild, premeditated murder scene. Not too probable. I think you've watched too much C.S.I."

Jack and Racy exchanged exasperated looks.

"Right now we're interviewing her clients to check on her active cases," Mike continued. "We'll match our findings with the lab results when they come back in a few weeks. We'll know a lot more then."

"Since you're here, and you hired her," Fuller said, "I'd like to ask you a few questions to help our investigation."

"I'll be glad to cooperate. I already have a suspect for you to check out."

"All right, give me a name."

"I'm not sure I can trust you. Do all you fraternity boys in blue protect each other?"

"Are you suggesting a cop may have killed her?"

"Damn right, I am."

"What would motivate a cop to murder someone?"

"He's trying to cover another death he caused in a hit-and-run accident."

"Go ahead, Jack," Racy interrupted, "tell Mike your suspicions. I'll personally vouch for your story."

"Okay," he hesitated. "I believe Steve Baxter, a cop who works in Desert Valley, killed my wife in a hit-and-run accident last year. I am certain of it. Sarah told me she found evidence to link him to Taylor's death, and I think he went after Sarah to destroy it."

"Hard evidence?" Fuller asked.

"Yes, Sarah collected broken glass shards from Baxter's vehicle she found at the crime scene and planned to take them to the FBI for analysis this week."

"Really?" Fuller frowned. "That throws a different light on it. Okay, here's what we'll do. I'll send forensics back to her office to search for the glass shards and then check with the FBI to see if she already dropped off the evidence. Then, I'll pay a visit to Officer Baxter and see if he can account for his whereabouts at the time of her death."

"And what should we do?" Racy asked.

"Nothing for a while. These things take time. Until we find some answers, stay out of sight as much as possible."

"My thoughts, too," Jack said. "If Baxter stole the evidence, he may still want to take us out as well. He played bad cop the other night and it scared the shit out of us."

"We'll move on this thing as fast as we can," Fuller added. "Racy, thanks for the heads-up on this one."

For several minutes, the couple sat in Jack's vehicle and stared blankly into the darkness. Each of them silently internalized their conversation with Fuller and searched for answers. Jack reached across the console for Racy's hand, and she gripped his tightly.

"I'm sorry I got you involved with this," he said.

"It's not your fault he found us together," she responded. "I was frightened before, but now I'm really scared. I think Steve may try to kill both of us."

"You're probably right. We'll stay together until Fuller and his team link Baxter to Sarah's murder."

"God, Jack," she laughed nervously, "that's probably the worst pickup line I've ever heard."

Her quip broke the tension, and he glanced at her with a weak smile. "Not a pickup line, dear, just a genuine expression of concern. I don't want to lose another woman to him."

"I know, bad joke," she said. "What do we do now?"

"Like I said, let's stick together."

A week passed with no news from Fuller or the FBI. Jack believed Baxter successful took the glass shards from Sarah's office and provided Fuller with a tight alibi. The tension of the unknown lay heavy on the couple's minds. Although Racy talked to Fuller every day, nothing new emerged in the case.

To support each other, Jack and Racy spent days and nights together. Jack picked her up from work, and they'd drive back to his house or stay at her apartment in town. Frequently, the couple stopped for dinner at one of the downtown restaurants. Their closeness forged a strong bond. They anticipated Baxter might pounce at any moment, but he didn't show.

Chapter Forty-Three

Two weeks after Sarah's death, Baxter's still failed to materialize. The couple began to behave like two regular people in love. On Friday, Jack and Racy met with some of her friends at the Rock Bottom Restaurant for dinner. The weekend crowd packed the establishment, and their laughter added a pleasant din to the evening. The couple engaged in animated conversation, filled with work-related events. Racy's friends became enthralled with Jack's ghost stories and his life as a writer. They speculated about the reality of Pandora and her messages. The party ended after dark and people headed home. Jack and Racy drove the thirty miles back to his house.

They pulled onto the gravel road a mile from Jack's driveway and noticed a faint orange glow on the horizon. Curiosity quickly changed to trepidation as he realized the glow was actually a fire burning close to his property. He accelerated and raced toward his home. To their horror, flames engulfed his detached garage and licked at the night sky like a gigantic bonfire. Racy's vehicle, still housed inside, had been turned into a charred lump of metal. The couple heard glass windows explode and watched the flames devour the locked storeroom containing Taylor's possessions.

"All of my memories of her … gone!" he lamented. He removed his light jacket and helplessly waved it at the fire eating the remnants of a garage door. The intense heat mocked his futile gesture and forced him back.

Racy yelled, "Please, please, there's nothing you can do."

They stood in silence and helplessly watched the destruction. Someone must have reported the blaze because the sound of fire trucks rumbling on the gravel road could be heard. Too late to save any part of the garage, the firefighters contained the inferno and prevented the flames from spreading to Jack's house. The couple watched as the garage collapsed in one final explosion and sent burning timbers skyrocketing into the night sky. The garage had been transformed into an unrecognizable pile of water-soaked rubble.

Stunned by the catastrophe, Jack tried to comfort Racy, who cried about losing her vintage Mustang. From the safety of Jack's front porch, the two watched firefighters walk the area looking for hot spots. Finally, the battalion chief approached Jack carrying two burnt canisters.

"I hate to tell you this, Mr. Weston, but I know for sure an arsonist started the fire. One of my boys found these two empty gas cans around the back of the building. You got any neighbors who have a score to settle with you?"

Anger replaced lament. Jack yelled, "What neighbors? I don't have any neighbors, but I do know who did this." He trotted toward his vehicle.

"Jack, where are you going?" Racy shouted.

"After Baxter! The son-of-a-bitch torched the place!"

"I'm coming, too. He destroyed my car!"

"Buckle up tight. This will be a fast trip." Jack wheeled his vehicle back onto the gravel road and headed for the Desert Valley Police Department. They hadn't gone far when a dark sedan pulled onto the road and cut them off. Jack slammed on the brakes to avoid a collision, swerved and passed the car.

The near miss had not been caused by an errant driver. The dark vehicle accelerated and closed the gap between the two cars. Jack looked into the rearview mirror and saw the trailing vehicle. It seemed as if the driver wanted to hit him. Racy turned and watched the car accelerate, intent on its collision course.

Within seconds, the sedan crashed into Jack's back bumper and caused his car to slide out of control. Jack overcorrected his steering wheel. Even though his Honda swayed, rocked and wobbled, it successfully stayed on the road. He looked into the mirror as the vehicle hit him a second time and sent the car into another tailspin. Jack fought to make the adjustments and regain control. Again, Jack found the road and steadied the Honda.

Jack slowed enough to negotiate a sliding right turn onto another gravel road. "It's got to be Baxter," he shouted. "The bastard's trying to kill us. Well, it's not going to be easy, you asshole!"

Jack sped to eighty miles an hour — much too dangerous for traction on gravel. However, Baxter's car closed in and slammed into the back of Jack's vehicle. This time the loose gravel made it more difficult for Jack to maintain his course.

Steve aimed his pursuit car at Jack's taillights in an attempt to create a glancing blow. The maneuver, designed to send Jack's vehicle into a spin and make it careen out of control, was a common practice in police chases. Ironically, Steve learned this technique at the Colorado police training conference, but had no time to practice it before tonight. His lack of experience helped the couple stay alive.

"We've got to outrun him, Racy," Jack shouted. "If he gets us off the road, he'll kill us both."

"Step on it, Jack," a frightened Racy yelled. She turned around and watched the chase vehicle close in. "He's gaining on us. He's going to hit us again."

Jack swerved and fishtailed onto a narrow, dark gravel road. Steve missed the sudden turn and stopped to back up. However, within seconds, his car threatened to collide with Jack's fleeing Honda. Jack jumped on the brake long enough to make another sharp turn onto a more remote road. This time, with little effort, Steve followed his prey and closed in for another assault.

Jack accelerated down the lonely stretch of gravel. Out of the corner of his eye, he spotted unlit utility poles flying by the window — lonely tin soldiers beckoning the driver with unheard voices. Distracted by the unexpected sight, Racy quickly read painted letters glowing on the sign: *Coming soon — Vista View Subdivision.*

Somehow their car had recklessly plummeted down the same road where Taylor had died the year before. Jack pushed his vehicle to a speed close to a hundred miles per hour. Steve followed close behind. The car twisted and swayed down the road, and Jack's mind feverishly hatched a plan — a plan requiring Steve to keep pace with him.

Jack visualized the indelible image of the curve where he found Taylor. Perhaps he could now make her death scene fool the assailant.

"Hold on, Racy, this will be tight!" he yelled.

As his car approached the hairpin turn, he accelerated and instantly slammed on the brakes. The car spun around four times as its wheels desperately tried to find traction on the loose gravel. Steve didn't anticipate Jack's maneuver and lost control of his car.

For the second time in a year, he missed the sharp left turn. This time, however, his vehicle catapulted off the road, flipped over twice and landed upright against one of the newly installed utility poles. The sudden impact and excessive speed sheered the pole at its midpoint, and the heavy metal top fell directly onto Baxter's car. The full weight of the metal pole penetrated the car's roof as easy as a hot knife entering a Jell-O mold. The impact drove part of the vehicle's top through the driver's skull. Steve died instantly.

Jack and Racy jumped out of the Honda and ran back to check Baxter's condition. They were greeted by the gruesome sight of Steve's head impaled by a section of metal. Racy turned away and vomited in the weeds. Jack gasped for air and looked for signs of life — none. He turned away, as well. For an instant, the faint scent of roses hung in the air. Jack looked for the source and saw Steve's vehicle had crushed a wild primrose bush growing at the base of the light pole. The squashed petals had adhered to the car's front wheel and released a gentle fragrance into the night air. Jack shook his head. Finally, he understood.

He turned to comfort Racy, "Are you all right?"

"I've never seen anything like this before in my life. I'm going to have nightmares for months."

"I know, but he had it coming. Steve's death fulfilled Taylor's prophecy."

"What are you talking about?"

"All the clues, the signs, the things Pandora said — Steve was blinded by the light! This is the spot where Taylor died. Remember, the song lyrics ... leave a light on when I'm gone ... get it? The city had been installing streetlights. Steve could have killed us if the light didn't fall on his car and permanently blinded him."

"Oh, god, Jack, that's really creepy. Taylor got revenge for her own death."

"I finally figured it out. The scent of the crushed roses let me know."

#####

The wheels and axle of Jack's car had been twisted into a tangled, bent mess. All four tires had gone flat during its acrobatic spin. They abandoned the vehicle and began the hour-long hike to the paved highway. By daybreak, the Desert Valley police arrived on the scene to take care of the accident and remove Baxter's body.

Chapter Forty-Three

Within a month, the FBI completed its independent investigation. More shards of glass were found in the road and lab analysis connected them to Steve Baxter's cruiser. Frank had a letter of reprimand placed in his file for not reporting the work he performed on the squad car, but didn't lose his job. Frank's age, experience and loyalty saved his position.

Reporters from *The Arizona Republic* conducted an investigative study of the Desert Valley Police Department. Unfortunately, none of the employees in the department broke rank and came forward to testify against the chief or reveal knowledge of any cover-up. In spite of the missing evidence, all reports had been properly documented and filed in accordance with department procedure. Two months after the story broke Chief John Thompson announced his resignation. He had been hired as the new police chief of a small community in Kansas. He told the Desert Valley City Council he resigned to live closer to his aging parents.

Steve Baxter's connection to Senator Sam Williamson became an inconsequential oddity to the case and no evidence linked the two to Taylor's death. "The Teflon-politician," a new moniker created by the media, dismissed his relationship to his stepson as nothing more than an unfortunate coincidence. In November, Williamson won re-election to his Arizona senate seat and, based on the popularity of his victory, announced plans to run for the House of Representatives during the next term. His election would be guaranteed.

Jack continued to date Racy for another year. His articles about life in the southwest added more loyal readers to his following and captured their imagination. However, he grew restless and expressed a desire to get back on the road. He wanted to have his articles reflect the soul and passion of people who lived in remote areas.

To fulfill his need, he asked Phil to send him on assignment to isolated areas in California, Nevada and Utah. He planned to write a series of articles about unique hiking trails near small towns and villages. Pleased with Jack's ghost stories, Phil's endorsement came easily.

One evening, he and Racy enjoyed dinner at Zendejas. Jack knew he wanted to be closer to his new love and no longer enjoyed traveling alone. He also had no further need to communicate with ghostly spirits for guidance or inspiration.

"Racy, before this relationship goes deeper, we need to explore our compatibility."

"What do you mean by compatibility? We've been dating for over a year. You still don't know if we're compatible?"

"Not really. I once read an article making the claim you had to travel with another person to really know if the two of you can enjoy life together. Travel creates a lot of stress."

"You don't think our experience with Steve Baxter offered enough stress for one lifetime?"

"Our experience with him gave us plenty to deal with, but the stress I'm talking about is different. You know, the daily stress of driving, reading the map, getting lost, finding a place to stop, selecting a restaurant … typical things."

"Okay, okay, I get it. So, you want me to go on vacation with you?"

"More than that. I'd like you to take a leave of absence and spend the next few months hiking the backcountry with me."

"Hiking? Like in the wilderness? With a back pack?" With an incredulous look, she added, "Don't you remember, I'm a city girl. I have no idea how to do those sorts of things."

"Don't worry. I'll teach you everything and promise to be patient as you learn. C'mon, Racy, it'll be a new adventure … much safer than the city."

"It may be safer, but there's a practical reason why I can't go. I have no money. I haven't saved enough to enjoy the luxury of a leave."

"I don't expect you to pay for anything. It will be a kind of working vacation for me, and I'll pay you to add a feminine perspective to my stories. Some of my best writing has been motivated by the voices of female spirits. Who knows, it could be better if I listen to a *live woman*."

"You mean you want this female's voice in your life?"

"Exactly. Your voice and your body. I get paid a lot of money to write articles. And, my sweet Racy, I love to hear your voice, especially when you snuggle up with me."

"It sounds more like you want to have someone keep you warm in a sleeping bag," she teased.

"Well, yes, but the last time I left town the soft voices of spirits made my writing glow. This time I only want to hear the voice of a warm-blooded redhead whisper words of love in my ear."

Racy looked into Jack's sincere eyes, smiled and said, "Okay, I have absolutely no idea what I'm getting into, except I love you and will have fun. Let's go play in the woods and listen to different voices."

On the way out of town, Jack took a back road through Walsenburg. They drove through town and simultaneously spotted a slightly built, female hitchhiker on the side of the road. Instinctively, Jack slowed down and took a long look at the woman. Racy glanced out the window and then back at Jack.

"No, dear. Don't even think about it."

A Final Thought:

So do we pass the ghosts that haunt us later in our lives; they sit undramatically by the roadside like poor beggars, and we see them only from the corners of our eyes, if we see them at all. The idea that they have been waiting there for us rarely if ever crosses our minds. Yet they do wait, and when we have passed, they gather up their bundles of memory and fall in behind, treading in our footsteps and catching up, little by little.

— Stephen King

About the Author

I worked in the public arena as a history teacher for twenty-five years. I became an apprentice storyteller by spinning tales of historical characters whose lives were more interesting than the flat *who, what, when, where* descriptions in dry textbooks. These enhanced stories added luster to my classroom presentations and offered students an insight into the human traits and foibles of historical characters. This kind of storytelling prepared me for my second career as a fiction writer.

The educational career I pursued turned me into an administrator, and I learned to follow the professionally, sanctioned art of near-fiction writing. An unspoken, rule of administrators is this: *If you don't know the answer, use your best professional guess. People will believe you. Power and authority create an impregnable façade that permits you to smudge the edges of reality when necessary.* If you make a mistake, it's easier to seek forgiveness than ask for permission. I also learned another simple axiom along the way: *If you say something often enough and state it with total conviction, it becomes the truth.*

Now as a writer, I often ask readers to suspend belief, withhold judgment and accept what they read as a possible truth. Such acts of generosity from a reader add flavor and zest to the essence of a story. After all, *Voices* is fiction, or is it? Is it possible voices, invisible and unheard by others, could make a difference in your life? I invite you to explore the thought on your own.

I currently work out of my house in Glendale, Arizona, and choose to travel or camp whenever the temperature in the Valley of the Sun goes above 110 degrees. These road trips offer the opportunity to market my books and listen to the voices of strangers as they share personal stories. Of course, I sequester their voices in the back of my mind or record them in a notebook. That way I can tap into them whenever I decide to write the next novel or short story.

Other Books by the Author

Non-Fiction Book:

Making Change Happen: Shared Vision, No Limits. Lanham, Maryland: Scarecrow Education, 2005. This book explains how a group of educators redesigned an alternative high school and turned it into a national educational model. The book outlines more than sixty strategies the staff used to modify its program, motivate students and garner support from the community and district administrators.

Fiction Books:

Bar Exam: Tavern Tales and Reflections. Bloomington, Indiana: iUniverse, 2009. The novel presents a fascinating dialogue between ordinary people, regulars who frequent a tavern in the Benbow Inn, a hotel tucked along the Eel River in Northern California. Their discussions range from the meaning of life to how to make love last. Their stories are filled with humor, sadness and hope. The reader joins these folks weekly and eavesdrops on their conversations. Each person attempts to live a fulfilled life and make a difference. Their stories contain all the elements that lie at the heart of the American Dream — finding happiness.

Depositions. Bloomington, Indiana: iUniverse, 2009. A prominent citizen of a small Illinois community dies in a one-car accident. It's a routine investigation for the police until they discover the victim, dressed in a three-piece suit, is still wearing his bedroom slippers. The twisting tale of suspense and mystery creates trouble for a nosey writer looking for an idea for his next novel. Co-authored with the spirit of Leon Palles, a man who died in 1996, the novel emerged in book form when it was converted from his original screen play.

The Attendant. Bloomington, Indiana: iUniverse, 2010. The idea behind *The Attendant* was originally posted on the Internet as an April fool's joke by the Bristol Evening News near London, England. The joke grew into a novel when the author decided to create a story adding life and motive to the fictitious parking lot attendant who thought he successfully scammed the system. The novel provides readers with mystery, suspense and romance and turns into a manhunt that begins in New York City and ends in the Greek Islands.

Out of the Zone. Glendale, Arizona: New Visions Publishing, 2011. A novella dedicated to my high school classmates for our 50th reunion, held in September, 2011. *Out of the Zone* is the story of a man who decides to return to his high school reunion to resolve past sins. While a senior in high school, his class turned against him because of a disastrous incident. Now, fifty years later, he wants to know if he made the right decision to leave the comfort zone of his hometown. Who is happier with life: Those who stayed in the zone or those who lived out of the zone? Vignettes in the book answer the question.

All books can be ordered from the author (blamperes@gmail.com), New Visions Publishing or special ordered through your local bookstore.

For more information, examine the author's website: www.blamperesauthor.com